TELLING Truths

— A Novel —

Susanne Bacon

SUSANNE BACON

authorHOUSE

AuthorHouse™
1663 Liberty Drive
Bloomington, IN 47403
www.authorhouse.com
Phone: 1 (800) 839-8640

© 2017 Susanne Bacon. All rights reserved.
Cover Photo by Susanne Bacon

No part of this book may be reproduced, stored in a retrieval system, or transmitted by any means without the written permission of the author.

Published by AuthorHouse 12/19/2016

ISBN: 978-1-5246-5630-0 (sc)
ISBN: 978-1-5246-5629-4 (e)

Print information available on the last page.

This book is printed on acid-free paper.

Because of the dynamic nature of the Internet, any web addresses or links contained in this book may have changed since publication and may no longer be valid. The views expressed in this work are solely those of the author and do not necessarily reflect the views of the publisher, and the publisher hereby disclaims any responsibility for them.

Preliminary Remark

The town of Wycliff is entirely fictitious. So are all characters in this novel. Any similarities with living or late persons and operating or former businesses, except those mentioned in the acknowledgements, are totally coincidental.

Susanne Bacon

To Katja "Tinka" Capito,
supportive friend from the very beginning.
And to Donald –
always with love.

Contents

Prologue 11

Chapter 1 15

Chapter 2 43

Chapter 3 77

Chapter 4 110

Chapter 5 145

Chapter 6 178

Chapter 7 208

Chapter 8 237

Chapter 9 263

Chapter 10 301

Epilogue 325

Acknowledgements 333

Prologue

The clear liquid was dripping slowly into the water puddle, creating a colorful rainbow from which an acrid stench wafted off almost immediately. A bird in a nearby bush shrieked and fluttered from its perch to fly deeper into the forest, calling out what seemed to be warnings. A lazy fly that had been sitting on the verge of the puddle started to move, but suddenly tottered and ended up tumbling onto its back. A few convulsive movements of its legs – then it stiffened for good.

The drum from which the liquid was leaking looked harmless enough. It was one of those blue plastic ones with a removable lid. It was labeled for its contents, but half of the sticker was ripped off, and another label made it clear that whatever was oozing from the drum was highly hazardous. The lid had loosened by a fracture, and the drum's contents were slowly seeking their way through the aperture to the rim. Drip. Drip. Drip.

Another drum bounced against it, then rolled back. And another. And another. Besides the dull sound of them hitting the forest ground, there was hardly anything else to be heard. Well, a few bird twitters. And the rushing of the constant sea breeze playing with the branches of the fir and spruce trees. Sometimes a rustle in the underwood, maybe caused by a rodent or some busy insect. And the heavy breathing of the person who was working hard to unload the drums from the truck bed.

When a dozen drums lay discarded on the ground, the process stopped. A few shovels of soil were spread halfheartedly over the site, neither covering nor hiding the insult to Nature.

A few moments later, the truck motor was revved up, and the exhaust fumes added to the stench from the rainbow puddle. The bluish cloud hovered over the ground for a while, filling the air like a ghostly fog. Then it got carried away in whiffs by the wind. The forest ground showed the pattern of some off-road tire profiles that had imprinted themselves into the muddier parts. Otherwise, everything looked idyllic if you turned away from the drums.

But the stench stayed. And it grew more intense by the minute.

Drip. Drip. Drip...

*

From "The Sound Messenger":

Tulip Parade Benefits Hiking Community

***judo*. The 50th Tulip Parade of Wycliff featured over 20 floats presenting various local organizations. The Wycliff Fire Department made Float of the Year and beat the Police Department's float by only a narrow margin of 2 % of the spectator votes, thereby winning for the fifth time in a row. The Tulip Queen and her court dedicated this year's donations to the upkeep of the hiking path system in and around the Wycliff community boundaries.**

Maybe it was still a bit chilly, but this year's Tulip Parade made the Victorian town of Wycliff look like an ambassador for summer already. And it truly turned into some big-time support for the tourist season when Tulip Queen Mary Hanson (Wycliff High School) announced that she and her court had decided to dedicate this fest's donations to the local hiking path system. Of late, there had been more and more complaints about paths getting overgrown and benches rotting. Further suggestions were the installation of "raccoon-safe" garbage cans along the main paths and new bark to be spread especially in areas prone to muddiness. "We all want healthy activities for our leisure time," Queen Mary, 16, announced. "This is the time to give the community the means for optimizing something that everybody can benefit from, regardless of age or income." (…)

CHAPTER 1

The Green Maven's Tip of the Week:
To clean tarnished silver, use aluminum foil, salt, and hot water. Cover the inside of a bowl with aluminum foil. Put the tarnished silver in. Cover silver with salt. Add some hot water. After about an hour your silver should be looking as if new again. Rinse and wipe dry.

Thora Byrd was humming as she walked along one of the wider paths in the forest east of Wycliff. Her black one-year-old Labrador, Bear, trotted next to her and looked at her every once in a while as if wondering about her thoughts. Thora loved April in the South Sound region. And especially in a place such as Wycliff, a quaint Victorian small-town somewhere on the coast between Olympia and Seattle. During the week, when she returned home from work as a secretary in Town Hall, she usually just grabbed Bear's leash and walked him on the beach near her tiny cottage a little outside Wycliff. But on weekends she drove into the residential area of Wycliff. It was also called Uptown, as it literally sat on a bluff which separated it from the businesses in Downtown. There she usually chose one of the trail heads into the forest, which stretched wild and lush until it was cut off by I-5. There was a pretty extensive network of paths, the widest even allowing for trucks since forest workers needed to be able to access the area.

Yes, April was gorgeous in the South Sound, all mild and filled with stunning colors. Even in the forest. Bear, of course, was way more interested in anything that moved or smelled. A patch of skunk cabbage in a marshy patch by the path was inspected as intensely as the legs of one of the old benches or the remnants of a plastic tote that somehow had ended up in the middle of the forest. Thora frowned. She put on an old garden glove and picked up the tattered tote to place it in a small garbage bag she used to bring along on her dog walks. As she had to have an extra bag with her for scooping up Bear's turds anyhow, she had made it her habit to carry an even bigger sack for anything people simply trashed out in nature. Not that she felt she was a better person for doing this, but it made her feel better about the environment. Today she had already found an empty box of cigarettes, an empty soda bottle, half (!) a Swimsuit magazine, and a tossed cassette tape out of which the ribbon was hanging in knots.

Bear was straining on the leash happily. Thora looked at the velvety ears, one flopped forward, the other turned inside out as if that got him better hearing. She had called her dog Bear because, when she had bought him at age four months, his paws had seemed to outsize his body in an impossibly cute manner. Clumsy and playful, Bear had been making her laugh ever since, and she didn't know how she could have done without him before.

Before … Thora sighed at the thought. She had turned forty-two last month, and it had been a very lonesome birthday. It wasn't so much that she didn't have friends. Well, let's call them acquaintances rather. Her family was spread over the entire country, and she hardly ever contacted them. Her own fault probably. But then she had met her cousins only as late as a teenager. Apart from the customary Christmas card and a personal one-sentence addition inside, they didn't tell each other much and, over the years, had grown more and more apart. Her dad had passed away some five years ago. That hadn't been much of a surprise. Scottish by birth, he had chosen to join a deep-sea fishing crew, and the tough life had finally taken its toll. Her mother had outlived him by a couple of years. She hadn't been that old, but she had seemed to have lost the gist of life without her husband even though he had been away so very often. As Thora had neither brothers nor sisters, she was pretty much on her own these days.

There had been men in her life. For sure. Thora was not unattractive. She wore her dark thick hair short in a way that complimented its waviness. She had large hazel-colored eyes, a nose neither too big nor too small, sprinkled with some jolly freckles, and a shapely mouth that almost said "come hither". At five foot six, she felt comfortable about her height, too, and apart from a couple of pounds too many that sneaked on her during the winter season with all its goodies she couldn't be called fat either. But none of the men whom she had cared about seemed to have been able to bear with her for long. After a first few passionate weeks, the frequency of their dates had dwindled to zilch, and the excuses ranged from "I have too much business on my hands to see anyone right now" to an honest "You are way too exhausting for me". It was frustrating, and sometimes Thora wondered whether Bear would be the only reliable male to stay by her side.

In a way, Thora had come to grips with her partnerless life. She had acquired a beautiful little cottage at the outskirts of Wycliff where the coastline became mellow and featured some sandy beaches that were only reachable on foot. She liked working alongside Mayor Clark Thompson, whom she secretly found quite attractive, if at times irritating. She sometimes caught herself thinking of him during meals when she was all alone. She knew he was a widower – did that make him even more lonesome than herself?

She dedicated part of her leisure time to environmentalist education at the Maritime Center that had been newly founded next door to "The Flower Bower" at the Wycliff Yacht Harbor. There she taught children of almost all ages about the direction water flows from divides through the countryside and through towns along the way to the Sound and how pollution at any place impacts maritime life and drinking water quality. She also contributed a weekly column to "The Sound Messenger", the newspaper of Wycliff. She had chosen the pen name "The Green Maven" and was hoping to make her fellow citizens more conscious of healthy alternatives to some everyday habits. She didn't know or care whether anybody knew that "The Green Maven" and the feisty town hall secretary Thora Byrd were one and the same.

She quite liked cooking, and when she did groceries, she favored the Wycliff Farmers Market over any supermarket because of the freshness of produce and because she knew where it all came from. She was a fervent reader, and more often than not the light from the reading nook in her living room shone into the dark outside until midnight. In order to get some exercise, without being able to make excuses not to, Thora had bought Bear one especially bleak Saturday morning. But Bear had soon become much more than her reason to go for daily walks. His comical puppy playfulness as well as his faithful and undiminishing dog love had conquered her heart in a way she would have deemed impossible before.

At the moment, she had to admit that she didn't even think of any partner in her life at all anymore. Which her friend Dottie McMahon, the owner of "Dottie's Deli", the beautiful German store on Main Street, had actually warned her of.

"Don't get too taken up with Bear," Dottie had said, while stroking the silky coat of the panting pup at her feet.

"There are still some very eligible men out there, and you are a beautiful woman inside and out. Don't ignore your heart. Bear is only so much of a confidant. There will be times in life when you will be glad to have someone who does more than just look at you and bore his nose into your hand..."

Thora smiled to herself. Right now her life was running smooth and without any complications. She had a purpose and she had sound circumstances of life. What more did she want?!

Anyhow, here she was walking in utter bliss on a beautiful April afternoon. Her dog, Bear, was pricking his ears every once in a while or sniffing at another interesting spot on the path. The birds were singing. And the air was balmy.

After a while they reached one of Thora's favorite spots. Here the woods grew less densely and retreated a bit to leave a colorfully blossoming, natural clearing. Sure, there was a crossing with a rough road wide enough for forestry vehicles. And there were also a picnic table and benches which were used mostly in summer. But what Thora really treasured was a map that showed the hiking path network in Wycliff Forest and explained what was blooming around the clearing.

Bear strained against the leash. Then he growled. A short puppy bark followed, and he dropped on his haunches, whining.

"Oh for Heaven's sake, Bear!" Thora exclaimed. "We are only half-way done with our walk and in the middle of nowhere, and you are balking?! What's the matter with you?" Bear tilted his head and looked at her. Then he started growling again.

Thora looked around. Bear had never behaved as weirdly as that before, she realized. And the thought gave her the goosebumps. "Hello?" she called out. "Is anybody out there?" But nobody answered, and nothing stirred. Thora called out again. Then she shrugged her shoulders. "Nobody around, Bear," she stated. "You must have seen a ghost. Come on, boy!"

She wanted to walk on, but Bear started pulling her into a different direction. "Bear!" Thora protested. "This isn't our way back home!" But Bear didn't give up. Finally, Thora gave in and followed him a bit further up the forestry road. Only then did she see the tire tracks that had plowed into and out of the meadow. Only then did she realize the acrid smell, so unlike the fragrance of flowers. Only then did she glimpse something blue and plastic farther away in the meadow. Bear whined and plopped on his haunches again.

"Good dog, Bear," Thora said in a soothing, low voice and stroked his silky head. Bear looked at her and flopped one of his ears inside out. Thora laughed. He was too comical. "Now, you stay here, Bear. Okay? I'll just walk in a few yards and have a look what's in that meadow there."

She laid down the leash, and took a couple of steps forward. Bear's whining increased. Then he barked and started coming after her. "Stay!" Thora insisted. Bear obeyed. But he was visibly unhappy and watched his mistress warily.

Thora strode purposefully into the meadow. The vapors started getting to her eyes and nose, and she finally stopped, quickly taking in the scene. "Unbelievable!" she exclaimed to herself in shock. Then she turned and walked out of the meadow even more quickly. She grabbed Bear's leash and gave it a slight tug. "Come on, Bear. Let's walk back as fast as we can. You discovered something gross and awful. And you deserve a big doggie treat as soon as we get home." She began to jog. Bear took up the urgency in her voice and fell into a slight run.

*

Julie Dolan, a 27-year-old journalist at Wycliff's only newspaper, "The Sound Messenger", was sipping a cup of coffee at the police station in downtown Wycliff and talking to her new step-father, Luke McMahon, the Chief of Police. He had married her widowed mother, German Deli owner Dottie, only recently. It felt still a bit strange to get the police news from a family member now instead from "just" another police man. But Julie suspected that sooner rather than later she'd get used to it. Luke seemed to be comfortable enough as he gave her the latest reports. A traffic accident outside Wycliff on the road to Lacey, involving a bicyclist and a wandering and disoriented cow. Also, there had been a burglary at a farm, another theft at Nathan's (the regional supermarket's) drug store department. And then Friday and Saturday night's DUIs. The usual things accumulating in a small town the size of Wycliff. Julie took notes busily.

A sudden commotion in the front room made her and Luke listen up and stop their conversation. A woman's voice was asking to see the chief of police immediately because of an emergency. Yes, please, it really was an emergency though there were no casualties. Yet.

Luke rose. "I'll have to see to this," he nodded at Julie. "Enjoy the rest of your coffee, dear. And take your time. If this is a real emergency, you might even want to stay around to get my report for your paper." He winked.

When he walked through the door, his face became sober at once. Thora Byrd was standing in front of the reception desk, talking to the officer who had Sunday daytime duty there. Luke knew that Thora, the serious-minded town hall secretary, would never come for pure attention seeking. She was a conscientious, dedicated person with a hang for environmental issues. And he suspected her to be "The Green Maven" of "The Sound Messenger". She'd never steal anybody's time over a mere whim.

"Hello, Thora," he greeted her. "I hear there's a problem?"

Thora nodded briefly. "A serious emergency, as far as I could make it out. That's why I came here at once. There is a chemical spill in Wycliff Forest."

"A chemical spill? Are you sure?"

"Pretty sure," Thora confirmed. "It was definitely not normal garbage."

"What makes you so sure about it?"

"A biting stench irritating eyes and nostrils," Thora described. "The source seem to be a number of drums dumped into a clearing. I counted six, but there could easily be more. I wasn't able to walk up more closely. The air was too poisonous."

"Would you be able to show me the exact place?"

"Oh sure! I'll gladly lead you there."

Luke jotted down some notes. "You would have to come back here with me afterwards again, as I will have to take a full report on this."

"No big deal,' Thora said. "This is important enough. I'd rather do something useful like this than lollygag on my deck."

"May I come, too?" Julie had entered the room unnoticed and overheard the main part of the exchange.

Thora raised her brows at Luke. "I wouldn't know why not. Julie will have to report this in her paper anyhow, right?"

Luke nodded slowly. "There is nothing that says she couldn't come."

"Then what's keeping us?" Julie asked brightly, shouldering her tote which held an iTab for just such purposes.

Thora winced at the chirpy note in Julie's voice. There was nothing to be happy about an illegal dump, much less a chemical spill. On the other hand, the young woman was a passionate and admittedly thorough journalist who would do her very best to tell the story and comment on it in an appropriate manner. Her presence might even help looking into more detail.

In the police department's visitor parking lot behind Town Hall, Bear was hanging his head through a back window of Thora's car, pressing his throat down on the door frame, wheezing. His eyes shot Thora an expectant look as she walked up to the car.

"May I ride with you?" Julie asked hopefully.

"Sure," Thora replied. "If you don't mind smelly, hot doggie breath on the back of your neck..."

Julie laughed and slipped into the passenger seat. "Not at all. Bear is such a cutsie. Labradors are simply wonderful. And such fun!"

"Until you have to take care of them," Thora grumbled as she started her car. But she wasn't really serious about it. Bear was the most important person in her life right now. And she couldn't imagine any differently.

*

They finally stood at the forestry road crossing where Bear had spotted that something was wrong earlier on. He had been left in the car, whining unhappily and trying to catch her attention with mournful puppy eyes as Thora walked off with Julie and Luke. She didn't want to expose him to whatever was lingering in the air, surely had already soaked into the ground, and was maybe even spreading as they were walking toward it.

"Over there?" Luke McMahon asked and pointed a direction.

"A bit more to the left. Let me show you where the tracks are leading into the meadow." Thora took the lead, and Julie readied the camera on her iTab. When they reached the indicated spot, she started taking pictures, general ones of the clearing, then close-ups of the tire marks.

Luke started walking into the meadow and soon covered mouth and nose with his sleeved arm. Finally, he stopped and looked at the scene. Julie, who had followed him, had bound the neck scarf she had been wearing over her face, so only her eyes were peeking out. She took picture after picture. Then she slowly walked a wide circle around the site and took even more. After a few minutes both returned.

Luke was coughing, Julie's eyes were streaming by now. "Are you alright?" Thora asked her. She had felt confident about the younger woman's work ethos, but she certainly hadn't wanted to endanger her.

Julie nodded and pulled the scarf off her face. "Dang!" she said. "That's a vile stink. Real bad. As in toxic, acid, etching ... you name it. Gee, and I counted an entire dozen of drums, not just the six you were able to see from the one direction."

"I might ask you for copies of your photos later," Luke told his step-daughter.

"Sure," Julie said. "What now?"

"Site evaluation," Luke stated, more to himself. "Can't let anybody walk into this without knowing what substances we are dealing with."

"You mean it could be a mix?"

"Most likely we are dealing with a variety of chemicals. They may have been carried separately. They may have mixed, if several drums are burst. They may be a mix already inside those drums. We don't even know yet how many drums have burst."

Julie frowned. She checked her photos, but she couldn't come up with an answer. She had clearly seen one lid askew, but none of the others seemed to have come off.

Thora nodded calmly. She knew, although this was an entirely new situation here in Wycliff, that Chief McMahon was on top of it and already had a plan. "Hazardous Waste Operations," she said quietly.

"What?" Luke asked, startled from his train of thoughts.

"Hazardous Waste Operations," Thora repeated. "Meaning, you are involving a whole lot of people to secure the site and have it cleaned up."

"Yes, yes," Luke said, and took out his work cell phone.

"I mean, I know that this will take up the rest of your day most likely. Therefore, I will gladly come into the police station tomorrow and make my report then. So you can work on this without distraction," Thora offered helpfully.

Luke nodded, visibly relieved. He didn't let on how the situation angered and stressed him. Who dumped hazardous waste anywhere it didn't belong?! Who was putting the health and life of his or her fellow citizens at risk like this? And was he up-to-date on all the details that were constantly changing in investigations like this, even though only in small ways?

"May I stay a bit longer?" Julie asked. "I can push the deadline a little and still place the article and a couple of pictures into tomorrow morning's edition."

"I know I can't persuade you not to," Luke answered grimly. "But keep from underneath our feet. It might get ugly. And don't endanger yourself. I wouldn't know how to explain it to your mother if anything happened to you."

"I hear you," Julie chimed and started opening a new document on her iTab, typing in her initials to start a new article. "judo", as in Julie Dolan, had been her acronym ever since she had started her career as a journalist in Seattle. She had been using it ever since, even though she had left her employment there a few years ago. The abbreviation almost sounded like a war name, she thought. And then she started writing away.

"I'll let Dottie know you'll be home late," Thora offered.

"Great," Luke said almost absently as he was dialing a number. Thora nodded and walked off with a little wave to Julie. "Hey!" Luke suddenly called after her. Thora turned around and looked at him, her face a question mark. "Thank you!"

She smiled. But her smile felt all wrong. This was major. Somebody was poisoning the environment without any thought of the consequences. She had known immediately what the motive was. No matter whether somebody legally built a plant that would cause more damage than benefits or whether somebody dumped hazardous materials illegally – it always came down to the money that went into somebody's pockets. The question in this case was: Whose pockets? Was it the same person as the one who had dumped the drums? And how many more illegal dumps might still be around? The thought was sickening. There might be time bombs ticking out there nobody knew about. And what were those substances that made breathing almost impossible? Where did they come from? What damage had they already caused? What lay in wait yet?

As she returned to the parking lot, Bear started barking out of the window. "Shhh!" Thora made. "Everything is alright." But she knew it was not. And Bear sensed it too.

Julie had been able to take down some more information as the securing of the dump site had begun. She had raced home to shape all of the notes and quotes she had managed to gather into a newsworthy article and shot it over to her editor's office in an email. John Minor, editor of "The Sound Messenger", was a scrupulously conscientious journalist, always on time, always reading or listening between the lines. If Julie had told him on the phone that she had a story, but was not able to deliver until after tonight's deadline, he would have pushed the deadline farther out. But Julie knew that her story wasn't finished anyhow. That she would probably write more than a couple of further articles on the illegal dumping of hazardous waste. So she decided to send in her short feature right on time and to create a bigger article with a background box on hazardous waste operations, on labeling hazardous waste, and on proper disposal a day or two later. Maybe she would even be able to tell readers about first suspicions of who had unloaded a dozen drums with toxic waste into the idyllic clearing in Wycliff Forest.

John hadn't called her on the surprise article. Instead he had spent an extra-hour on overhauling the lay-out of the Monday newspaper's front-page. This article was small, but important. It concerned the people of Wycliff directly. A dramatic looking photo came along with it, showing people dressed in full body suits with special face masks, handling drums. Inset was a photo of a half-ripped label that showed a date, some numbers, and abbreviations, but not the source of the barrel. It would be difficult to place the origin of these drums. But it might not be entirely impossible.

Later, Julie had returned to the site and interviewed some of the people who had handled the toxic waste. She had asked Luke McMahon when he thought they'd receive the results about what substances had been spilled and whether further danger was to be expected from the leaks.

"Could you tell me anything about those drums that were not spilled?" Julie asked him, hope gleaming in her eyes.

Luke looked weary. "Julie, I'm not a clairvoyant. I can see for myself that the labels have been partly ripped off to obscure the source of the contents. I see numbers that might give some clarification about what's inside. But the labeling might be wrong. We will have to wait until the lab has analyzed the liquids. From there we may conclude about a source, and even then it might take weeks until we have narrowed down the field to a number of suspects that is workable in more detail." Julie looked disappointed. "I know that is not what you want to hear, but it is all I can say with a clear conscience for now."

"Anything else you could tell our readers?"

Luke's eyes narrowed. "M-hm. Unfortunately, there might be more such sites out there. Anybody who spots a similar place – don't go anywhere near it, as you might harm your health. Call the police immediately, and don't be afraid that it could be a false alarm. In fact, I prefer a false alarm about hazardous waste illegally dumped over a real site not reported. And so should everybody out there."

"Would you let me know when you have a hint as to where the drums could have come from?"

Luke sighed. "I know you love investigative journalism, Julie. But remember: The people who dropped off those drums are criminals. Don't dig too deeply, or you might get hurt yourself. Those people have no conscience at all. They might be willing to kill."

"Sounds like a real cool detective story," Julie answered.

"Rather a totally uncool reality involving some hot mess," Luke countered.

*

It was a chilly morning. Fog was still lingering over the sea and downtown Wycliff whereas Uptown already started enjoying the first sunbeams biting through the clouds. Mathilda Barton felt even chillier in her tiny office container at the wharf she had inherited from her father. The little furnace in the corner blasted out furious waves of heat that hardly reached farther than a couple of yards and left her freezing behind her desk. She was rubbing her cold hands. Her sandy hair was shoulder length and kept straying into her face again and again as she was scouring her books for the latest orders and payments.

Business had been slow last year, but it seemed to be picking up with the new season and a bigger run of salmon as well as an increased population of bottom feeders. Whatever caused the curiously repetitive pattern of years filled with great catches and others with dwindling numbers that left fishermen in debt, she didn't know. The fact was that, right now, she needed to keep her head above water businesswise. She must not be daunted by the long line of boats that was waiting to be taken care of by her wharf.

"Barton & Son". Her father had always been a dreamer. The big wharf he had been imagining had stayed small fry and never made it on the list for anybody but the Wycliff fishermen, some local boaters, and maybe a few tourists who were looking for a small wharf, as they thought the prices would be smallish, too. The son the company firm boasted had never been born either. Mathilda's mother had died of pneumonia in their drafty little house between the cottages on the outskirts of Wycliff and the poor side of town, which was just adjacent to the wharf. Mathilda had stayed the only child. Her father had never remarried; nor had he renamed the wharf. He probably thought the "& Son" invoked his customers' trust.

Mathilda had finished Wycliff High and Tacoma Community College. Then she had started an internship as a mechanic at a small wharf over in Tacoma. The family who owned it had hoped she might fall in love with their son who was rather an introvert and gauche to boot. Mathilda's friendly and ambitious attitude made everybody really like her. And she liked everybody back – except the son. She couldn't for the life of her imagine to date him, even less to spend a lifetime with him. After a year, the wharf owners and she separated in friendship. The son stayed solo. So did Mathilda. But at age 28 nothing was lost yet, and she wasn't really worried.

When her father had handed over the wharf keys to her on his hospice bed where he was dying of lung cancer she had straightened her shoulders and perceived the business as what it was: a challenge she could accept or walk away from. She had decided to stay. She hoped that one day she would be able to make her father's dream come true. That of a renowned wharf. With a solid office building and a nice breakroom for her workers. Brand-new repair and maintenance equipment instead of old or leased stuff. Maybe even a lunchroom with a café that she'd open for workers from the other harbor businesses around, too.

For now, she needed to be prepared for the new week with the testing of one fishing boat. Its motor had been burning and almost sunk the vessel while it was still out on the Sound. Another boat had needed a total overhaul of the hull, including caulking, paintjob, and varnishing. And one of the first boating tourists in Wycliff had asked whether

her people would be able to place more seating into his cockpit, probably so he could show off his motoring skills to female guests. Mathilda was grimacing. The man had looked rich and acted cheap. He had tried to haggle over the price. But she had insisted that she couldn't go down on hourly wages, material, and express service. He had finally given in and still made a good deal. Ugh!

Mathilda took a sip from her tea cup. She held it in both her hands to warm her chilly fingers and enjoyed the hot steam that rose fragrantly towards her face. Lady Grey was one of her favorite types of tea, and she made it a special treat for tough office mornings like these when things looked a bit overwhelming, she was cold, and she felt all alone.

To be honest though, of late she hadn't felt that lonesome anymore. There was that nice owner of Harrison Disposal Center in the vicinity of Yelm, Daniel Harrison. He must be a bit older than her and obviously took meticulous care of his business, which she liked about him. He was somber, but could be pretty humorous, too. He was good-looking, but not too obviously so, with an almost military haircut to his dark blonde hair, and a muscular, yet not over-trained build. Most important: He seemed to take her seriously and didn't smirk when she arrived in dungarees and a flannel shirt to discuss quarterly business with him. If she was honest to herself, just thinking of those meetings made her heart skip a beat and then race double the pace. Silly...

There was a knock on the door. None of her workers usually knocked. They rather burst through the door, especially on chilly mornings like these, to stand in front of the furnace or to help themselves to a mug of coffee or tea, while already throwing facts into her face. The knocking was for visitors from outside the wharf.

"Come in," Mathilda called friendly.

The door opened, and a woman pretty much Mathilda's age entered the container. "Good morning," Mathilda said friendly and business-like. "What can I do for you?"

Julie searched the woman's face with its big brown eyes, tiny nose, and full lips. Probably the secretary, she thought. "Mmmh ... I would like to talk to Mr. Barton or his son," she ventured.

Mathilda sighed. "There's neither nor. You want to talk to me. I'm Mathilda Barton."

"Oh," Julie said and blushed. She stroked an auburn strand of hair behind her ear. "I'm sorry. I had no idea. Well, I'm Julie Dolan from "The Sound Messenger", and I was wondering whether you'd have some time to talk to me, please."

Mathilda scanned the clock that hung on the wall across from her desk. "Might as well," she said. "But I only have a few minutes, as I'm expecting a customer soon."

"Oh, that's fine," Julie said breezily. "It won't take long."

"Please, have a seat," Mathilda offered. "Would you like a mug of coffee or tea?"

"Tea would be fine," Julie said, experienced with coffee standing too long on the burner of a percolator and simply tasting awful. She sat down on a swivel chair that had seen better days, but proved to be surprisingly comfortable.

Mathilda set a mug of hot water and a wrapped teabag in front of Julie. "Sugar?"

Julie shook her head and smiled. "No, thanks. This is just perfect on a morning like this." She unwrapped the teabag and dropped it into the mug. "I am researching some facts about wharves, and I was wondering whether you could help me with some background info."

Mathilda smiled vaguely. "Sure. I should hope so. What would you like to know?"

"What kind of maintenance and repair services do you offer?"

Mathilda started counting off her wharf's tasks, and every once in a while, Julie took some notes. It was an impressive list, and half of the terms were gibberish to Julie. She'd have to look them up. "Quite a few seem to involve chemicals, don't they?"

"Sure," Mathilda said friendly. "That's modern life for you. It makes a lot of things easier. And where does chemistry start anyhow?"

"Are there any hazardous substances you use in everyday work life around here? And if so, how do you protect your employees from them?"

Mathilda laughed. "You almost sound like the Health Department. But here you go. We use a lot of cleansers, solvents, and thinners, highly inflammable and acid liquids. Would you like to see?"

"Sure," Julie said.

Mathilda rose and led the way out of the container. "We have two locked storages. One contains all the original products." Julie followed Mathilda around and took care where she stepped. The grounds were uneven and dirty, and she was glad that she had decided against heels this morning, but rather chosen an old pair of sneakers. She peeked into one of the storage rooms and found everything in tidy order. "And then we have the storage room with all the hazardous waste," Mathilda said after locking up the storage room again and leading her towards another garage-like building. "Here's where we store the drums with all of those liquids that need to be discarded." Julie got a look into the room and saw a lot of blue plastic drums.

"How do you get all these liquids into the drums?" she asked.

Mathilda continued her tour around her wharf. She suddenly felt a special pride in her business. Everything was in order, looking spic and span. "My employees are wearing special suits and breathing masks when they work with hazardous liquids. Of course, we also have fire equipment in case anything goes wrong and we need to put out flames. And we do have a direct line to the Wycliff Fire Department and to the hospital. So far, we haven't needed any of these, as I see to it that our safety measures are up-to-date. I want my employees to feel secure."

Julie nodded. Mathilda seemed to be a very caring business person. Not like one of those people who sat in the office all day, sponging off their company without truly knowing what its business was about, but one who knew where was what and who was doing what at any time of the work process.

"We have special collection devices in which anything is ...," Mathilda laughed about her lack for words, "... well, collected. These are pumped out constantly, and the waste is gathered in drums such as those you have just seen."

Julie nodded. It made sense. "So you have all kinds of mixtures in those drums?"

"Can't be avoided. But as we are required to label the drums, any waste collection center will know how to deal with those."

"How often do you empty your storage room and get your hazardous waste drums to a collection center?" Julie wanted to know.

"About once a week," Mathilda said. "Last year's business was very slow, so we had a discard-on-demand policy with our partner. Made it easy for all of us, and cheaper too."

"May I ask who your partner is?"

"Sure," Mathilda smiled. "It's Harrison Disposal Center near Yelm. They have been working with us ever since my dad founded the wharf. – Anything else?" Mathilda had glimpsed the boat customer who wanted to talk to her about conditions for repairing a bilge pump on his 30-foot-yacht.

"No," Julie answered and smiled back. "That was awesome. Thank you!"

"If you have any more questions, you're welcome to call or come by any time during business hours. Just holler, so I'm sure to make time."

Julie thanked her profusely. "Let me give you this in exchange for your info. It's fresh off the press." She reached into her tote and handed Mathilda a brand-new edition of "The Sound Messenger".

"Haven't had time to get one yet," Mathilda appreciated the gift. She rolled the newspaper up in her hand, took leave from Julie, and approached her customer.

Hours later she sat at her desk, browsing the paper. She bit into her turkey salad sandwich and was just about to enjoy her quiet lunch hour when her eyes hit a smaller headline on the front page and she almost choked. Suddenly not all was right with the world anymore.

*

From "The Sound Messenger":

Mystery Drums Spill in Forest

***judo*. A dozen drums containing unknown toxic liquids were found in Wycliff Forest late Sunday afternoon. Police are investigating a related spill and had the area sealed off for further site cleansing. So far the drums' source is not clear.**

If it hadn't been for Wycliff citizen Thora Byrd walking her dog in Wycliff Forest yesterday afternoon, an illegal hazardous waste dump in Wycliff Forest might not even have been discovered in a long while. A short distance from a popular picnic area in a clearing, she spotted a dozen blue drums and noticed an acrid stench.

Closer inspection by the Police Department and experts, working as contractors for the Environmental Protection Agency (EPA), found that the drums contained cocktails of toxic liquids as they are used in the boating industry, e.g. ship building, repair, and maintenance.

"Unfortunately, we cannot trace the drums back to the source they came from," says Luke McMahon, Chief of the Wycliff Police Department (WPD). "The person or persons who deposited the drums made sure that the labeling on them was partially removed." According to him, the chemical substances contained by the drums were correctly stated on the labels, but the name and address of the source had been destroyed.

"This could mean that the original source is not even aware of anything illegal going on," said McMahon. "Yet we hope for co-operation from any business in the region using toxic liquids in bigger amounts." So far, the site has been closed off to the public, and cleansing measures have been started. EPA contractors would not make a statement as to the hazards that might ensue from the toxic spill, as neither the duration nor the exact depth of it have been confirmed yet.

WPD requests the citizens of Wycliff and anybody else to keep their eyes open for possibly more illegal hazardous waste dumps. It is not known for how long the drums have been lying in the clearing of Wycliff Forest nor how many similar sites there might be in the greater area. Citizens are being discouraged from getting close to such sites or to handle discarded drums themselves. In case of similar finds, please call WPD at phone number...

Chapter 2

The Green Maven's Tip of the Week:
To clean an oven, generously strew baking soda on the bottom of the oven and add vinegar. Let sit for some minutes, then wipe the mixture off. Repeat if necessary.

"The Sound Messenger" had its office on top of the bluff next to where the steps came up from Downtown. It was a plain, little white house with hanging baskets of blood-red geraniums, a tidy lawn, and a white picket fence with a small gate. It was also the publisher and editor-in-chief's home, which is why it looked more like a home than a business building.

John Minor had taken over the newspaper a decade ago and run it single-handedly until he had employed Julie Dolan a couple of years ago. He was known for his eclectic taste, and it always counted as a treat to get invited to his home. His small office held two heavy antique tables and a mahogany book shelf for his files. Otherwise it was as modern as need be with a PC, a printer, an express online-connection to the local printing house below the bluff, and a Keurig in case John had visitors – or he and Julie had a meeting as they did this morning.

"Anything new on your environmental story?" John Minor asked Julie as she sat opposite from him. It was Thursday, and Julie was checking the weekend calendar with her boss for appointments that she needed to put onto her agenda. As usual, John would take on anything cultural – an afternoon concert at Wycliff High, a photography opening night at Main Gallery, and a ballet matinee at Lawrence Hall, a venue that had been built by one of the town fathers back in the 1880s, hosting any event that might draw a regional crowd.

"Well, I have narrowed down the field to five companies in Wycliff who might be the drums' source," Julie said.

"Doing police work?" John asked slightly amused. "You sure you didn't miss your vocation?"

"Duh! You should see how dry my new step-dad's police reports read. I certainly wouldn't want to do such write-ups. Not for the life of me," Julie countered. "But I have to admit that I find it quite exciting to work alongside him in my little ways. People talk to me differently than they would to him."

"Which businesses did you go to? And what results do you have?"

"Well, I went to Wycliff Airfield, the Marina, the Boatbuilding part of the Maritime Center, the wharves, the car shops, and the gas stations. They were all pretty keen on showing me around and letting me look into their work stations and storage rooms. I told them I was writing an article for Earth Day."

"Does anybody know why there is only *one* Earth Day, by the way?" John asked. "Rhetorical question, of course."

"Of course. - Turns out, some businesses have special vehicles with tanks that kind of vacuum up the stuff, so the liquids never even go into anything like a barrel or a canister. Others have contracted special service companies who do this for them. And the gas stations are getting taken care of by their respective chain. Oh, and one business only uses yellow metal drums."

John nodded. "You were looking for blue plastic ones, of course."

"Exactly," Julie said. "I hope the lab results will be out by Friday. They promised to accelerate their work, as the contamination is so very near inhabited areas."

"Hear yourself speak, Julie," John warned her. "Please, see to it that you write it down in simpler language. We want everybody to understand your story, not just people with a college degree."

Julie blushed. She had obviously read up on too many scientific and environmental papers this week. Also, she had only discussed the case with Luke, whose "police speak" would have to be modified to newspaper language. Ah, the perks of meeting so many specialists in such a short time ...

"So will there be another story about the spill this week?"

"I should hope so," Julie said lightly. "It might be worthwhile considering a big space for the Saturday edition."

"Front page, of course," John teased.

Julie stayed serious and returned his stare. "Of course," she said.

*

Thora was standing in the cookie and candy aisle of "Dottie's Deli", the German store on Main Street in downtown Wycliff. She was comparing the ingredients of two packages of Bahlsen cookies and trying to make a decision.

"Why don't you take both?" a cheerful voice from behind tuned into her thoughts. "They will be gone pretty quickly anyhow. They are so delicious."

Thora laughed and turned around. Her friend Dottie, a few years older and a lot shorter than she, stood holding out a shopping basket to her. "Thanks," Thora said. "I'm getting these not for myself, but for a group of visitors our mayor is expecting this afternoon. And I'd also like a pound of your terrific German coffee."

"Sure," Dottie smiled. The tiny German store-owner had come to Wycliff a bit over three years ago, opened the store a year later, and conquered the hearts of her fellow citizens by storm with her cheerfulness, her business ideas, and – above all – the delicacies she sold. "You better also get hold of a few of the pretzels for your guests," she recommended." They are extra-crisp on the outside today, and they are selling quickly." Dottie had these flavorful pretzels delivered by Hess Bakery & Deli in Lakewood, who used traditional Southern German recipes for their delicious baked goods. After Dottie had introduced Wycliff to them, the town's foodies couldn't believe how they could ever have done without them. "May I ask who your guests will be?"

Thora frowned. "I don't know myself yet. I was only told that there would be five people coming for a conference, and that I was supposed to take notes. I've got no clue so far. Which is strange. Normally, Clark doesn't make a secret of whom he is expecting."

"Oh, I'm sure we'll all know soon enough," Dottie smiled.

Thora nodded. "I'm sure."

*

Peter Michaels was leaning his wiry, muscular body against his dark-gray Dodge RAM as he lit a cigarette and gazed into the flame of his lighter a bit longer before he let the button go. It was his first smoke after work hours, and that one tasted always the best. He inhaled the bitter, rich smoke deeply and enjoyed it a second time as he breathed it out. To hell with those people who held their rules above you everywhere. Wasn't the US the land of the free?! So he would smoke in public places as long as he felt free to do so.

One of the wharf workers passed by and nodded. He nodded back and spit. One of those family fathers who earned enough to rent a small house that grew smaller by the year, as his wife delivered baby after baby. Hadn't obviously heard of birth control. That guy was said to bring his own food for lunch breaks, too, and to roll his own cigarettes, as he insisted they tasted better. Hah, as if cheaper ever was better! Plus you got an extra chew on the tobacco leaves you hadn't tucked in tightly enough. Nasty. Peter spit once more. His longish brown hair flopped over his face, and he tore his hand through it to get it out of his eyes. Emerald green eyes. He squinted.

Another guy passed by. "Join me at the Harbor Pub later?" he called over.

"Nah," Peter responded lazily. "I need to gas up the truck and see my lady tonight. Haven't been with her in a couple of nights, and she gets kinda jealous."

"Give her a smack from me," the other guy teased. "Must be a hottie if you choose her over a beer."

"Nice enough ass," Peter commented. Then he realized that Mathilda Barton had locked her container door and was approaching across the wharf yard. He frowned. She had looked at him this morning as if she was in doubt about him. Maybe he was wrong. But his gut feeling told him that she was watching him more closely and critically this week than she had ever done before she had employed him half a year ago.

"Ma'am," he acknowledged her with a mock military salute.

"I hope you don't ever smoke near the drums," Mathilda said drily.

"Wouldn't dream of it," he replied.

"Good." Mathilda walked on, then she turned around again. "Tomorrow, I'd like to talk to you about the next transport. Come into my office at nine, please." She didn't expect an answer. She knew that she had been heard and that her words had been accepted as a work order.

"Yes, Ma'am," he mumbled and spit. He took another long drag of his cigarette. Then he tossed it to the ground and crushed it with his boot heel. He had suddenly lost the taste for his smoke. It was good to be his own employer. But some people seemed to think he was their slave rather than their service provider helping them get rid of their industrial waste.

Ah well, gas the car up and drive over to Lakewood. As soon as he would see Alice, he knew that the world became a better place. His girl was one of a kind. Pretty, though not as hot as the wharf boss. And almost clever, too. At least clever enough to keep the guys who wanted to get too near her at the fitness studio off her back. Not smart enough to know how to stop him from roving though. Every once in a while, Peter simply had to have some change. And he found it in a small dive near Towne Center, one that looked as if it were just a beer lounge, but had a willing extra-bartender or two.

Alice might know or not. She was clever enough not to make a scene. She knew she'd lose him if she kept him on too tight a leash. Maybe though she didn't even know about his little adventures, after all. His work – collecting hazardous waste from all kinds of businesses in the region and then discarding it at Harrison Disposal Center – made a splendid excuse for irregular hours, especially with those drives over to that place near Yelm.

But tonight he'd have some fun with Alice and let off steam. They might even barbeque some burgers. He'd down a few cans of beer – he'd found a new microbrewery nearby that also canned its strong drinks. They'd make a night of it, and tomorrow was tomorrow. His boss was probably just going to talk another change of schedule for delivering the next dozen of drums, as business was picking up and liquid waste was increasing weekly.

He still couldn't believe his good luck that he hadn't been recognized by anybody in Wycliff so far. True, he had left as a scrawny teenage boy. And look at what had become of him! His parents had been indulging him. Though later his mother had left his father. Maybe, because she couldn't stand life with him anymore. Definitely, because she couldn't bear what had become of their son. A small criminal, later a drug dealer and a robber. A few times he'd even shot some people who had gotten into his way. He had changed his name every once in a while, but always kept his initials, so he was able to use old signatures and what came with such things. He had grown his hair into a mullet, then cut it super-short. Now it had lost its shape entirely and hung in long strands around his head. When he was working, he sometimes wore a bandana around his brow to keep it from getting into his way. In a bad fist fight some years ago, somebody had smashed his nose, and it had grown together in a slanted way. And he wore emerald green contact lenses. A scar on his left cheek had also changed his looks.

He laughed mirthlessly. He was back home, and while the FBI were chasing him for various things they had on him in their files, he was making money where they least expected him to be. Good money that enabled him to have an apartment, a rather new Dodge RAM, plenty to eat, booze, and any girl he could charm into being with him. And sometimes a good snort of Blow. Of course, he had to be careful not to be found out, but as long as he could cash in checks – more than he earned in regular work, too – he was good. He would know how to make sure he wasn't found out. Sneaky little bitch of a journalist! What did she think, pestering Mathilda about the ways of the wharf?

*

Thora nodded friendly at the gentlemen who entered her town hall office punctually at five in the afternoon. She rose from her comfortable swivel chair, quickly saving her computer data and closing the window she had been working on. Though nothing was really secret in her document on screen, she didn't want anybody unauthorized to read it, while she was sitting in the conference room taking more notes.

"Mr. Thompson is expecting you," she smiled. "Would you please come with me?" She led the men out of her office, down a long hallway, and into a conference room that was overlooking the yacht harbor. Its furniture was modern, but heavy. A big screen was pulled down from the ceiling for a power point presentation, and on a sideboard there were pretzels, cookies, an icebox with sodas, and a couple of coffee jugs.

Mayor Thompson rose from his seat. He had chosen a chair that was facing the door rather than the window. He preferred it to have the light from behind and have it shine into other people's eyes. He knew that gave him a slight psychological advantage.

Clark Thompson was indeed a very handsome man. He was six feet tall and still slim for his mid-fifties. His eyes were deep blue, his features could be called aristocratic – though that would have bothered him, as he was certainly proud to come from a family who had fought the British in the Revolutionary War. His hair had whitened early in life;

he kept it neatly cut and combed back. Usually, he wore a sports coat and jeans into office when nothing formal was on the schedule. But today he had changed into a business suit and white shirt to underline the importance of the meeting.

Mayor Thompson started shaking hands and introducing his visitors to Thora. "Mr. Anvil Sr. from AnCoSafe Oil," he said.

The obvious leader of the group was a small, thick-set man with the face of a bulldog, even more so when he bared his teeth to smile at Thora. "How charming of you to grace our meeting with your presence," he snarled.

Thora had to suppress she didn't know was it an urge to laugh or to puke. Instead, she gave him her brightest smile. "Someone will have to take down notes on the important issues you are going to talk about, right?"

Another man, slightly taller and slightly slimmer, was – Thora had already suspected it – Mr. Anvil Jr., Senior's son. The other three rather colorless, very sober elderly men were part of the board of AnCoSafe Oil: Mr. Jefferson, Mr. White, and Mr. Gepetto. After everybody had found a seat, Thora quickly took down the names on a fresh note pad.

"First, I would like to thank you that you have traveled up the coast all the way from California to talk business with me," Mayor Thompson said. "If there is anything that might make your stay in Wycliff more comfortable, please let me know." The men acknowledged his words with curt, slight nods. "So far, my secretary is the only person I am drawing into our confidence. I simply would like to have 'ammunition' enough to shoot my points for our project in the next town hall meeting. I am pretty sure we will be able to convince everybody of the advantages of your company starting a branch here in Wycliff."

Thora looked at her boss expectantly. When would he let the cat out of the bag and explain what this was all about?

"Maybe we could watch your presentation first, before I start peppering you with questions." Mayor Thompson leaned back in his chair comfortably as Thora got up to close the blinds, and Mr. Anvil Jr. slipped a DVD into his presentation lap top. Thora switched off the light, and the disc started whirring before it opened on the logo of an anvil above which a yellow drop was hovering – AnCoSafe Oil. Then some classical music started playing as the camera flew over a rainforest towards an oil platform in the ocean.

"Millions of years ago, the resources for our modern world were created," a male voice droned into the silence. "The primeval forests of yore turned into what keeps our nation running a step ahead of everybody else." Here the film switched into mind-blowing speed as it showed stills of chemical labs, cars, medicine bottles, cosmetic jars, plastic toys, fabric, and a flame burning in a brass ship lantern.

Now the camera zoomed in on a drilling platform. To make everything more authentic you could see the shadow of the helicopter grow bigger as it was flying lower and lower. Helmeted workers were watching the landing as the voice went on. "For three generations, AnCoSafe Oil has been working offshore drilling operations with the most current equipment in the market. Specialists control the environmental friendliness of the process. For every thousand gallons pumped up from under the sea, AnCoSafe Oil donates shares to environmental projects."

Thora almost coughed up her coffee. Clark threw her a questioning look. Thora blushed and concentrated on the film again.

"... healthy food for the workers produced in greenhouses that are operated on the platform with AnCoSafe Oil. So are the restaurants at AnCoSafe Oil refineries on shore." Here the camera clipped into a buffet that could have been anywhere, except the eaters all wore working clothes and helmets. The latter didn't make sense to Thora, but she presumed that it was to show that the restaurant was really on a work site.

"AnCoSafe Oil refineries are your clean neighbor next door who helps you get your oil cheaper. Because we can be right where you need us. Next to your airfield or your ferry terminal, next door to your manufacturing company or whatever else you need us for. We provide work places for you, and we train specialists with a safe vocational future. AnCoSafe Oil is the neighbor who sources your oil for your well-being. Choose AnCoSafe Oil!"

A happy family was shown - the mother harvesting tomatoes from a green house, the kids riding on plastic toy cars and tractors as the father was waving from the garden gate, dressed in an oily overall and a helmet. The sun was transforming into an oil drop hovering above the now happily united family fading into an anvil.

Thora was speechless. Not that she was expected to say anything. After all, she was only meant to write down what was being said. She knew advertising language when she saw it. She never fell for any of it. Actually, she had been raised on the principle that "If a product needs advertising, you don't need it". Thora was glad she was able to turn her back on their guests for a moment as she opened the blinds again.

"Wonderful," she heard Mayor Thompson say. "Now let us talk what those refineries look like. How much space would you need? How many workers would you be able to employ?" He added another question and another. He must have been thinking over that project for a long time. It turned out he wanted to have the refinery at the fringe of Downtown near the ferry terminal. They would have an extra railway depot for the delivery of crude oil. And Wycliff might be able to build a passenger station right outside the refinery premises and enjoy the perks of an AmTrak connection. AnCoSafe Oil would certainly support such a venture.

Thora scribbled hectically, wondering whether she'd be able to decipher her own code later on. Numbers flew around her head. She had a tough time keeping in step with the discussion. The men were clearly oblivious of her. They talked all the advantages a refinery would have for Wycliff. The ferries would be maintained and tanked in Wycliff in the future, which would save them time and cost and entail more business for the local population. Gas could also be delivered to the local gas stations, provided they were willing and able to cancel their contracts and become AnCoSafe Oil gas stations. There would be work places not just for oil specialists, but also for janitors, kitchen personnel, and guards. Even the Wycliff Fire Department would have to stock up on personnel. So might a special burn unit at the hospital. Thora shuddered at the thought.

"In short," Mayor Thompson summarized with enthusiasm, "this would put Wycliff on the map. Not just as a South Puget Sound tourist destination, but as a town capable of serious business. We'd attract people who are looking for jobs, a true blessing in these days."

Small talk began to ensue. The men joked about all kinds of topics, firing each other up over the project they were intent on setting up together. Thora busied herself with refilling cups, offering more cookies and pretzels, and handing the guests Wycliff souvenirs - mugs with the silhouette of Wycliff Light (which was a landmark, but automated these days), golfing visors (left-overs from the last regional competition at Wycliff Golf Course), and Wycliff Pebbles, a lavender-candied chocolate specialty created by the newly founded Lavender Café on Back Row.

It was about two hours later when Mayor Clark Thompson accompanied his guests to the town hall foyer and unlocked the heavy doors for them. Thora was cleaning up the conference room when he returned, enthusiasm all over his face. He was rubbing his hands. Thora evaded eye contact.

"Now, what do you think? Isn't this splendid?!"

Thora took a deep breath, then she looked him into the face. "You simply cannot be serious about this," she stated calmly.

Clark looked at her full of bewilderment. "But then – why didn't you say anything?"

"It wouldn't have been my place," Thora replied. "I was just the secretary taking notes."

"Yes, but I thought we were telling each other what we thought about town projects."

Thora looked at him sadly. "I had thought so, too, Clark. Until you burst this one on me. And I'm not sure you really want to know my thoughts." She wrapped up some left-over pretzels and offered them to him. "Want those?"

He shook his head and looked at her as if he didn't understand what she had implied. "You enjoy them!" he said.

"I'm not sure about that," Thora said.

*

Thora was sitting on a big boulder on the beach below her cottage, watching Bear run happily after the softly lapping waves. What had happened to Clark to come up with the terrible idea to build a refinery in Wycliff and thereby destroying the entire vibe of this beautiful Victorian town? She was totally bewildered. This was an undertaking that sounded so unlike the Clark Thompson she knew. But then – how much did she know about him?

She knew that Clark had been born in Wycliff, had studied law, and settled as a lawyer in his home town. Thora also knew that he was living in the home of his childhood and that he had brothers and sisters, some little nieces, and a few nephews. He had met his late wife, Vicky, at the Wycliff Golf Course, but then things became rumors and hearsay. Nasty ones about her having been an alcoholic. Thora preferred sticking to facts. And those facts were that the couple had stayed without children. A few years into their marriage, on a Christmas Eve, Vicky had died in a car accident through no fault of hers. Only the week before, Clark had been elected into office as the new mayor. Clark had taken up his task as if unshaken, but he had never remarried.

He rarely mentioned Vicky to anybody. Thora knew that he still had a picture of hers in his town hall office.

She had once caught him looking at it. As soon as Clark had realized he wasn't alone, he had slid the frame into his desk drawer and shoved it closed.

Thora really liked Clark. He was a kindly boss and usually very clear-headed. Under his leadership, Wycliff had blossomed into the popular tourist destination it was now. He was liked by almost everybody in town, and most town council members found his suggestions and ideas well-founded and helpful. Clark was also very charming. Thora sighed. He was certainly one of the most handsome men she had met in her life. But, of course, as her boss he was off limits.

Bear ran towards her, his fur all salty wetness. He stood right in front of her, panting and – if dogs can do this – grinning. Then he shook his coat extensively until Thora was wet.

"Bear!" she scolded. "You naughty, naughty dog!"

He whined and clamped his tail between his hind legs. But half a second later he grinned again, then ran off to search for something that would make Thora play "Fetch" with him. Thora sighed once more. She felt really uncomfortable in the fresh evening breeze now, but Bear needed the workout. So she indulged him for a while, throwing the stick he'd found and laid at her feet. As the sun vanished behind the summits of the Olympic Mountains, she called Bear and walked back to her cozy cottage.

She loved her home, though she would need to put a lot of work into it yet to make it look really good. The walls needed a coat of paint. So did the deck. She wanted to plant some boxes out of reach from the deer. And she wanted to set up a greenhouse to grow her own berries, herbs, and vegetables. The roof needed to be cleaned of a winter's layer of moss. And the windows could surely do with a washing. She intended to put new hardwood floors in the kitchen and the dining area. And she needed a new shelf for her reading nook.

Ah, that nook. It had been one of the reasons she had bought the cottage. It was a deep bay window with a view across the Sound. Thora frowned. If Clark's dream of a refinery came true, the starry nights on the Sound would have seen their last, soaked in the illumination of a large plant that would be working night and day.

*

Clark Thompson had closed up his office and walked up Main Street. He had hardly eaten any of the food that Thora had laid out during the meeting. Not because he didn't like it. For who didn't like German baked goods?! He had been way too excited about the facts he was able to gather for his presentation to the town council the following week.

But Thora's reaction had quite dampened his mood. What didn't she like about a company that obviously would bring so many working places, taxes, and benefits to the community? They even sponsored environmental projects, which must be totally in Thora's line.

As Clark strode towards "Le Quartier", the little bistro restaurant next to "Dottie's Deli", he was greeted by a few Wycliffians, but he nodded only absent-mindedly. He sensed that Thora had felt insulted, but couldn't fathom why or how. Maybe a glass of that wonderful Viognier that the young bistro team was serving lately might help clear his thoughts about his secretary. Accompanied by an appetizer, that might be just the right thing to lift his spirits.

But as he sat in his favorite niche at "Le Quartier", the table decorated tastefully with a cluster of whitish-pink rhododendron blossoms and a white candle in a candle jar, courtesy of "The Flower Bower", he found that his wine tasted sour. And the escargots in herb butter felt as chewy as the slices of baguette tasted like saw dust. Of course, he knew that the wine and food were really exquisite as always. Tonight he simply found he had lost his appetite. And he knew the reason were Thora's sad and upset huge eyes.

Véronique, the French-Canadian slash Swedish co-owner of the bistro restaurant and tonight's host, realized that Clark sat at his table a bit forlorn and approached him. "Is everything alright with your order?" she asked carefully.

Clark looked up and felt guilty. "I find it delicious," he lied.

Véronique smiled at him impishly. "Not true, Mr. Thompson. Our food never has people look sad for long. So you obviously don't have a taste for it tonight. But I tell you what. Christian and Paul have cooked up a specialty today which they intend to put on the menu next week. Let me talk to them and send you an amuse bouche – I'm sure your mood will lift immediately."

Clark blushed a little that she had been able to see through his fake enthusiasm. He gratefully looked at the pretty, young blonde and raised his arms in surrender. She laughed. "I guess that's a yes." She turned with a charming little swing to her skirt and walked swiftly to the kitchen window. A couple of minutes later, she stood in front of him again, holding a cappuccino cup on a saucer. Something hot and fragrant wafted into the air, and despite his lack of appetite Clark's mouth began to water.

"I knew it would work," Véronique exclaimed happily and set down the cup with a crisp cheese puff pastry cookie on the saucer. "Bon appétit," she said and left Clark to his thoughts again. Curiously he lifted his cup and breathed in the spicy, pungent steam that rose from it. Then he carefully placed his lips on the rim. "Le Quartier" was known for European-style hot soups and stews, fresh from the kettle. Nothing ever left their kitchen lukewarm.

"Ah," he smacked his lips after he had swallowed some of the concoction. He tasted beef and actually even had a tad of meat between his teeth. The flavor lingered warm around his taste buds, a mix of sherry and bay leaf, a bit of onion, celery maybe, and a pinch of pepper. It was light, it was playful, it was drawing him in. It seduced him to want more.

"Oxtail clair," Véronique explained in passing by, her smile even more impish. "I see it helps already."

Clark smiled back and slightly waved his cookie at her. "You are magicians, all of you!"

He actually felt his mood rise after this and enjoyed the rest of his snails in herb butter after all. Still, he wondered whether he had somehow brushed against Thora's grain.

She had hinted that she was utterly surprised by his plan. But it was not a mayor's duty to inform his secretary about his ideas or plans. Nor to ask her about her opinion about them. Wait! That sounded so not like himself. Actually, Thora Byrd had become so much more than a mere town hall employee with dedication to everything she did. Not only did he admire her prettiness and her straightforwardness. She had become a confidante in many things, if not his non-existing private life. She always knew when he needed a special item to be dealt with first, when he needed quiet, or when he was in a talkative mood, but didn't want word to leave the office.

Yes, he should have talked to Thora about his ideas before the meeting, just as he usually sought her out when it came to a meeting with strangers. Or when his former mother-in-law had died and he was not sure how to react properly, as he hadn't seen his father-in-law in a decade. Thora was always honest with him. So why hadn't he let her in on this one? Because he secretly feared she might disapprove? But what was there to disapprove of?!

And after all, why did he care so much? This was a truth Clark had been prancing around like the proverbial cat on the hot tin-roof. He couldn't imagine the office with any other secretary. He couldn't imagine talking about his most private thoughts, few as they were, with any other woman or – make it more general – any other person than her. In short, he knew he was falling in love with Thora more and more every day, and he knew it was not appropriate. He looked at her and felt his fifty-something heart skip a beat and then race as if he were a teenager. But it was simply not done. He was her boss. He couldn't take advantage of her. Besides, would she return his feelings at all?

So, yes, as a mayor he had done all the right things. As a friend and someone who quietly loved Thora he had done her wrong. Actually worse. He had managed to hurt her by not trusting her enough. That must be the clue. He would try to make it up. She would look at him with a smile in her beautiful eyes again.

*

Daniel Harrison was sitting in his office at Harrison Disposal Center, rubbing his temples. He ignored the views across the beautiful prairies of Yelm and the snow-white gleam of Mt. Rainier. He couldn't see any of his yard from his desk without getting up. It was a puristic, but warmly furnished office with big windows, comfortable chairs and arm chairs, and an air of "groundedness". He had a migraine coming on, and not just because there was obviously a change in the weather forecast over the next 72 hours. His business was declining. Not in a foreseeable way. Not in a remarkable way. But somehow steadily. Though with the beginning of the boating season there should have been a slight plus. He couldn't make out the reason. Maybe the wharves were picking up more slowly than usual. He'd have to ask Mathilda Barton.

He smiled to himself. Ever since Mathilda had taken over the wharf business from her dad, he had been looking forward to their monthly meetings. Her dad had been nice enough, for sure. But Mathilda had this charm, this look, this voice. She was all business. She was all woman. And she seemed unaware of either. When she came to talk about schedules, extra conditions, better labeling, or new laws, he gladly pushed off any other appointments and had someone bring in doughnuts and coffee from Dunkin' Donuts. He assumed she liked sweets, and he knew that many people said that the Dunkin' Donuts coffee was special. They didn't have any Olympic Beans coffee shops around Yelm yet. He usually scheduled meetings with her in the late afternoon so he could invite her out for dinner. But so far he had lacked the courage to do so.

He stared at the books Mr. Teal had brought him in earlier. He looked at the numbers, and they looked good. But he knew that his bank spoke differently. They had only sent him his monthly records this morning. He was flustered. He knew that his bank didn't err. He saw that every single check was noted down in his books. Daniel rose from his chair and walked over to the window that overlooked the yard. Some of his employees helped unload a truck. Others were pumping out a tank. It seemed as busy as it should be.

Well, he'd surely look at the books again and then talk to the bank and to Mr. Teal. Bummer, this was no perspective to offer to Mathilda. He wouldn't ask her for a real date as long as he couldn't offer her better than this. Mathilda …

*

Another man was thinking of Mathilda at this moment – Trevor Jones, the attorney. After Kitty Kittrick from "The Flower Bower" had turned him down, he had suffered in silence for a few months. He knew it had been his fault that he hadn't stood up in her behalf against his mother, who thought a relationship with a "shop girl" was beneath their family honor. And he hadn't shut up a socialite who had been publicly ridiculing Kitty and her now fiancé Eli Hayes with his little daughter Holly. Sure, they were still friends, as he had finally shown some backbone, rescuing Holly from her mother's kidnapping and restoring her to her father's custody for good. But he was still missing the times with Kitty. Or, maybe, as a man slowly approaching his thirties he simply missed dating a woman in general these days?

Trevor Jones lost himself in a little daydream about Mathilda. He had helped her with a lot of legal advice when her father had handed over the wharf business to her. She had sat in his office, reading endless contracts and changes in the will. He had been to her container office only once. It had been chilly and uncomfortable in there. After that he had made sure the appointments with her were in his Uptown office. That workplace was part of his parents' home, facing away from the panoramic view. Maybe that had been intentional when the first Joneses had opened their law firm. The view would have been too distracting – and earning money came from working hard and successfully, not from having a vista. Trevor's office was similar in size to Mathilda's, but it was so much more comfortable.

Mathilda had seemed a little awed about entering the Victorian mansion at first. But Trevor had charmed her and made her laugh. He had set her at ease, and they had celebrated the handing over of the keys and the final signatures with a nice business dinner at "Le Quartier". Trevor couldn't even remember what the town had done before that beautiful and innovative bistro had opened its door. They obviously had all gone for the heavy fare of the Harbor Pub with its burgers, chowders, and sandwiches. Or to the slightly more elegant food of "The Ship Hotel" with an additional, equally high-caloric fish and steak menu. The dinner at "Le Quartier" had been relaxed and friendly, but Trevor had failed to invite Mathilda there ever since. Or anywhere else, come to think of it.

"Found the papers you were looking for?" His father popped his head into his office. James Jones was proud of his son's capabilities as a lawyer. And he was glad that Trevor had somehow managed to escape both, a relationship with flower shop manager Kitty Kittrick as well as one with that uppity Seattle lawyer Patricia Carson, whom his wife, Theodora, had wished for as a daughter-in-law and actually almost managed to put in place. His son deserved better. He knew that Trevor was far from perfect. Well, maybe he just needed to be a bit more robust and learn how to stand up for anybody he felt close to. Women still secretly dreamed of a hero and prince in their lives, didn't they? Trevor had it all – blue eyes, blond hair, and charming dimples at the corners of his mouth, a good job, an honest mind, a future. The only thing he was lacking was chutzpa sometimes. But he was still young. He'd learn.

"I hope the paperwork will help you, Dad," Trevor said, as he handed over a file. "Mathilda Barton's case was probably a bit less complex than the one you are working on though."

James smirked. "When brothers and sisters fight over inheritances, it always gets a bit nasty. Even for the lawyer who manages to settle the case. That's why I consider our fees as compensation for personal suffering." He was about to close the door again.

"Dad?" Trevor ventured.

"Hm?"

"Is there any paragraph that says a lawyer cannot date a former client?"

"Not that I know of," James Jones said. Then he paused. "But there is always the Theodora book of law…"

*

Thora had dressed with special care for the town council meeting. She always did this. More often than not they had guests from out of town. And sometimes they even had people from Wycliff sitting in on the public part of a session. "The Sound Messenger" also usually turned up and produced an article for the next day, sometimes longer, sometimes shorter, depending on the contents of the meeting. Thora felt she was co-representing the town of Wycliff, even in her very unobtrusive role as the note taker.

Tonight, she was sure Clark Thompson would introduce the town council to his latest idea in making Wycliff even more progressive. Thora wasn't sure what the town counsellors would say. She was very apprehensive that some of them would get sold on the idea from the first.

There would also be environmentally aware people. But would they have arguments ready against building an oil refinery near downtown Wycliff? And then there would be those who were undecided and who could and would be swayed either by considering their own popularity or by their desire to make history. They were the unknown factor in this equation. Plus there was the new member, a doctor. She had no idea what his mindset would be. She liked his quiet ways, and she admired the diplomacy he had revealed in the two meetings he had participated in so far. His name was unusual, and he must have roots at some place in Asia with his dark hair and milk-coffee colored skin. India or Pakistan was her guess. His English was without any other than a Washingtonian accent, by the way. Which made Thora very curious about his story. But that was not her business at all, she reminded herself.

She would be sitting there, taking notes. As a secretary she was not entitled to utter an opinion. Discussing the refinery would be the task of the counsellors and the mayor. Would Clark come to his senses when somebody, anybody spoke to him about the negative consequences the project he aspired would have on Wycliff and surroundings? On the people as well as on nature?

Bear sat by the cottage door and was breathing heavily as she was about to leave for the meeting. He pressed his head against her thigh, and she gave his head a last good rub. "I'll be back soon, boy," she said. "Wish this meeting were already over and I knew where we are standing." Bear whined and woofed shortly, then he laid down next to the doorway. Thora smiled. It was so good to know that her puppy would be waiting for her when she came back. Bear's true affection had become an anchor in her life.

*

Clark Thompson sat in his office, shifting papers, feeling antsy. Tonight he would introduce AnCoSafe Oil's offers to Wycliff. He knew he'd have to make his arguments as transparent as possible. They must be understood by all of the citizens later, and he wanted as many counsellors as possible on his side in this. Nobody should be able to claim later that he had blindsided them by not telling them everything he knew. And he needed to lay enough enthusiasm into his suggestion to make others catch on. Or should he be very unemotional instead? Because he was only putting out an idea?

He wished Thora was in his office now, so they could discuss the way he should present the project. Instead, she would enter the big conference room on the second floor probably just in time for the meeting's beginning. Not, as usual, with a few minutes to spare for him. Normally, she would check that he had all he needed at hand. Normally, she would tell him whether his tie sat straight and that he would do a great job as always.

Clark sighed. A few more minutes and he would face his town council. They came of all kinds of occupations in Wycliff. James Jones, the attorney, was one of them, a member he could pretty much always count on having his back. Walter May, retired army, a rather humorless, but thorough man who was straightforward and to the point. Bill "Chirpy" Smith was apparently representing retail, although his interests went far beyond downtown business. Philip Nouveau was a firefighter and senior high school football coach, a conservative, but open-minded youngish man, widely popular amongst the Wycliffians. And then there was Dr. Ajith Katkar, MD, a town doctor who also practiced at the hospital one day a week, usually Sundays. He was still quite new in town and had been voted in to represent the hospital. Sometimes Clark wondered whether he wasn't also the fig leaf of political correctness towards ethnic minorities. He didn't know much about Dr. Katkar, as the doctor was a very private person. But he had found him to be meticulous, conscientious, with a fine sense of humor, and a wide knowledge of philosophy.

Clark threw a quick glance towards the clock. Time to go and present his proposal. Later he'd make some time for Julie Dolan from "The Sound Messenger", as she might have some questions as to facts and motivations about building a refinery. He knew she'd write a well-founded article without any personal evaluation. Something that might help him get the right vibe out to his fellow citizens.

Also, Clark hoped that he might catch Thora after the meeting and talk to her. Why did he realize only now that she was so much more to him than his secretary? And that he missed her voice and her thoughtfulness?

*

From "The Sound Messenger":

Secretary Quits over Controversial Industry Plans

judo. **Yesterday's monthly town council meeting at Wycliff town hall ended with an éclat. Secretary Thora Byrd handed in notice after a heated discussion amongst the council members about the building of an oil refinery in the vicinity of the ferry terminal (see text box below).**

The town of Wycliff might become the location of another oil refinery in the South Puget Sound region. Mayor Clark Thompson proposed a contract with national company AnCoSafe Oil, which would translate to refining crude oil, but also to distributing the finished products and to fueling the Wycliff ferries. Thompson emphasized the assets to the Wycliff economy such as an increase in jobs, a financial upsurge of the construction industry, and a direct connection with the national railway system, as a harbor depot for crude oil transports would also give room to a passenger station outside the refinery.

Town counsellor Bill "Chirpy" Smith instantly vetoed the proposition, reminding his fellow counsellors of environmental risks. Counsellor Walter May held against him that the abundance of safety measures in the modern oil industry would prevent any incidents. The debate ended after more than an hour in an aggravated stalemate. New council member Dr. Ajith Katkar requested to adjourn the meeting, as they had all been surprised by the unforeseen project and needed to do their homework on refineries and their impact – positive and negative, as he stressed – on communities.

At this point, town hall secretary Thora Byrd rose and announced that she would hand in notice with immediate effect. As a reason she indicated the incongruity of supporting work on a refinery proposal with her conscience as an environmentalist. She further announced that she would start rallying against the plans and intended to get an information campaign under way, "including marches to the state governor if necessary". Mayor Clark Thompson didn't want to comment on this development. (...)

CHAPTER 3

The Green Maven's Tip of the Week:
Apply your used coffee grounds as fertilizer to roses,
rhododendrons, azaleas, and other plants. Wait until
the grounds are cooled off. Then pour them around
the plants, and slightly mix them with the soil.

"Oh Bear, what have I done?!" Thora moaned from her pillows as she opened her eyes to her tail-wagging friend. Bear was standing next to her bed, starting to nuzzle her right hand, and Thora couldn't help but laugh. "Your mistress got herself into an emotional ditch. And you will have to bear the consequences with her."

Bear whimpered. He seemed to know that Thora was upset about something. He turned around and went to his dog basket. When he returned, he had a well chewed-on, but still recognizable teddy bear between his flews. He offered it to Thora. For a moment she looked at him. Then he became somewhat blurry, because Thora was tearing up. "Oh Bear, my Bear! You know, I'd love to hug you right now if I didn't know that it would freak you out. But you are the best doggie ever. And you deserve a treat for giving me such comfort."

Bear obviously only understood "treat" for his tail started thumping the floor in expectation. "Okay," Thora laughed, wiping away her tears. "You got me there. Now I'll have to get up. How about one of those nice crunchy, crumbly dog cookies that I bought at the Farmers Market the other day? You like that?" Bear wagged an affirmative, at which Thora tossed her cover aside and flung herself out of her comfy Queen-size bed to cross the room barefoot. "What?" she looked back at Bear, who was still sitting there, the teddy at his front paws. "No treat? Come on!" Bear grabbed the teddy between his teeth and almost ran her over in order to reach the kitchen and his doggie bowl.

While Bear was chewing on his cookie and Thora was eating her cornflakes doused with Greek yoghurt and home-made strawberry jam, her thoughts wandered off. This time yesterday, she had had a job with benefits. Today, she found herself all on her own. No more salary. No future insurances after the paid-for quarter ran out. No way to pay off her mortgage. With Bear to care for into the bargain.

Had she really been that stupid to toss in her own fate because of a refinery that might yet be built in spite of the efforts she would make to avert that project? Was her conscience worth risking her livelihood and even as much as her creature comforts? How many other Wycliffians would side with her and protest their town becoming an industrial center? Who would give her a job she felt qualified for? One that set her life straight again?

A knock on her front door roused Thora from her thoughts. Who was coming at this early hour? Bear padded over to the door, wagging his tail. Then he barked.

"Shhh, Bear," Thora soothed him and shoved him aside to open the door. On the patio stood Clark Thompson, looking slightly sheepish. He was in jeans and a faded T-shirt, just like so many other men on their time off.

"Good morning, Thora," he said meekly.

"Good morning, Clark,' she said somewhat coldly. "You're up early."

He nodded. "Couldn't sleep really well after what happened yesterday. You resigning and all."

"I guess I should say I'm sorry about that," Thora replied. "But the fact is that I'm not. I'm certainly sticking with my decision."

The hopeful look in his eyes disappeared. "Listen, Thora. May I come in and talk to you? As we always used to? As friends?"

Thora frowned. "My friendship for you has nothing to do with sticking with my resignation. I thought you knew that much. But come in anyway." She held the door open for him. "Want some coffee?"

"I could do with some," Clark admitted. "The walk from home over here has quite chilled me. The wind is nippy."

"You walked?!" Thora said, taken by surprise. "That's quite some early morning activity!"

"Should do it more often," he said with an almost mischievous grin. "It's not bad when you're sitting down with a friend afterwards to chat about this and that."

Thora busied herself with the percolator and a bag of ground coffee. "You know you really hurt me," she scolded him, but her voice was soft. "You usually let me in on all of your projects. You even used to ask for my opinion. As a friend, I supposed, not in my position as your secretary, of course. This time you simply clammed up and expected me to go along with you all the way. But I'm an environmentalist."

"Maybe that is why I didn't dare talk to you," Clark said. "I knew that you would question the motives I have for setting up a refinery in the first place."

Thora rubbed her neck. "You know, I understand part of the plan. The one that means jobs and taxes. But this is not all. We are living in a world that gets endangered because more and more people are living 'the good life' every day. Those who experience it for the first time, second-world countries or people on the rise, are not ready to give up on things. Imagine somebody getting their first car. Or flying for the first time. Or whatever luxury has become such a part of everyday life in our part of the world. Well, in the western world we are well informed about the destructive consequences of such a lifestyle. And it's about time that we act accordingly. Wycliff has it all … even without a refinery."

Clark nodded pensively. "Pretty idealistic, don't you think?"

Thora blushed with anger. "You know what, Clark? Maybe I am idealistic. Why don't you call me emotional and naïve, too? I don't give a fig. But I want this world to survive for a little longer. Sea stars are already dying in the Sound, and the salmon run last spring was awfully low. They say that blue fin tuna will soon be extinct off our Pacific shore. And once the life in the sea is gone, life in the air and on the ground will be badly impacted as well. I'm not willing for this to happen. And I'll put up the fight against a refinery near such a sensitive eco system."

Clark hid his eyes behind one hand, then slowly looked up again. "Sorry that I rubbed you all wrong again. I really am. Here I've come to make peace, and look how I got to you without intention. I guess I'd better be leaving." He rose.

"Stay!" Thora said firmly. "I made you a cup of coffee. Now have it." She placed it in front of him.

Clark sighed. 'What will you do without the job at town hall, Thora? Have you thought about that? Is there really no way of getting you back?"

Thora shook her head and sat down. "I don't know right now." Bear pressed his head onto her thigh and she stroked his brow. "It won't be easy to find any job at all around here. Maybe I will come up with an idea. Maybe

I'll just take up enough odd jobs to tide me over..." Her voice faded.

"Listen, Thora," Clark gulped down a sip of his hot, bitter brew. "I know we are not on the same page in the refinery business. But I still consider myself as your friend. So if there is anything I can help you with, let me know, okay?"

Thora shrugged her shoulders and gave him a wan smile. "Sure. Thank you. Something will come up though, I'm sure."

Clark rose, chugging the rest of his coffee. He gave her a half-hug, patted Bear on the head, and went for the door. "See you soon, Thora. I'll look out for you."

The door closed behind him, and Thora looked at his empty cup. "I'm not sure what to make of this," she said finally. "Do you, Bear?"

*

John Minor was staring at a letter he had received this noon. It consisted of a single sheet of letter-sized paper, covered with singly cut out newspaper words that shaped the short text directed to him: "John Minor, stop digging into the drum story. If not, we will out your sexual preferences."

The envelope had no return address, of course. And his address was type-written. The stamp was from the post office in Wycliff though. A hint that one of the employees there had manually stamped it, not the stamping machine letters ran through usually. So the sender might be a fellow Wycliffian. Or an employee in Wycliff.

John sighed. When he had started as a journalist with a big Seattle newspaper, some of his more conservative colleagues had made sure to make his life hell as soon as they had suspected he was gay. They had whispered behind his back, some not even low enough for him not to overhear. His bosses hadn't intervened. He had been searching for a way to live with his sexual orientation for a long time. But he had found it to be tough. He was not the kind of gay man who participated in rainbow parades or visited clubs. He hadn't even ever outed himself to his mother. She had somehow known quite early though and, rather than be estranged, accepted him as he was without lamenting.

As luck would have it, one day he had found "The Sound Messenger" for sale. He had grabbed the chance, walked out of the Seattle office, and moved to Wycliff. Here he had been leading a quiet and peaceful life as the only newspaper staff until young Julie Dolan had rushed into his life. At first he hadn't been enthusiastic at all to let her in on his enterprise. Or into his beautiful office in his quaint home. He was a reclusive person, after all. But Julie hadn't taken his "no" for a no. He had to admit that he was glad now she was on board his newspaper. She might be a bit complicated as a person. But she had brought truly good articles from the beginning. A couple of years ago, her series about the Victorian Christmas event that had almost failed because of some fraud had been a genius stroke for the circulation of "The Sound Messenger".

John sighed again and stared at the paper.

"Bad news?"

He looked up and saw Julie leaning in the doorway. He hadn't even heard her enter the house. "Here," he said and held out the blackmailing letter to her.

Julie read the lines and frowned. "What will you do?"

"Don't you even ask whether it's true that I'm gay?"

"I don't think it's my business what's going on in your private life unless you say differently. Do I care whether you like men or women? No. Do I care when someone blackmails you? Yes."

John smiled at the young and eager face across from his desk. "Thank you, Julie. - Yes, I am gay. And no, I won't stop digging into a story that needs to be covered for the better of our community. But I won't let anybody else do my outing for me. Do you have more on the drum story?" Julie nodded. "Fine. Then, please, place a textbox placeholder into the page lay-out. I'll have something to say to the people of Wycliff."

Julie's right hand flew to her mouth. "But this is so utterly unfair!"

"Whoever claimed Life was about anything being fair? I didn't even have a choice to be gay or straight. And who in their right mind would *choose* to be gay in the first place, as we get discriminated against by so many who still think we had made a wicked choice and believe we should either forego love or simply become straight again."

Julie's eyes filled with tears. "I'm sorry," she whispered. "It must be so tough …"

John gave her a lopsided smile. "It helps a bit to be able to talk to somebody whom I appreciate not just for her splendid work, but also as a confidante."

Julie blushed. "I won't let you down, John. Promised."

*

The post office on Back Row was slowly quieting down. The shadow of the bluff had fallen across the street early in the afternoon. Now the neon lights were switched on inside, and one of them was flickering nervously, while humming discernibly.

"Maybe, we all can go home early today," Gary joked with one of the customers in front of his counter. "I can hardly make out the address on your letter in this light. Or maybe it's just that calligraphy of yours?" Gary and his colleague Arnie usually worked the post office in Steilacoom, but they had rotated schedules with the Wycliff staff for a couple of weeks. Their place was filled in by another colleague. Postal services rotated staff sometimes for the sake of staff vacations.

But whereas the people of Steilacoom very much appreciated the jokes and puns that the two postal employees came up with, the old lady standing in front of Gary right now was not amused. Her hair was an almost incredible shade of ruby-red, and the rhinestone top she wore with her tight leggings would have looked out of place even on a woman half her age. Her face looked as if she had bitten into an extra-sour lemon. "It is amazing somebody like you is able to read at all," she hissed. "Now sell me the stamp for this, Mister, and don't steal my time with your impertinence."

Arnie, who had been ready to add to the fun and to include the young Asian in front of his counter into the joke, swallowed down his remark and rolled his big brown eyes. Gary just tossed him a look and went about his work in silence. Finally, the woman turned her back and left.

"Was I really that bad?" Gary asked the next person in line, who happened to be Julie Dolan.

Julie shrugged her shoulder. "No matter what you do, you'll never get the approval of Angela Fortescue."

"Oooh, that even rhymes, though probably without a reason," Arnie called over, and Julie had to laugh.

"But you need to work on the number of syllables to your lines yet," Gary added. "It sounded awfully bumpy."

"You are really something, the two of you," Julie exclaimed. "Do you always have an answer to everything?"

"Unless someone calls us impertinent," Arnie admitted.

"Big word for a small joke," Gary countered. "And what disservice may I serve you with today?"

Julie shoved an envelope across the counter. "Do you by any chance remember who brought this here to send it off?"

Gary threw a short look at it. "When I last saw it, it wasn't open," he began, but he realized immediately that Julie remained serious this time. "Something bad?" he asked.

Julie nodded. "Someone trying to blackmail the newspaper. - Now, would you remember by any chance who came in here and sent this off? Obviously it was stamped by hand in here …"

"Wasn't it that small boy the other day? Shortly before closing time? Came in and had it all in dimes and cents?" Arnie threw in.

"Right," Gary said. "About this high," he held his hand a few inches above the counter. "Was barely able to see his entire face. Couldn't describe him really though. Blond hair, I guess. Rather a shy kid."

"He had a slight limp," Arnie said.

"Yeah, right," Gary added. "Not like in a sports injury either, but something wrong with his leg."

Julie's face lit up. "That's a pretty good description. Thank you."

"Listen," Gary said. "That kid didn't look like a blackmailer to me though."

"He doesn't have to be him either," Julie said slowly. "Rather a messenger than the blackmailer, I guess. And probably totally in the dark of what he was doing to boot."

"What was the blackmailing about anyway?" Arnie asked curiously.

Julie lifted her hands apologetically. "Not my place to talk about it, sorry. Which is why I need to ask you to keep quiet about this until we know who is behind this thing, please."

"Sure," Arnie and Gary answered.

"Do you need any stamps or cash?" Gary returned to business to emphasize how serious he was about keeping the talk to himself.

"No, thank you. Not tonight," Julie said. She gave them a smile and a little thumbs-up as she turned around and left, stuffing the envelope back into her shoulder bag.

*

"Hello, Daniel?" Mathilda Barton was sitting in her office chair, cradling the phone receiver between her shoulder and her left ear, while leafing through a file.

"Hi, Mathilda!" Daniel Harrison's voice sounded surprised. "How's it going?"

"Good," Mathilda answered. Then she hesitated. "Well, actually not really that good." She reverted to silence.

"Anything I can do for you?" Daniel inquired cautiously.

"I'm not sure," Mathilda said.

"Hmmm," Daniel made. "I can't help you if you don't talk."

Pause.

"I'm not sure how to put it," Mathilda started over again. "I had our newspaper reporter at the office this morning. She claims that the dumped drums in Wycliff Forest contain exactly the chemical waste mix a wharf like mine produces."

"There are dozens of wharves along the South Puget Sound shoreline."

"I know. But why would anybody from Olympia or Tacoma or Federal Way or anywhere else want to go way out of their way to drop their waste here of all places?"

"But you can prove that the drums are not yours. You have all the paperwork, after all."

Mathilda laughed mirthlessly. "I do. But the insinuation that it could be our drums creeps me out. Tell me – did you receive our last delivery?"

Daniel coughed away from the receiver. Then he spoke again. "I certainly should have paperwork here that says so."

Mathilda breathed in deeply. "Why do I have this feeling that something is still dead-wrong?"

Pause.

"Maybe you want to meet me for dinner tonight and we can talk it over? I'll bring my delivery folder, and we can go through it together. Dinner is on ... my company. We can make it a working dinner. How about it?"

Mathilda rubbed her brow. "Make it lunch, and I say okay. Fine. Thank you. When and where?"

*

"So what was the outcome of your school visit today?" Julie asked Luke, taking another bite of chicken and rice.

"Don't speak with a full mouth," Dottie asked in only half-serious aggravation.

They were all sitting around the dining table in the McMahon house. Dottie had made one of her family favorites, chicken fricassee with white asparagus and mushrooms in a tarragon gravy with a side of refreshing green salad. Luke complimented his wife with a loving gesture. Then he swallowed and turned to his grown-up step-daughter.

"Your research was a great help, Julie," he complimented her. "I went to see the principals of all schools in Wycliff and asked them about boys that fit your description. I ended up with four with walking impediments, but only one of them had about the right height and fair hair."

Julie straightened up. "Wow! That sounds pretty exciting."

Luke nodded, and even Dottie, who had been in her own thoughts about her deli and ways to make further small changes there, listened up. "Of course, I didn't talk to the kid right then and there at school. It might have given a wrong impression to his classmates."

"Of course," Julie nodded, but looked a bit disappointed.

"You understand, the other kids might think he had committed a crime or bully him about being sought out by a policeman in school." This time, Julie looked more persuaded. "So I had the principal give me his home address, and I drove over there to talk to his parents first."

"Anybody we know?" Dottie asked curiously.

"Is there anybody in and around Wycliff you don't know, Dottie sweets?" Luke joked. Then he became serious again. "I cannot reveal the name, of course. You already know more than anybody else about the case, as it is." He took a sip of water from his glass and sighed. "The parents weren't too happy to see me at the door and my car parked right in front of their house, of course. As a matter of fact, I saw one of those old gossips pass by and turn around when their front door opened. I shooed her off waving my arms. I simply cannot stand people putting their noses into matters that are not theirs only to spread rumors." He took another sip of water. "Anyhow. I talked to the boy's parents, and we waited for him to come home, which he did soon after."

"He must have been pretty upset when he found it was about him," Dottie stated empathetically.

"He was," Luke confirmed. "And he was in full denial at first."

"How so?" Julie asked, spearing a piece of white asparagus and licking her lips.

"He was obviously afraid," Luke answered. "I mean, he must have realized that it was strange getting asked by a person he didn't know to post a letter for him or her when the person could easily have done it himself." Luke ladled another scoop of fricassee onto his plate.

"Huh," Julie beamed.

Dottie turned to her. "What do you mean by 'huh'?"

"So now we know the person who handed the letter to the boy was a man. Luke just gave it away."

"Didn't," Luke muttered and blushed slightly.

"Did!" Julie grinned.

"Duh," Dottie said. "Continue with the story."

"Not much of a story there," Luke claimed. "The boy finally admitted that he had been approached by a man on his way from Fifty Flavors back home. The man had actually given him ten bucks for taking the letter into the post office and having it stamped manually as a guarantee that it would reach the recipient as soon as possible." Luke wiped his mouth with a paper napkin. Dottie always put pretty napkins next to the plates when laying the table. "Ten bucks is a lot for a kid."

"Sure is," Julie nodded. "So he took the money and went on his errand…"

Luke chewed vigorously and swallowed to be able to continue his story. "He was in tears when he realized what kind of letter he actually had sent on its way."

"But if it hadn't been him, it might have been any other kid," Dottie threw in.

"Exactly. That is what I told him, too," Luke said. "So I asked him whether he was able to describe the person who had given him the blackmailing letter. And he said he could. Actually, his description sounded so interesting that I will have him come over to the office tomorrow and have him sit with one of our forensic artists to draw a resembling picture of the guy."

"Wycliff has forensic artists?" Julie asked totally thrilled.

Luke shook his head. "We don't. But we have some in the County and can apply for their service. I was lucky to get one assigned so quickly."

"So you think you will be on to the blackmailer soon?"

"We may, we may not, depending on whether he is still around."

"But blackmailing John only makes sense when that person is still in the area and fears to be found out. I mean, obviously the person who did that illicit dumping in Wycliff Forest and the blackmailer are one and the same." Julie was all fired up.

"I didn't say that," Luke warned her. "Don't make any assumptions until we have the guy and his statement. And, for heaven's sake, don't write anything about it yet."

Julie slumped in her chair. "Of course, I wouldn't," she pouted. "That would be unprofessional. Spreading rumors is so not my thing. Leave that to the yellow press... Still, you have to admit it would make sense." She scrutinized Luke's frowning face.

Finally, he relented and winked at her. "It would, wouldn't it?"

*

"Do you sell the ends of your sausages and cold-cuts cheaper?" Thora was almost whispering, leaning over the top of the counter, as she didn't want to be overheard by the other customers at Dottie's Deli.

Dottie stood behind her deli counter and was ready to serve her. Her face was a picture of surprise at Thora's question, but she stayed calm as always. "As a matter of fact we don't," she answered. "You were surely thinking of Bear, right? But that kind of meat wouldn't be healthy for your cute doggie anyhow."

Thora blushed and nodded. "Of course, you are right."

Dottie saw from the look of Thora's eyes that her friend had had something different on her mind though. And then it hit her. Having given notice on her job for her environmental cause had cost Thora the freedom of shopping as she wanted. She still tried to shop locally, but she must be on a budget. "Actually, come to think of it, it makes sense – instead of simply giving away the meats to people who already bought perfectly nice cold cuts. Right now I don't have any sausage ends, but in about an hour – at the rate we are moving through our sausages today – I might be able to come up with some."

Thora's mien relaxed a little. "This would be wonderful," she said, almost shy. "I'll run some more errands and will come back then. How much would a pound be?"

"It'll be reasonable, I promise," Dottie said. As she watched her brave friend walk towards the door, she sighed. Life was never easy. A slight twist, and everything could fall apart. And if you didn't have friends, you were left to your own devices. Dottie had been through that when she had lost her first husband, Sean Dolan, without any warning. Freshly widowed and new in town, she had been only too grateful to have found a friend such as Pattie May, her neighbor, who had helped her set up her German deli and kept working by her side ever since.

"Maybe it's my turn now," Dottie thought to herself and planned there and then to make Thora proud of her stance and not embarrassed about the consequences.

"Maybe it's my turn now," a sharp voice interfered with her thoughts, and Dottie looked into Angela Fortescue's overly made-up, aged face with a hairdo that shouted home-dyed.

"I'm sorry, Angela," Dottie said and smiled especially warmly. This woman had been her nightmare since day one when she had won the first deli Christmas raffle and been uppity about delivery. Back then, Dottie had only had a glimpse of the poor circumstances in which Angela was living, in a run-down housing complex near the wharves. Ever since, Dottie had tried to be extra-nice, but it also took an extra-effort every time. Was there nothing that could soften the old hag?

"Asking about sausage rests, uh! Not too long ago, she was filling her basket to the rim with all that high-falutin stuff from your shelves when Nathan's at the mall has the same brands at lower prices."

"They buy in bulk," Dottie tried to explain.

Angela waved her off. "I'm not brainless. But I would feel it were beneath me to ask other people for a favor like she just did."

"It's not in everybody's capability to ask for favors," Dottie replied calmly, while seething with anger underneath. "Maybe we all should be willing to ask for favors more often. It might make it easier to return them as well."

"Hmph," Angela retorted. "Be that as it is. I overheard your deal with her though. I guess what's good enough for one customer is good for all, right? Will you have sausage rests for me sometime today, too?"

Dottie swallowed before she answered with a very mellow voice. "It will be a pleasure, Angela."

"Good," the woman huffed. "And mind – I don't like that pistachio bologna. And for heaven's sake no blood sausage or headcheese." Before Dottie was able to reply anything, she turned around and walked down the aisle, head held high.

Dottie sank against the back counter and almost laughed out in despair. Leave it to Angela to ask a favor and make it look as if she were entitled to more. Some people simply needed to be taken down a notch or two. But it wasn't for Dottie to do so. Something would surely though. One day. Hopefully soon.

Meanwhile, Thora was walking down Main Street, mulling over what her next steps should be. She'd have to budget her household tightly until she would be able to come up with another job. For the time being, she needed to follow up on her words during the town hall meeting and do something. That refinery project was threatening to turn her beautiful hometown into another industrial place, which somehow left a wrong flavor in the mouth just at the thought of it. She knew she wouldn't be able to handle things alone. So she needed to rally her fellow townspeople for meetings and marches to make their voices heard. And she would go all the way to the governor of Washington State with her arguments if need be.

Her stomach roiled. As a political and ecological matter, protesting the refinery was an obvious step to take for Thora. But at the same time she was in danger of losing a wonderful, long-standing friendship. To be honest, her feelings for Clark Thompson had been a lot more for a while now. But she had known to stop herself from giving in to them, as he was her boss. Now he wasn't anymore, but he was even less attainable. The future looked very bright if

Thora wanted a public career as a spokeswoman for Nature and sustainability. But very bleak when it came to her own personal dreams.

"You look like you need something to cheer you up," Kitty Kittrick called out to her as she was driving past with her farm delivery van headed for "The Flower Bower". The very young manager of the flower shop on Front Street had become engaged to a farmer from Medicine Creek Valley, Eli Hayes, only a short time ago and accepted his little daughter, Holly, as if she were her own. She had her heart in the right place. "Why don't you drop by for a short chat? I need to know some more about that refinery thing. And what it implies for our businesses."

Thora, roused from her thoughts, waved briefly and nodded. "I'll be around", she called after the car. That was when she knew what her next move would be.

*

Kitty had placed her elbows onto the kitchen table in the Hayes Farm kitchen, cradling her face in her hands. A candle threw its softly flickering light over the raw wooden table surface and illuminated Eli, who sat across from her. It put some odd red accents to his dark short hair as if it were glowing. They both looked pensive.

"She's quite a courageous person," Kitty said. "You know, I wonder how she will manage once her last pay check is used up. She didn't say anything about any worries, but I saw it in her eyes."

Eli reached for his young fiancée's hand. "You are a sweetheart," he said softly. "And I know how you feel. So you gave her flowers and potatoes for free ..."

Kitty smiled wistfully. "It was the only thing that came to my mind at that moment."

"I guess she is out of the loop as to what's going on in town hall right now. What their steps will be. What has she planned next though?"

Kitty drew invisible lines with her fingers on the table top. "She wants to organize a big protest in front of town hall. She said she is creating an information leaflet that she will have copied for every household and business in Wycliff. She also wants to go from door to door to convince anybody who needs convincing."

Eli whistled softly. "That is a Herculean task indeed. By the time she's reached the last of the households in Wycliff with her message, the refinery will have gone into construction."

"Aren't you ever the optimist?!" Kitty half scolded him. "Of course, she will need people who do this with her."

Eli picked up his half-empty can of beer and sipped from it. Then he grimaced. "It's stale."

"You only opened it."

"Well, I'll still toss it. I lost my taste for it."

"Keep it. It is great for making snail traps in my lettuce beds. Another tip from the 'Green Maven'. Do you know I suspect it's really Thora behind that pseudonym?"

They sat in silence.

"I think Thora should only try to speak to the businesses and to some of the more influential people of Wycliff first, not every single household as well" Eli said after a while, ignoring Kitty's last remark. "That way she can set up a solid protest leadership and spread her information during a protest march or whatever she plans."

Kitty took a sip of ice tea. "That sounds like saving a lot of time and energy," she agreed."

"She will need every bit of both against a giant as AnCoSafe Oil and the mayor, I'm sure," Eli answered. "And she will need some sponsors too."

"You mean as in food and such?" Kitty asked eagerly.

Eli smiled. "I was rather thinking as in posters, ads, buttons, and what not."

"Oh," Kitty said.

"We can't give much, as we need to consolidate both, your business and the farm. And there is Holly's summer camp to think of, too. I don't want to cut her off from that activity."

Kitty shook her head. "Of course not. But say, if I were helping her with the door-to-door canvassing, would you mind much?"

"Go ahead," Eli said. "You sure have my blessing. Especially after today's find at the little plot of no man's land between our farm and our neighbors'."

Kitty leaned forward. "What find?"

Eli was looking grim now. "You wouldn't believe it. Somebody dumped a load of a dozen or more hazardous waste drums in the slough."

"They what...?!"

"Exactly. Juan spotted them when he was chasing one of our calves back into the pasture. The drums looked just like those in the newspaper photo. While Juan was mending the pasture fence, I called the police. The officers were pretty upset about it. There's no knowing how many illegal dump sites like that are to be found around here yet."

"That is horrible!" Kitty exclaimed. "Why would anybody do this?!"

"Money," Eli said drily. "I guess somebody is saving or gaining money by not having the poisonous stuff recycled or burnt properly. If you look on crime, in most cases it comes all back to money issues. Well, almost all..."

"All the more important that we take a stand alongside Thora and her cause," Kitty said. "These dump sites are only comparatively small, but dangerous stuff. How much worse will a refinery be here in Wycliff?!"

They sat in silence again. Then there was the light patter of small bare feet on hardwood floor. A tiny girl with huge blue eyes and straight black hair stood in the doorway.

"I can't sleep," Holly said.

Kitty rose with a smile. "I think it's the full moon shining right onto your nose tip, hm?" She took Holly by the hand. "Let's go upstairs together. I'm sure I know an old fairy tale about why the moon is getting bigger and then smaller again all the time..."

*

The knock on John Minor's office door was so timid he didn't even really hear it. It was rather the sudden sense of intrusion that made him look up from a pile of invitations, letters, and manuscripts of would-be journalists to perceive a small, lanky boy on the threshold. Big brown eyes with long lashes looked at him through thick glasses, and the soft mouth was slightly agape.

"Yes!" John Minor said.

The boy shrunk and took a tiny step backward. He made a little noise like a wounded animal, but then pulled himself together again. "Are you Mr. Minor?" the boy asked timidly.

"And who would you be?" John frowned at the boy with the fair hair.

"I, I ..." The boy stammered, then he shut his mouth. "I'm Eddie Beale," he started over again.

John Minor had a hunch now who he was talking to. "Eddie Beale," he repeated. "Why don't you step over here and have a seat?"

Eddie followed suit. He had a noticeable limp coming from a flawed hip that had probably never been set right after his birth. John Minor sighed. He knew there were other countries in the world where this would have been taken care of pretty soon after birth and made a significant impact on a person's life. He mellowed.

"So... What can I do for you?" he asked.

Eddie hardly dared look him into the face, and when he finally did, his own was full of misery. "I'm the one who sent off the awful letter," he whispered.

John Minor was taken aback by the blunt statement. "Did you write it?" he asked, though he knew better. Julie had briefed him right after Luke had let her in on the police investigation.

"No!" the small boy exclaimed. "Oh no! I would never do any such thing!"

"So you only sent it off?"

"Yes," Eddie said. Then he slipped his right hand into his pant pocket, took something out, and placed it on John's desk. It was a crumpled ten-dollar-bill. "And I want to apologize. And I don't want that money that I got for it anymore."

John reached out and took the bill. He carefully smoothed it out and studied it intently. "So you think by paying me the money everything is fine again?" he murmured.

The boy fidgeted in his chair. "Yes. No. I mean ..."

John sighed. "Ten dollars are a lot of money for a kid, right?" He looked at Eddie whose eyes had started filling with tears. "And an incredible lot for posting a letter for somebody who probably could have done it by himself so easily, too." The boy nodded silently. "Ever thought of the proportion between the difficulty of errand you were asked to do and the amount of money you received for it?" Eddie looked clueless. "When somebody offers you more than a job is worth, Eddie, there is always a hook. Either the job is wrong or somebody wants to have you on their beck and call. Either way, you will always end up in a place you don't want to be." This time Eddie nodded.

John handed the bill back to the boy. "Keep it, Eddie. And apology accepted. Actually, it takes a pretty brave boy to come here all by himself and stand up for what he did." He smiled benignly at the kid. "A lot of grown-ups wouldn't have owned up this way."

Eddie rose from his chair. "So you really forgive me?"

"No more questions asked," John nodded, and the boy shyly smiled back at him. "Oh, well, yes, just one more. Did you already make that portrait with the police artist?"

"I did," Eddie suddenly bubbled over. "And it was so cool! He had me choose from all kinds of different facial parts and put them together on a computer screen. And then he painted in details with the mouse. I really think the picture looks like the man."

"Good," John said. "See, that was worth a lot more than ten dollars."

Eddie nodded slowly. "I see. I wouldn't have wanted to take any money for *that* though. It was simply the right thing to do."

John chuckled. "You're a good kid, Eddie Beale. Now run off and leave me to my work!" And he immersed himself again into a pile of papers.

"Sir?"

"You're still here?!"

"Thank you."

John stared at the boy as he turned around and limped out. He rubbed his brow with his hands. "I might as well go for it," he muttered to himself. Then he took an old-fashioned fountain pen and a sheet of paper and started to write.

*

"Hallo, Mattie?" Trevor Jones paced to and fro in his small office with his mobile phone as he gazed through the window.

"Hi, Trevor."

"Do you have a moment?"

"Is anything wrong with any paperwork?"

Trevor was laughing nervously. "No. Goodness, no."

A sigh of relief on the other end. "You had me worry for a moment. What is it then?"

Trevor cleared his throat. "I was wondering whether you could make time for lunch some time. Or dinner?"

"So it is about paperwork after all?"

"What makes you think so?" Trevor was puzzled and vexed at the same time. "Can't a guy just ask you out?" Silence. "Well?"

"Well... I wouldn't be good company these days, Trevor. I have too many worries."

"So that is a no?"

"Don't be angry, please."

Trevor hung up slowly. "She said no to me ..." He stroked his chin, while laying down his mobile phone on his desk. "I can't believe she said no to me."

*

From "The Sound Messenger":

Out with the Truth
A Commentary by Julie Dolan, editor

Everybody has a corpse in the closet, some people bigger ones, some smaller ones. At least, that is what I presume, and you may feel free to protest this assumption in a letter to the editor. Very recently we stumbled across a huge ugly corpse … and we are still looking for the person out of whose closet it came.

To put it in plain words: *The Sound Messenger*'s publisher and editor-in-chief, John Minor, has been blackmailed. He was demanded to stop investigative journalism in the Wycliff Forest illegal dump. Otherwise somebody would out his sexual orientation. As you can see, John still printed the latest article on another illegal dumping site in Medicine Creek Valley. And he also outed himself to you, his readers.

I keep asking myself what the blackmailer wanted to achieve by his threat. We are living in a society that is more and more accepting that sexuality is everybody's private business as long as it is legal and consenting. Here, in Washington State, being openly gay or lesbian is not only lawful, it is also no more a social flaw unless your religion goes against it. But would anybody find a journalist less credible because they are gay or lesbian? It was big news when Anderson Cooper outed himself a while ago. Probably even more so because of his female audience's disappointment that he is not their secret dream material anymore. He is still on TV. He is still cherished for his work. Who couldn't care less about his private life?!

Is John Minor a less worthy and less credible editor and publisher now that he has outed himself? Or isn't his courage to do so and to present his most vulnerable self to public scrutiny another reason to believe that his work is well-grounded? Doesn't it even make his dedication to report on an environmental crime and try to find the culprit in spite of a blackmailing letter more credible?

The blackmailer is obviously very closely involved in ruthlessly dropping drums of hazardous waste in ecologically vulnerable areas. He needs the silence of the press and the closed eyes of the public to continue his life-endangering crime. He thought John Minor would put his private life before the public's need to know, just as the blackmailer himself put his private greed before the public's interests. John told the truth about himself. Because he also wants to out the truth about a criminal. And whereas he will be able to retreat into his privacy again, the blackmailer better watch out, because he will soon be a very public person.

CHAPTER 4

The Green Maven's Tip of the Week:
Sticky tree sap (resin) on your clothes? Apply some cold pressed olive oil on the spot and gently rub it off. After that, treat it like a normal fat stain and wash.

Mathilda sat at one of the tables towards the back of the room at The Bair Bistro in Steilacoom, waiting for Daniel quite nervously. They had agreed to talk about business where nobody would know them. Steilacoom was none too far out of the way for either of them. So it had been a done deal.

The restaurant was quite an unusual place. Being part of the town's historical museum, it had been a drugstore at one time as bottles, vials, and other paraphernalia indicated. There was also an old-fashioned fountain at one end of the room-length counter. The display was filled with a few scones and pies; this morning's clients must have enjoyed quite a share already. And near her, at the end of the room, Mathilda spotted a post office with ancient mailboxes.

"Enjoying yourself?" owner and Chef Sarah Cannon asked Mathilda, handing her a menu. She was very busy, but she always made it a point to take care of her customers personally. "I've never seen you in here before ..."

Mathilda took in the young chef with the jolly smile and beamed back. "That's because it's my first time here. As a matter of fact it will be a work lunch. I'm still waiting for my business partner."

"Then I'll leave you to yourself and check with you again when your party is complete. How many will you be?"

"Just two," Mathilda answered. "Oh, and there he is already."

"Good for you," Sarah smiled. "I'll give you some time to study the menu, and I'll be right back with you."

As she walked back to the kitchen, Daniel approached the table. "Sorry I let you wait," he said. "The roads here were a circus. Construction sites everywhere as soon as summer is near."

"I know," Mathilda said. "I got stuck too." They smiled at each other, a bit awkwardly. "Why don't we simply have a look at the menu and have lunch first. We can talk about what we have discovered while we're eating, and look at the books afterwards."

Daniel sat down and scoured the menu. "Mmmh," he said. "Chowder, salmon salad ... Doesn't look bad at all."

"I thought it was always us women who are supposed to go for soups and salads," Mathilda teased.

Daniel chuckled. "I'm alright with soup and salads when they feed my weakness for seafood."

Mathilda nodded. "I'm totally with you there. Makes it an easy order for the kitchen, too."

Daniel turned around and, catching the eye of a waitress, signaled her over. After they had placed the order, he confidentially leaned across the table. "I'm so glad we are finally having a meal together. It was about time."

Mathilda smiled at him. "I hope you still find it nice once we are done talking business."

"I'm pretty sure," Daniel said, not knowing where his sudden bravado came from. After all, it seemed to have been only yesterday that he had mused about and discarded the thought of taking Mathilda out in his state of financial disorder.

Sarah appeared again with two bowls of hot, fragrant clam chowder. "I hope you will like it," she said cheerfully. "I wish it were a bit warmer outside, today. You could have enjoyed our patio. Maybe next time?"

Daniel nodded. "Sounds inviting," he said. "If the clam chowder is as good as your interior design, we'll gladly be back." He dipped his spoon into the creamy dish and tasted. "It's a done deal," he stated. Sarah gave him a huge smile and went back into her kitchen.

"You certainly won a heart today," Mathilda remarked and found herself sounding a bit jealous. She regained equilibrium, pushed a strand of sand-colored hair behind her ears, and started tasting the chowder as well. "Mmmh," she said. "Quite remarkable."

They ate in silence for a while, furtively eyeing each other.

Finally, Daniel spoke again. "I have to admit that not all is well with my business either, Mathilda."

"Mattie," she said softly and lifted her eyes from her spoon.

"Mattie," he repeated. "I have looked over my books. According to them, all the checks that came in were handled through correctly. So on the surface I seem to have in the bank what I should have. Except a few things, Mattie."

"What?" Her eyes filled with expectation, and she put her spoon down.

"For the life of me, I have been finding entries on deliveries and checks of yours during the past four months, but no entries in the disposal book or in the company's bank accounts. And maybe other people's, too."

Mattie gasped. "What?!"

"You heard me right, "Daniel said." I really double-checked. I have no entry in the books saying any waste from Barton & Son was disposed of in the past four months. None of it went off to our treatment plant or the furnace either. I wouldn't even have realized, because I never looked at whose deliveries or checks came in. Until you called and told me about that dreadful suspicion against you and your business."

Mathilda had turned pale. Only two tiny red blotches showed on her cheeks, a sign that she was highly alert and upset at the same time. Her hands started trembling. "But Dan, I mean Daniel ..."

"Dan is fine," he said and almost felt elated, though the situation was anything but great.

Mathilda seemed to ignore his input. "That means that I don't even know where my drums with the waste have gone to!" She put her hand over her mouth and stared at Daniel in horror. Then she started fiddling with her napkin. "That means that Julie Dolan could have been right about those drums being ones that belong to Barton & Son. And that means that there are more illegal dumping sites in more than this one space."

Daniel drew in his breath and let it out very slowly. "This is becoming a biggie," he said. "Who is usually delivering your drums to my place?"

"I should have entrusted an employee of my own with it. There is that Collection Services guy from somewhere around Lakewood. He made me an offer when I was short on personnel and didn't want to send one of my men. He always seemed to do it right on time, and he delivered me a receipt from your Disposal Center every single time as well."

"And the checks?"

"Were redeemed at different banks in and around Yelm. I never thought more deeply about why you would go to different banks all of a sudden. I thought that maybe it was more convenient for you or your bookkeeper for petty cash at your Disposal Center, while you were running other errands."

Daniel laughed mirthlessly. "My bookkeeper is supposed to mail in all checks on a bi-weekly basis to one and the same bank in Yelm. And they deposit the money into a company account. They are not supposed to be cashed in at any bank. Dang!" He banged his fist on the table, then he looked at her apologetically. "Sorry, Mattie. This is so not me. It angers me beyond anything."

A waitress removed their now empty chowder bowls and replaced them with two huge plates of salmon salad. Neither of them picked up their forks when she left, as both were too shocked by their discoveries.

"That means I'm getting betrayed by my own service provider," Mattie said almost tonelessly.

"Wrong. It means we are both getting cheated. The service you get is criminal. And I am probably cheated by my own employee," Daniel stated.

"How so?"

"Well, it looks like your service provider takes your drums, dumps them some place, then goes to my place, and has my bookkeeper sign a receipt for delivery that looks all legal. The check that is intended for us ends up at a bank to be cashed in, but doesn't ever end up in an account it belongs in. You get all the paperwork you need. I get almost all the paperwork I need. Your drums simply disappear into Nirvana at one point. I have your check receipt copies, and the delivery receipt, but no entry in the disposal books. The drums are simply 'lost' between the fake delivery and the furnace. And there are certainly no check deposits in my company account either."

"Everything looks legal, unless somebody is taking a closer look," Mattie continued breathlessly.

"Exactly. Nobody is any the wiser, and your collection service provider and my bookkeeper split the checks." Daniel frowned. "Unfortunately, Julie seems to be right about your drums. I wonder what other deals my employee might have cut with either other people or that same service provider of yours. After all, it's not just *your* checks that are missing in my account."

"But this is awful!" Mathilda said. "Just imagine the environmental disaster that those people are causing. And they are ruining your business as well."

Daniel grimaced. "Not much longer, you bet." He picked up his fork and started on his salad, adding some of the tart lemon vinaigrette it came with. He chewed and mused, his face betraying grim thoughts. "And all of this because they are greedy for money."

Mathilda stabbed at a piece of lox. "I could throttle the man!" She stopped the fork mid-air. "Now everybody will think that it was me behind it. My wharf will be ruined."

"No, it won't," Daniel interrupted. "He is not your employee after all. And we will simply both do the right thing.

"Go to the police ..." Mathilda stated it more than she asked.

"Go to the police," Daniel nodded. "Isn't that Dolan woman somehow related to the Wycliff Chief of Police, too?"

"She's his step-daughter," Mathilda said. "So that is probably why she puts so much fervor in covering the news story. To have his back in the investigation. And, of course, professional ambition."

"Well, can't be wrong to let them both in and help us catch them red-handed. What do you think?"

Mathilda swallowed. "I cannot believe we are caught up in such a mess and neither of us realized. But I guess we are in for it. Either we help getting this cleared or we can both say good night to our businesses."

"That's the spirit, dear," Daniel said and toasted her with his half-empty glass of Green River soda.

She lifted her glass as well. "Let them choke on their greed," she agreed.

*

Thora was proud of the flyers she had created. They were printed on glossy white paper and looked like some official paperwork. The layout program on her PC had given her some pretty attractive solutions, and the printing house on Back Row had cut her a good price for the order.

She wondered whether they knew of her financial worries and had accommodated her so kindly because of that. Or whether they had read the flyer and were all set against the AnCoSafe Oil refinery as well. She hadn't dared ask, as she didn't want to emphasize the straits she was headed for.

For now, she stacked the two big boxes on the floor of her car's passenger side. Bear was sniffing curiously and tried to make his way up front, but Thora gave him a strict "No" on that.

"You stay where you are and behave, Bear," she admonished him, while stashing a small pile of flyers into a beautiful fabric bag she always carried with her. "I'll be back in a few. Let's see how my friends will react to this paperwork."

Leaving the window partly open so Bear could still put his nose through, Thora locked the car and walked off with her print-outs in the bag.

"Dottie's Deli" was amongst her first targets. She arrived at a good time. Business had just slackened from the breakfast rush. Dottie and her staff were preparing the displays for the noon run. They were cleaning the display windows and the meat cutters. One of them was prepping a Swabian sausage salad made from a mix of blood sausage and bologna with an onion vinaigrette. Dottie had started that as an experiment, and it was working out quite well. Funny enough, as most of her American customers still found the concept of blood sausage disquieting.

"Good morning," Thora called out cheerfully.

Dottie looked up from her jars of dill pickles that needed to go onto the shelves yet. "Good morning, Thora. How are things?" she replied.

"Good," Thora said. "Depending actually. You do know about the AnCoSafe Oil refinery that Mayor Thompson seems to be keen on having built here in Wycliff, don't you?"

"And such a shame too," Pattie May said, coming out of the office. She was curious what brought Thora today. Pattie had a sixth sense when somebody entered the deli and had a purpose other than buying.

"Exactly," Thora said. "And that is why I'm coming here this morning. I think that we can't just let this go. If we don't agree with these plans, we need to open our mouths and say something. We need to protest this business."

"I thought you and Clark were friends," Dottie threw in.

Thora's face betrayed discomfort. "We ... kind of still are. But that doesn't mean we have to agree about everything, does it?"

"It might make a big difference once you step out into the open and make your point publicly," Dottie pondered. "He might not find it amusing at all."

"Well, neither do I," Thora said.

The other staff had gathered around now and were listening intently.

"It might mean some cool jobs for people in the area," Sabine said.

"That is exactly one of the points Mayor Thompson makes," Thora replied. "And I can't ignore it. But do we really need more jobs in our beautiful town? Doesn't everybody have good job opportunities here already? And do we want people to move into Wycliff and have more houses built and prices going up just because of a disfiguring landmark that is going up next to the ferry terminal?"

Dottie nodded thoughtfully. "You have a couple of good points there, dear. So what might we be able to do to support you?"

Thora lifted her little pile of papers out of her cloth bag as in an afterthought and showed them. "This is an invitation to join a protest in front of town hall on Friday. We need to show Mayor Thompson and everyone on the town council who are for this project that we have to be considered as well. I will paint signs. I will deliver flyers to all households in Wycliff. I will..."

"Wait!" Pattie said. "You cannot do all of this on your own. It will cost quite a bit of time and money."

"Time is not the issue now," Thora laughed bitterly.

"Hey," Sabine said. "I can help. I can stick those papers into the mailboxes up my road and the neighborhood."

"You wouldn't mind?" Thora asked surprised.

"Heck, no!"

"Well, thank you!"

"You might also want to leave some of those flyers at our cash register," Dottie suggested.

"But is that legal?" Thora asked. "It's like a political statement of a business. No business in Wycliff is supposed to offer a political opinion as far as I remember the town statutes."

"True," Dottie smiled. "But this is not uttering an opinion. This is informing about and inviting to join an event. It could just as well be a book signing or a "Clean the Park" activity, you know?"

Thora chuckled. "Explain that to Mayor Thompson. - You really sure you want to do this?"

"In for a penny, in for a pound," Dottie confirmed. "I'll also spread flyers. Do you have any more anywhere?"

"In the car," Thora said.

"Well, you better get some to me then. And you might want to ask our next-door-friends as well. I know they are environmentally conscious."

"So you mean I could succeed with that rally?"

Dottie laid her hand on Thora's arm. "You bet. Most of us like the tourist business and the ferrying well enough. But as soon as they'd build even as much as a huge cannery over here, they'd be on the barricades. And this is talking about a refinery with all its consequences. - How do you pay for all this additional promotion material anyway?"

A shadow flew over Thora's face. "I'm not sure. I guess the time will come I live hand to mouth unless something comes up."

"That sure is a pretty bag you got there," Sabine interrupted. "I've never seen anything like it. Did you make it yourself?"

Thora blushed. "Thank you. And no. My late mother used to sew quite a bit for me, and this cloth bag made from patchwork fabric is pretty much the last crafting I have from her."

Behind the little group, she heard a slight harrumphing. Turning around, she spotted Angela Fortescue approaching them with a curious look in her eyes. "May I see, too?" she asked, and everybody was tensing up. Thora cautiously held out her bag, and Angela reached for it to inspect it. "Neat piece of work," she said. And Dottie thought she'd misheard. Praise from the lips of Angela Fortescue? From her most feared customer?

Thora smiled weakly. "Thank you."

"Nothing to be especially proud of though," Angela went on. And everybody was almost relieved that she was back on her old nagging track. "All straight seams and just very few of them, but still clean workmanship." She handed the bag back to Thora. "You're really an environmentalist, aren't you?"

Thora blushed even more. "I just try to do my little thing."

Angela nodded almost regally – a strange sight, as she looked so out of place with her bright ruby-red hair, another glitter shirt underneath a fake leather jacket, and leggings that betrayed her thinness. "You could make those yourself, you know."

"As a matter of fact ... I cannot sew," Thora said sadly.

"Easiest thing in the world," Angela countered.

"Easier said than done," Thora ventured. "I'm a dunce with sewing machines. And hand-sewing takes a long time."

Angela scanned Thora's face slyly. "You should look for someone who knows how to sew." And with that she turned around, grabbed some pumpernickel from a shelf, and went to the cash register. "Heavens, I am sewing a lot of things for my home!"

They all watched her, stunned.

"Is nobody going to charge me for this?" Angela mocked, holding up the bread.

Pattie May rushed towards the cash register. "Of course. Sorry, Angela."

Thora still stared at her bag. Then her eyes followed Angela out the store. Some of the words Angela had said had stirred something in her. She wasn't sure yet. But she had a feeling there might be more to it once she sat down by herself and pondered the situation. For now, she had business to do.

When Thora came back to her car a couple of hours later, having canvassed all of the Main Street businesses, one of the big boxes on her car floor was already empty. Bear was wagging his tail happily at the sight of Thora; she smiled and patted his back. "Looks like things are coming together better than I dared hope for, my friend," she said to the dog. "Let's just hope that there will be enough people coming together and making their voices heard. Can you imagine an oily stink hanging over Wycliff all day long and all night too?"

Bear woofed.

"Me neither," Thora said and started the car. "Me neither."

*

"Listen, man," Peter Michaels said in low urgent tone. "We gotta lie low for a while." He paused.

A male voice sounded through his smartphone, obviously angry and upset.

"No, no, listen," Peter tried to calm down the person on the other end of the line. "I'm not trying to get out of this. I'm not dodging anything. I don't even have any proof. It's just a hunch, dude."

More aggravated speech from the other side.

"I know we've had a good run so far. But maybe we need to take a break for now and make different plans. My gut says that some people are getting too close for our own good. We just need to play it by the rules again for a little. And then we are back to normal."

The other person muttered something.

"I know. Those checks come in handy, and I could well use some of those greenbacks to sort myself out. Gotta set some things straight with my girl, too. Anyhow. Let's play it safe for now. They will stop looking too closely after a while, and when they think they were mistaken after all, we hop back on our game."

He listened into some more arguing. Then he nodded grimly.

"Okay, one more time. But I have a bad feeling about this one. I won't do it with the Barton load either. They are too close on that one. Let's do it with today's haul from University Place instead."

They exchanged some more words. Then Peter clicked off and put the phone back into his shirt pocket. He looked around. The wharf lay quiet. The dry dock held a boat the hull of which the crew had been sealing and painting for the past week. They had finished the job an hour ago and left for a celebratory beer or two at the nearby Dock Tavern. Peter had promised he'd be with them in a few.

But then he had seen Mathilda come back from wherever earlier on, and she had been carrying a folder. A folder that Peter knew held delivery and check receipts. He had become too tough years ago to feel anxious. But he knew that either he upped his plans or laid them to rest for a while. He knew that they had covered their activities thoroughly. Every check had been carefully confirmed by a receipt from an official receipt pad of Harrison Disposal Center. Every delivery he had been supposed to make had been accounted for by a receipt form letter with the company's letter head. Even if Mathilda looked closely enough she wouldn't realize where he and his partner came in. There was simply no proof.

Mathilda had looked over to him, nodded curtly, and continued walking to her container office. Peter smirked. If that bitch thought herself better than him she was mistaken. She had been handed a silver spoon. And what did he have apart from a very migratory life?

It didn't occur to Peter that he had made his own bed. Nor did he care whether Mathilda really did well with her business. He needed money, and she was a means to come by some. End of train of thoughts.

*

Daniel was pacing his office above the delivery yard of Harrison Disposal Center. It had been a busy day. It often was on Fridays, as many businesses delivered what waste they had accumulated over the working week, tidying up for the weekend.

A delivery from Barton & Son had been due also. Mathilda had let him know, and he had been curious whether it would happen. If Mathilda's collection service provider arrived as expected, they would have a hard time proving that he was in cahoots with one of the Harrison employees. Daniel had almost hoped there wouldn't be any delivery from Barton & Son, but another fraudulent receipt instead. He would have loved to catch those guys red-handed.

But then the truck with the drums from Mathilda's wharf appeared in the delivery court and was unloaded. One of his employees took notes and accompanied the driver into the office building. Daniel had been almost disappointed.

Now it was evening, the premises were closed for the night, and Daniel was waiting for Luke McMahon to come by. Technically, he wondered whether he should have also invited the Chief of Police of Yelm to tell him his strange story and have them take a look at his books. On the other hand, the deliveries involved a Wycliff company, and therefore McMahon was most probably in charge. In the end, Daniel thought that the police would figure it out amongst themselves. All he wanted was catching the guys and putting an end to their crime.

He heard a car arrive, and a few moments later a side door in his building was opened.

"Mr. Harrison?" a strong male voice called.

"Coming!" Daniel strode to the top of the stairs and saw Luke McMahon together with his step-daughter.

Julie Dolan gave him a tentative smile. "I hope it is okay that I came along?"

Daniel nodded. "Come on in. The more the merrier," he said without a smile. "In the end, you are going to write your piece anyhow, and I want you rather to have the facts right."

They all shook hands, then they went into Daniel's office. As dusk was setting quickly, the room was lit by the last rays of sunshine and some cold neon tubes. The sitting area in a corner by the windows held a number of folders. A can of coffee was steaming on a side table, and a plate of cookies was set out.

"I thought we might as well snack on something while we're working," Daniel said and invited them to take a seat.

Luke gave him a brief smile. "Coffee will do for me, thanks." Then he leaned over to grab one of the folders. "So tell me: How did you come to suspect some fraud is happening in your company?"

Daniel told Julie and Luke that he had been worried about a steady decrease in his company account whereas his books spoke a different language. He also mentioned that he had finally realized that he hadn't seen some of his regular customers in a while. "It's not like I keep track of who is coming in when. But when Mathilda Barton called me about being a suspect for illegal dumping, I put two and two together."

"Has she any proof that she isn't involved?" Julie ventured.

"She has all the right receipts and form letters from us. And her checks have been cashed in every time she wrote one."

"Cashed in?" Luke frowned.

Daniel sighed. "Obviously those checks were not sent in via company mail as usually, but she and I traced them back to a number of banks in the area. None of them our house bank, by the way."

"And she never got suspicious?"

"Not really," Daniel shrugged. "Every company has some petty cash somewhere. She simply assumed that hers went towards that stash and that it was more convenient for whoever cashed it to simply use a bank wherever."

Luke opened a folder. He started reading, then he turned a leaf. Then he went over the next. He took his time, and Julie started leaning into him and reading over his shoulder.

Daniel watched them somewhat impatiently. "Everything is listed just as it should be," he remarked.

"Hmmm," Luke murmured without looking up. He turned another leaf.

"Wait!" Julie suddenly said.

Luke lifted his face in surprise. "Back a page?"

"Yes, and then some."

Luke complied. Daniel was craning his neck to discover what it was about. Julie scoured page after page. Then she turned pages over forward again. She used her finger to compare specific parts of the forms. Finally, she looked up at Daniel and smiled. "I found it!" she breathed.

Daniel was almost choking. "So there is truly a case of fraud?"

"There is definitely." She sat back as Luke placed the open folder onto the table, so they were all able to see what Julie had found. "Your bookkeeper uses numbered receipt pads, obviously."

"Right," Daniel confirmed. "Of course."

"Well, he or she blundered big time with the receipts for Barton & Son."

"How so?"

Julie smiled secretively. "It's very obvious, but on the other hand probably the last thing anybody would look for."

"Out with it, girl," Luke said impatiently now, too.

"It's the pad numbers. Most of the receipt forms in this folder are from the same pad. Not so Mathilda Barton's. Hers are from a totally different set of numbers."

"How do you mean ..." Daniel blurted. Then it became clear to him. "So that darn fraud used another pad for all those checks that went into his own pocket."

"Exactly that." Julie pushed the folder towards him. "See this and that?" She pointed to a few forms with consecutive numbers. "Then, all of a sudden, there is the Barton receipt with a totally different number. And the next receipt is from the other pad again."

Daniel rose and paced his office in agitation. "I can't believe this. My own employees stealing from me!"

"Just one – your bookkeeper," Luke said calmly.

"Isn't that enough?!"

Luke nodded. "May I have a copy of this, please?"

"Sure thing," Daniel said, emptied the folder onto a copier nearby, and started the process. "What are you going to do with it anyhow?"

"I'll go over Mathilda Barton's books and check the receipt numbers she has. If they are all consecutive, we have made one case. If her receipt numbers show gaps in between, we have other fraudulent cases. Then everything is back in your ballpark to check who the receipts were for and in what amounts."

Daniel took a deep breath and sighed. "Meaning that might also be the path to more illegal dumping."

Julie held her breath. "Oh my God, I completely overlooked that for a moment."

Luke grabbed the folder and rose. "I guess we are onto something bigger here. Don't alert your employee yet, Mr. Harrison. He needs to continue until we get a hold of his accomplice who is probably doing the dirty work all by himself. We do have a pretty good idea, but no proof for now as to who he might be. You don't want your bookkeeper to warn that guy off."

Daniel shook his head vigorously. "How long do you think it will take?" he asked.

"To be honest, I don't know," Luke said. "We have to figure out who else might be sending in checks and get charged for alleged delivery of their hazardous waste. And then we'll have to find out whether it's the same person who is behind the scheming."

"My step-father is usually finding out things pretty quickly," Julie consoled Daniel with a wink.

"Don't raise expectations I might not be able to fulfil," Luke warned her. She shrugged with a comical smile. "I'll be doing my best, I promise," he added for Daniel's benefit though.

They shook hands, and left.

"Hey," Daniel called after them. They turned around. "Thanks!"

They smiled. The real work was still lying ahead.

*

Eli Hayes was checking the fences in one of his cow pastures that same night. One of his calves had tried to escape, and its mother had bellowed anguished "Moos" all across the meadow as her young one got caught in the melee of wire and underbrush. The damage had just been skin-deep to the scared calf, and a hoof had landed on Eli's foot, leaving it black and blue. Juan, one of the farmhands, had got a head-butt from the animal, but otherwise had held on to it until the metal scissors had cut through the wire and freed the little dude.

After they had driven off the herd to another fenced-in area and Eli had put some cooling ointment on his swollen foot, they had walked back to mend the hole in the fence. That being finished, Eli had sent Juan back to the house to take a rest and have his dinner. "Tell Kitty I'll be just another 15 minutes to see whether there are any other parts in the fence that need to be seen to. I don't want our cattle back in there before everything is safe."

Now he was walking the fence line, checking the wire, and stopping every once in a while to listen to the sounds of his land. Ah yes, his land. He loved it dearly, although his father had been worried whether he wasn't force-feeding farming down his son's throat. Yet from the very beginning it had been Eli's strong inclination to farm. He loved the detachment from the city hub, the slowness of Nature, the change of colors, the waxing and waning of all things living, the smell of the rich soil of Medicine Creek Valley, and the comforting sounds of animals and humans getting nourishment from it.

All the more disturbing was the noise of a strong-motored vehicle rambling through the backwaters of his farmland. It didn't sound like the farm truck his neighbor used. Nor any of the other cars he knew he drove. This one sounded like one of those oversized off-road pick-ups workers or people who liked to look rough usually used.

Eli strained his eyes, trying to penetrate the fast falling dusk. A little later the noise changed from moving to running in neutral. And then Eli heard a dull "Thump" in the dark.

"What the ...," he muttered under his breath. All of a sudden he had a vision of what was happening right in his backyard. He lifted the wires of the fence with his thick leather gloves and slid through to the other side. Then he started moving as softly as possible to the area from which he had heard the sound.

Another "Thud". Eli shuddered. He was no coward, for sure, but he also knew that he was entering a danger zone. This might be the person the entire area was looking for, unloading another load of drums filled with hazardous waste. Encountering a criminal in the dark on purpose was not one of the things anybody untrained should venture. He knew it well. Just in case, he took out his smart phone. He wished now it had been a revolver. The thought made him smile grimly.

Then he saw the back of a large gray RAM, and standing in the truck bed was a man wearing gloves, rolling over another drum toward the rear. Eli was not able to make out the man's face, as the head was covered by the bill of a baseball cap and a hood. But he could clearly see the truck license plate. For a moment he had to steady his hand, as his hand holding out the smartphone was wavering in an almost ridiculous way. Suddenly the flash went off and lit the dark – Eli hadn't taken the time to figure how to shut that function off – and he rushed back into the underbrush.

"Hey!" he heard a startled gruff voice from the vehicle. He perceived that the person jumped down from the truck bed and ran a few steps towards him. Then the man stopped with a curse as his foot got wet.

Eli ducked down in the slough by the fence. It was just as well that he knew his land well enough. Sloughs were treacherous, and they could suck you down quickly. But he knew well where to step, and the deepening dusk was his friend now.

A few moments later the steps retreated, the motor was thrown in gear, and the RAM hurtled back on the rough path to its junction with the arterial road. Eli waited a few more moments; then he rose and made his way back to the farm.

Kitty was standing on the porch of the main house when he came in from the dark of the pasture, slightly limping, pants wet up to his knees. She rushed towards him. "What happened? Are you okay?" she asked anxiously.

"Everything is fine with me," he reassured her. "No need to fuss."

"Juan came in half an hour ago, and you said you'd be here shortly. I have put your dinner into the oven to keep it warm. What took you so long?"

Eli put his arm around his fiancée and climbed the porch steps. "You wouldn't believe what I found," he said. He pulled his smartphone out of his pocket and switched on the photo memory app. The picture showed the back of a gray RAM with a Washington State license plate. But Kitty gasped when she saw why Eli had taken the photo in the first place. The truck bed was filled with drums and a man who was in the progress of shoving off another drum to where a few already lay on the ground.

"The guy who is doing all the illegal dumping around here?" she asked incredulously.

"The same," Eli stated.

"That was totally dangerous!" Kitty said.

"I know," Eli admitted. "I guess I didn't really think it through."

"Is that why you are all soggy and muddy?"

Eli pulled off his shoes and socks and stared at them ruefully. "Had to hide out in the slough." Kitty's hand flew to her mouth. He folded her into an embrace. "Listen. Nothing happened, and everything is fine. The guy just saw the flash of my camera, followed me for a few steps, and then ran out of there. He never caught a glimpse of me."

Kitty's eyes were still filled with horror. "What will you do now?"

"Call the police and then eat dinner," Eli said calmly. "By the time they are here, my stomach will have stopped rumbling, and I will be able to lead them over to the dumping area."

"You know what?" Kitty whispered from inside the circle of his arms.

"What?" Eli asked.

"You are a real hero."

"I know," he chuckled smugly.

"And I hate it that I love you for all the anxiety you cause me!" Kitty burst out. Then she laughed. "Come on, my reckless man. Let's fill your plate and have you changed into something warm and presentable."

*

"Are you crazy? I can't keep going on with this!" Peter stared at his visitor wild-eyed and in disbelief. "What do you think I should have done?!"

"Shot him," the man said calmly.

"In the dark!" Peter snorted. "You are some idiot amateur, and I shouldn't even have listened to your plan.

"My plan?! Is it that now?"

"Well, you cashed in all the checks didn't you?"

"I gave you your cut."

"I took all the risk with the drums."

"Do you think the books were easier?!"

The two men tried to stare each other down and failed at the same time.

"Shit!" Peter's visitor said. "And what now?"

"I need to hide out for a while," Peter answered, scratching his stubbly chin. "Found this little cabin out in the woods near Mt. Rainier. Seems like nobody uses it. Might just as well go there and wait it out for a while."

"How about getting rid of the RAM?"

"Are you kiddin' me?! That's the best truck I ever had. No, man! I'll keep that with me. And sticking it out in the mountains for a while will make it drop from people's minds, you bet."

"What about your girl?"

"Her? Easy. I already sent her an email. She'll hook up with someone else. Would have done that sooner or later anyway. Bitch got a bit too clingy on me."

The visitor winced. "Well, I guess that's it then for now."

"I guess." Peter opened a can of microbrew and took a deep, long drink. "Hey, man. Do me a favor. Keep things on low, and we'll be in business some time again."

"Sure."

"Cool."

The visitor slapped Peter on the back and left the room without looking back. Peter gave the door a kick to shut it and collapsed on a chair. "Douchebag!" he said. "I bet they'll catch him yet."

He emptied his beer can. Then he went for his sports bag and started tossing in his belongings.

*

Mathilda was waiting in vain for Peter at the wharf the next morning. When there finally was a knock on her container door and she opened, she was facing Chief McMahon instead.

"Good morning, Mattie," he said and smiled. "May I come in?"

In answer, she held the door open for him and waved towards the chair across from her desk. "Would you like some coffee?"

Luke shook his head. "No thanks. It would be my third cup this morning and give me the jitters."

Mattie closed the door and sat across from Luke. "What can I do for you then?" she asked.

"May I have a look at your books, please?" Luke requested.

Mattie's face became troubled, and her voice quivered slightly. "Of course, you may. I guess you talked to Mr. Harrison already?"

Luke nodded. "Yes, I did. In fact, Julie and I paid him a visit yesterday night, and Julie was the one who found proof for his claim that he was betrayed by one of his employees."

Mattie opened a drawer underneath her desk and retrieved a file folder. Handing it over to Luke, she blushed. "I've never thought that I would ever end up in a situation like this. Having to prove that I'm not guilty of a crime."

"Easy, girl," Luke said, and his voice calmed her somewhat. "You haven't even been accused of anything yet. And as far as things look …" He opened the folder and quickly turned the pages, comparing them to pages in a folder he had brought with him. Then he handed it back to her. "May I see your bank receipts, too?" Mattie handed him another file. He scoured the pages, then returned the folder to the desk. "You are in the clear, Mattie."

"What?!"

"Actually, at this time my colleague over in Yelm is on duty at the Harrison Disposal Center. I'll give him a call in a few and let him know that our hunch was right. Your receipts come from a pad that was kept aside by our suspect for fraudulent cases. The "real" receipts come from a pad with a totally different set of serial numbers. Right now, we are looking into it whether you are the only victim or whether there were more."

Mattie had jumped up and was pacing the container now. "I cannot believe this! I cannot believe this!"

"You better. By the way – do you know a man who looks like this?"

Luke pulled out the police artist's drawing. Julie stared at it wide-eyed and opened her mouth. Then she closed it.

"Do you?"

"That is Peter Michaels, the guy who is my collection service provider. Did he do it? I mean dump the drums?"

Luke placed the drawing back into his folder. "We don't know that yet."

"I was expecting him this morning to talk over the next deliveries to Harrison Disposal Center. But he never showed up."

"That might be a coincidence. No, actually we are looking into a different matter that may or may not be related to the illegal dumping. It's too early to say for certain yet."

"I see," Mattie answered. Then she sat down again. "I'm feeling kind of shaky."

"Understandably so," Luke said. "It's not every day that you get so close to a real crime. Maybe you should simply take it easy on yourself today. Get a massage or have some nice lunch. Stop thinking about this case. It's out of your hands now, and we are onto it. No worries. We'll get it done."

Mattie's face cleared up a little and she lifted her hands. "I don't even know what to say."

"Then don't say anything," Luke chuckled. "Maybe your eyes already do it for you." He winked and got up. "Off to further business now. And don't forget – just relax."

He went outside and gazed over to the boats on the dry docks and the workers welding or painting. Barton & Son was a busy place even this early in the boating season. If he had a hand in it, he'd help keep it that way. He'd find the guy who dumped hazardous waste illegally and make him pay for the danger he put his town in. Luke straightened his shoulders.

*

From "The Sound Messenger":

One Arrest, Search for Accomplice in Illegal Dumping Case

judo. Police have arrested the bookkeeper of Harrison Disposal Center, Yelm. 27-year-old Julian Teal is supposedly connected to the illegal dumping cases that were discovered in Wycliff Forest in April and in Medicine Creek Valley early in May. The search for an accomplice still continues.

When Daniel Harrison, owner of Harrison Disposal Center, Yelm, checked his accounts earlier this month, he detected some flaws that had him on alert. "I had no idea I had actually found way more than a mere financial misconduct situation in my own business," he tells *The Sound Messenger*. "I only wanted to clear some doubts about my check disposals and customer satisfaction with one of my clients. Instead, I seem to have stirred up a hornets' nest."

Police are now investigating Harrison's employee, bookkeeper Julian Teal, for a particularly severe case of check fraud. Teal seems not just to have cashed in checks intended for Harrison Disposal Center over the past quarter of a year, he also falsified disposal receipts for hazardous waste that actually never made it to the company. Instead, the same hazardous waste was dumped illegally. So far, Wycliff Forest and Medicine Creek Valley have been found to have three such sites. Police are looking into possibly even more cases of check fraud and therefore further, so far undisclosed or undiscovered sites.

In connection with the illegal dumping, police are looking for a gray RAM pick-up truck with a Washington license plate. An eye witness was able to take the picture below that also shows the person committing the illegal dumping. The owner of the truck is Peter Michaels, 28, who has been providing Pierce County companies with hazardous waste collection services. Michaels might or might not be identical to the person in the picture, but was definitely identified to be involved in a case of blackmailing publishing manager John Minor earlier this month, in the attempt to squelch research on the illegal dumping case in Wycliff Forest. A police artist drew his likeness according to another eye witness description.

Meanwhile, one of the check fraud victims is Wycliff citizen and wharf owner Mathilda Barton of Barton & Son. "I had no clue that

I would ever be connected to crime scenes," she said, still visibly agitated. "I have always gone by the law in everything and made it a special issue to dispose of the wharf's hazardous waste in an appropriate manner. You cannot even imagine how shocked I am that the drums I thought had been delivered to Harrison Disposal Center were actually found in Wycliff Forest. This is not just about financial damage done to a small family business. This is about dragging the name of an honest company through the mire."

If found guilty, Teal faces jail time and an enormous fine for complicity in deliberately polluting the environment. Peter Michaels has obviously disappeared and is on a Washington State wanted list.

The Wycliff Police Department (WPD) requests the citizens of Wycliff and anybody else to keep their eyes open for possibly more illegal hazardous waste dumps. Citizens are being discouraged from getting close up to such sites or to handle discarded drums themselves. Also, WPD requests hints as to the whereabouts of Peter Michaels and/or his vehicle. You may contact WPD at phone number...

CHAPTER 5

The Green Maven's Tip of the Week:
Reuse old T-shirts by turning them into totes. Cut off
the sleeves and keep the side and shoulder seams that
already exist. Sew up the arm holes and neck hole. Add
two sturdy ribbons as handles to the shirt bottom, back
and front. These bags are reusable and washable.

Thora was driving down Main Street, which started at the Harbor Mall round-about. The mall featured the usual mix of chain businesses, but also Nathan's, a local supermarket. It was one of those windy, drizzly May days on the Washington coast, and Thora would have loved to go into one of the stores to browse. Yet, having no money, it was easier to abstain from such a plan entirely than to find herself inside one of the stores with the sudden desire to buy something she couldn't afford. Besides, she had an idea how to make money again. Actually, that was why she was out and about in the first place.

A hundred yards past the round-about, she found the entrance to a run-down housing area. A huge sign proudly announced "Maritime Palace". Thora wondered how the most repelling housing locations in Western Washington always came up with the fanciest names. It was past euphemism to give trailer parks or, in this case, half dilapidated houses a fancy name at all. It almost amounted to somewhat sadistic irony to call these narrow abodes with their sunk porches, cracking paint, and sagging doors and windows "palaces" at all. Yet here lived one of Wycliff's town originals who couldn't have comported herself more regally in an Uptown mansion.

Thora searched for a specific house number and parked her car right in front of the porch. She was trembling a little with anticipation. Angela Fortescue actually was scaring a lot braver townspeople than Thora. "You stay in the back and behave, Bear," Thora told her sweet-tempered Labrador. "I might come out within a few minutes. If she lets me in at all. But at least I can't say I didn't try." She stroked Bear's head and gave him a little treat. "There's more if you don't fool around in the car." Bear laid his head to one side and whined.

Leaving one window slightly open, Thora locked her car and cautiously walked up to the porch of Angela's house. There wasn't a sign of life in the run-down place, and Thora was in half a mind of turning around and leaving again.

As if she had sensed it, Angela suddenly tore open the door. "Look whom we have here!" she exclaimed. "Town Hall visits the poorhouse."

Thora was startled and shocked at the same time. "I'm not representing Town Hall," she managed to say. She left the other half of Angela's comment out, as it was too painfully true.

Angela suddenly gave her an awkward smile. "I know I said the truth when I called this a poorhouse. Even the owner has given up on us." She stepped aside. "I can't offer you much, but why don't you come in?"

Thora was surprised. She looked back at her car with Bear in it as if to tell him it was alright. Then she stepped through the door. There was no hallway, but she stood immediately in what was meant to be a sitting and dining room as well as a kitchen consisting of appliances from times before the Ark. The sofa in front of an ancient tube TV-set was well-worn, so was the arm chair next to a tiny coffee table. A camping table and camping chairs presented the dining room set. Another door went off to the back of the house. Thora thought it was probably leading to the bedroom.

"Welcome to my fancy palace," Angela mocked. "In fact, you are the first person ever whom I let inside."

"And why is that?" Thora asked. "You don't really know me at all."

Angela shrugged. "Maybe because you showed some guts the other day when you rather left your job than went against your conscience." She waved Thora towards the sofa. "Seat?"

"Thank you," Thora said and tentatively sat down. She had to admit that, though the house was filled with old and poor equipment, everything had been kept immaculately clean. "How did you end up here anyhow?"

For a moment Thora thought that her own question was pretty impertinent. It was none of her business where Angela came from nor what her living circumstances were. Yet everything she had on her mind also needed consideration of these facts. She needed to know that Angela was reliable and ambitious. Well, if Angela decided to, she could always throw Thora out again.

Angela sat down in her arm chair with a mug of coffee. "It's not a pretty story," she said and suddenly looked hurt and fragile. "Are you sure you even want to hear it?"

Thora felt a wave of empathy rise in herself. Was the most antagonistic woman in all of Wycliff really letting her not only into her home, but into her life? "Please," she said. "I would love to know you better. And I promise I won't judge."

"If I had thought so, I wouldn't have offered." Suddenly, Angela sounded haughty again. But it was with a hint of nostalgia and more than a pinch of bitterness.

*

Angela Meier had been born in Germany in the late 1940s. She grew up in an atmosphere of overcoming the wounds of World War II and experiencing that you can reap a lot from putting in a little effort. Her father was one of those people who made a fortune pretty quickly as a Volkswagen dealer. Everybody wanted a car, and the beetle was affordable. Her mother enjoyed entertaining his friends, some of whom became hers after a while, too. And his best friend became even more than that.

Angela felt more embarrassed by the fact that her parents divorced when she was still a teen and that she was now branded as coming from a dysfunctional family than she felt awful about her mother's betrayal. Her father paid her mother enough, so she was still able to live decently with Angela. But it was in an old apartment building near the main station inside the city of Nuremberg now, not in a smart little house out in its suburbs anymore. Gone were the days of entertaining, and Angela's mother started to miss it badly. Her lover had turned his back on her as soon as her circumstances had deteriorated. Everybody was looking to succeed in those days. Germany had had enough failure only too recently. Nobody needed a failure of a partner in a relationship to boot, did they?

After a while, Angela's mother started to look for work and ended up in the pencil industry, for which Nuremberg and surroundings are still world-famous. Every once in a while, Angela received a box of only slightly damaged pencils. Or, later, some cosmetic pencils, as those companies also produce for all of the great brands in the world. Angela appreciated the cosmetics more than the drawing pencils. And sometimes – to her mother's amusement – she looked almost as colorful as if she'd painted herself with the regular drawing products.

As her father was still living closer to the beautiful countryside of Franconia than the city, he took little or no influence on Angela's raising. Every once in a while he wrote her a letter, admonishing her to keep learning in school and to head for a career. More often than not, he even sent along a ten-Mark-bill along with it. But he never called, as he didn't want to get hold of his ex-wife accidentally. And he never invited Angela for visits to her former home as if staying with her mother had tainted her as well.

Angela craved her father's attention. As she wasn't able to get more than a letter and some money every couple of months, she started looking for the attention from men in general. She had learned to tone down her make-up meanwhile, though the fashion brought up quite dramatic styles soon enough. And as she was actually pretty with her slim, but curvy figure, dark pixie cut and a somewhat challenging nonchalance in her languid movements, she caught more than just one man's attention pretty soon. But Angela let them only look and maybe hold hands. School became less and less interesting, and after tenth grade, she simply called it quits and learned how to be a secretary. Her father, who would have wished her to go for more, was somewhat disappointed and stopped sending her money or letters. She'd only get Christmas and birthday letters until she was 21. Then even that would cease.

Her mother applauded Angela's decision. As a secretary, Angela might make a real catch. She might turn the head of a CEO of one of Nuremberg's bigger companies. She might even end up in a fancy villa and throw parties and travel. For the time being, they'd simply continue sharing the apartment and enjoying a girly life.

Of course, Life never plays along a parent's lines. One Saturday night, Angela encountered a smart-looking young American. He was a US soldier stationed near Frankfurt on the Main, and he was just visiting over the weekend to check out the historical places in Nuremberg and have some fun. She fell head over heels in love with him. Carelessness, a drink too many, and utter besottedness with the handsome, somewhat Italian looking young man led to some fateful moments on a moat meadow behind the ancient huge castle.

A month later – Angela had just turned 22 – she found herself pregnant. She was frantic. Johnny (that was the name of the GI) hadn't been back to Nuremberg. She had kept the scrap of paper he had given her. It was a bit crumpled by now, and she didn't even need it anymore, as she had learned the number by heart. But it was physical evidence that he had been in her life. Johnny Piccolini ... And now she had proof in unwanted abundance, too.

She didn't let her mother know about her predicament. She went to the local post office to make her call from there. To her utmost relief, Johnny actually answered the phone. He claimed he had had no time to call her. And, yes, he was thinking of her day and night. Angela sobbed with longing.

"Listen," Johnny said. "Why don't you buy yourself a train ticket and come over for the weekend?"

Angela took a deep breath. "But how do I find you?"

"I'll pick you up at the main station," he offered.

So Angela actually bought herself a ticket. If her mother wondered what this trip was all about, she didn't let on. Her sharp eyes had discerned some subtle changes in Angela lately. She knew the signs well enough when somebody was in love and when that love was not as happy as it should be. Ah well, didn't this happen to everybody at some point in time?!

Angela watched indifferently as the beautiful Franconian landscape swooshed past her train window. She was sharing the compartment with a middle-aged woman and her snoring husband, a nervous old lady with her 15-year-old niece, and a fat old man in Lederhosen, who was eating a liverwurst sandwich the smell of which grew stronger with every bite.

And then, there was Frankfurt. It wasn't beautiful at all, Angela thought. An ugly city at first sight, wasteland along the train tracks, some ruins from the bombings still waiting to be taken care of. The main station was huge and almost overwhelming. However, Angela spotted Johnny almost immediately. He was wearing his uniform and stuck out from the German crowd like a bump on a log. But who stuck out even more was the handsome tall stranger next to him.

"Angela!" Johnny called out and smiled broadly.

On the way to Frankfurt, Angela had contemplated how to greet Johnny and how and when to let him know that she was expecting his child. But now she wasn't sure whether she wanted to give the young man even as much as a hug. Who was that tall, serious looking man next to him?

"Meet my cousin Thomas Fortescue," Johnny said. "He's traveling across Germany during his vacations. Made some time for his cousin though."

Thomas nodded at her. "How do you do?" he said. Angela was flustered and found it difficult to answer him. All her school English seemed to fade under the stern look of the handsome stranger.

Johnny broke the tension by taking Angela's arm and firmly guided her through the crowd on the platform. He had parked his car outside, the green number plate already surrounded by little boys pointing at it and investigating the smart wooden accessories inside the vehicle through the windows. American cars were so much more exotic than the European ones they knew. And when the man in uniform turned up with a beautiful young lady on his arm and a man looking like a movie-star in tow, they respectfully stepped aside and gaped at them.

The day in the countryside near Frankfurt was beautiful. They had lunch in a beer garden, and in the evening they went to an apple wine tavern that also served rustic regional food. Angela held Johnny at arm's length. She didn't try too hard to pick up where they had left off in Nuremberg. Instead, she tried to be as interesting as possible to this cousin of his, Thomas. And she felt that she needed to play hard to get with him in order for him to catch on.

They had booked rooms at a tiny countryside hotel. At one time in the middle of the night, Johnny tried to visit Angela, but she had locked her door and pretended to sleep. After a while, Johnny gave up with a sigh and walked back to his own room, slamming the door in frustration. The next morning at breakfast, Thomas seemed way more approachable, and Johnny tried his best not to pout.

A week later, Thomas visited Angela in Nuremberg. He brought flowers for her mother and pralines for Angela. They walked up the castle hill and went inside Saint Sebaldus Church where an organ player was rehearsing for Sunday service. They ate tiny sausages in a bun. They took a look at artist Albrecht Dürer's home. They strolled across the farmers market in the huge market square. They held hands. They kissed. They talked about their dreams.

Thomas had lots of dreams. Angela listened to his and adapted hers so they might fit his bill. She didn't mention big suburban villas. She didn't mention large parties with champagne and chocolate fountains. She didn't mention cruises and Paris fashion. She left herself behind in a melee of wanting this man and accommodating his dreams.

Thomas Fortescue was half Italian, half American English. He had joined the Navy as soon as he had finished college, and he had started his career as an officer. He looked a bit like Gregory Peck, and he knew that women loved his appearance. He was career-bent, and he wanted to enjoy his life as best as he could. Traveling to Germany had been one thing that had been on his bucket list – he needed to impress the people back home with his geographical experiences.

When Angela told him a month later that she was pregnant, Thomas' world shook and came to a standstill for a moment. He knew what he had to do. He wouldn't have his career ruined by a woman with a baby in a foreign country. He wouldn't have his reputation ruined. He looked at her grimly, then he asked her to marry him. It couldn't be too bad to be married to a German woman, after all. So many other military people did it, too. She might even be an asset, pretty as she was.

Angela was soaring with relief. She became probably one of the liveliest pregnant women ever. Stroking her baby belly, her eyes were dancing with glee of having found such a handsome husband, an American at that. And she would not be shamed by having a child out of wedlock either. She would never let Thomas know that the baby wasn't his. It would be staying in the family, after all.

So Angela packed her bags, hugged her mother goodbye, and traveled to Washington State with a bump as big as a watermelon. The wedding ceremonial was a bit subdued. Thomas' mother openly disapproved of the sluttish girl who had lured her brilliant son into marriage with the oldest trick in the world – by having a baby. Thomas' father would have loved to flirt with Angela himself, but was confused by her pregnancy. Thomas tried to be thrilled, but failed. There were flowers, and there was a wedding cake. There even was a small wedding reception. But nothing was as big and glamorous as Angela had hoped for.

They called the slightly prematurely born, but full-sized baby Florence, because that was a place high on Thomas' bucket list. Angela liked it for the alliteration it made with their last name. They moved into a small rambler off Bremerton Naval Base. The suburb wasn't fancy. The house seemed nice enough, but certainly wasn't a villa. Angela started being home-sick. Florence was crying a lot. Thomas worked long hours and enjoyed each of his deployments in more ways than just being away from the family.

Angela started suspecting that Johnny would have been the wiser choice in the long run. At least, he had really wanted her. Thomas obviously didn't. Lipstick on shirt collars simply can't be explained away by "It isn't what it looks like" reasoning. And some phone calls that came in were certainly from dates who wanted to ask for a repeat arrangement, but hung up quickly as soon as they heard Angela's voice.

At first, Angela was extremely hurt. She would have loved to run away to go back to Germany. But she didn't have the money to do so. And she didn't have the guts either. Then came a phase when Angela thought she had brought it on herself. After all, Thomas had married her because he had believed she was with his child when it was really his cousin Johnny's. So she swallowed her hurt and anger and started pretending that she was fine with Thomas' conduct. She didn't encounter the women she got betrayed with in her neighborhood, and nobody had proof enough for what Thomas was doing when he was between base and home. If anybody did, they certainly didn't tell Angela to her face.

There was one episode going really wrong for Thomas' career one day though. Inadvertently, he had started having an affair with a woman whose marriage was going through a rough stretch, lingering on the verge of divorce. By a stroke of sheer luck, Thomas found out that she was married to a fellow officer and was able to jump ship before being spotted. After that he applied for relocation to a naval recruitment office in Wycliff. Angela never got to know the entire background to this sudden shift in career.

In Wycliff, they lived in a cute little Uptown rambler near the forest. Florence started going to school in their new hometown. Angela busied herself with sewing clothes for her girl. And Thomas came home each and every evening. No more deployments for him. After a while he stopped being in time for dinner. One excuse ran into another, and he was off to his old ways, this time charming the women of Wycliff and beyond with his Gregory Peck looks.

Wycliff was a smaller town than Bremerton though. And Angela soon heard rumors about whom Thomas favored and whom he had just cast off. Angela blushed, but couldn't do a thing. After all, they were only rumors, and Thomas had slick reasons for each and every absence, backed by clever little alibis. So Angela started carrying her head even higher than before, trying to ignore what was happening and concentrating on her daughter. She yearned to be her husband's one and only. But he had not just a roving eye, he actually cheated on her. It wasn't that he didn't do his duty towards her. But dispassionate was what it amounted to at most, and there were no further children added to their marriage.

"We have Florence," he stated, when she asked whether he didn't care to try for another child. "She is not even pretty. Why should I want another eye sore in my home?" It had been like a slap in the face to hear her child criticized so brutally and senselessly. But Angela had swallowed down her anger and just nodded. She loved Florence for the both of them.

Ah, Florence ... She didn't turn out to have Angela's looks at all. Neither did she have those of Thomas. Her build was more solid than either of theirs, and her looks were definitely on the Italian side. Angela was worried that at one time somebody might find the resemblance of her child to Johnny and mention it to Thomas. But then Johnny never visited – so who would see it?!

Then came the day that changed everything. One of the town gossips told Angela that Thomas had something going with the shop manager from "The Flower Bower", Bonny Meadows. Bonny was about Angela's age, a little mysterious, very pretty, and playful. And the town gossip also let Angela know that Bonny obviously was entirely unaware that Thomas was married. Angela gave the old woman a haughty look, but something inside Angela snapped. She didn't go to see her rival; she found that would have been beneath her. She waited for Thomas to come home and join her in the kitchen. Then she flung the accusation into his face.

"So – what are you going to do about it?" Thomas had asked her with a sardonic twitch to his sneer. "Do you want to raise a scandal, my dear? Because I've had it with your holier-than-thou-ways. Or do you really think I haven't long seen through your lie?!"

Angela blanched. "What do you mean?"

Thomas got a glass from a cabinet and poured himself some whiskey, then gulped the liquor straight down.

"You are a slut, Angela," he stated. "You are a shameless, lying slut!" He walked around her. "Just look at you. Does your own mother know about your little game? Did she encourage your plan? Was GI Johnny not good enough for you? So you simply went and fooled the fancier Navy officer? Because you thought he might make more money, right? And he wouldn't mind having your bastard for his daughter." He lifted his hand, and Angela shrunk. "Afraid I might slap you, aren't you?!" He laughed mirthlessly. "At least, you seem to realize you'd deserve it. - How stupid do you think I am? What with everybody asking me how a child as ugly as ours could be mine?"

"She's not ugly!" Angela protested.

"Maybe not," he conceded. "But she's not mine either, is she?" He stepped towards her, face red with rage. "Is she?"

"No." Angela's voice was very small.

They fell silent. The silence was interrupted by a low whimper. Florence stood in the doorway. She had overheard everything. She was pale and upset.

"Come here, sweetie," Angela said softly to the now nine-year-old.

"No," the girl said and hugged herself. Angela sighed. "Who is my real father?" Florence asked with a dead voice.

Angela bit her lips. Thomas looked at her. "Well, you better tell her yourself. It's been none of my doing, after all," he challenged her.

Angela nodded helplessly. Her world had started falling apart. She might as well face it. "Your father's...," she faltered under Thomas' icy look. "Johnny Piccolini," she finished.

"Uncle Johnny...," the girl said. Then she turned around and left.

"Great timing," Thomas mocked. "But that always seems to have been your special gift."

"I was so young then," Angela tried.

"Not too young for a lie as big as that."

"I loved you."

"And I am to believe this?!"

"Is there a way to apologize?"

"For more than nine years stolen from my life?"

"I tried to give back," Angela pleaded. "I did everything I knew to make you a home."

"From my money."

Angela didn't know how to answer this. She sank down on a kitchen chair. She wasn't aware that she had started to cry.

"I'm sick and tired of you and the child," Thomas continued. "After tonight you won't expect me to keep this farce of a marriage going. I will sell the house and have my lawyer send you some paperwork."

"Divorce!" Angela mouthed, her face as white as a dishtowel.

Thomas shrugged. "I'm sure you will find a way to deal with the situation. You have found your way around before."

"What will happen with Florence?"

Thomas thought it over for a moment. "You have been a good mother, so let her decide. I certainly have had enough to do with someone who is not mine."

"Will you tell Johnny?"

Thomas gazed at her coldly. "As I said: Florence is not my child. She's not my business."

Angela buried her face in her hands.

*

"And so it happened," Angela finished her story, staring in front of her. "We got divorced. Florence never forgave me and asked to be removed to her real father, Johnny. Thankfully, he and his wife accepted her at once. I wrote to her for a while, but she never answered. And then Johnny asked me not to write anymore, as my letters upset his wife a lot more than caring for his daughter by another woman."

Thora rose and walked over to the window. "How sad," she said softly. "To think that everything started so happily and ended here."

"I tried to find work as a secretary over here after that," Angela admitted. "But my English was way less fluent than today. I couldn't get the spelling right either. And it took me so long writing down things in a foreign language. Even the type writer keyboards were different from what I was used to. So I found work in a cannery a little south of here. I was still able to live in Wycliff, but didn't have to deal with the people on a closer level. It kept me alive. Of course, having been married for only a bit over nine years, I had forfeited my benefits as a military spouse. Should have waited with my accusations about Thomas taking a lover three years longer." She smiled bitterly. "When I got myself hurt at one of the big canning machines, I had to pay the hospital bill out of my own pocket. St. Christopher's here in Wycliff treated me great. But they ate into my life savings big time. I have finally managed to pay the last bill off a week ago. So, there may be a new beginning after all."

Thora turned around and smiled brightly at the older woman. "And what a coincidence! This is exactly what I came here about. To suggest something to you. Would you like to hear?"

Angela nodded. "I would. I also guess I have to apologize for having been so abominably stand-offish in the past."

"It worked as a shield for you," Thora stated.

Angela nodded. "I didn't want pity. And I didn't want anybody to know about my circumstances. If you act haughtily enough, nobody will want to get to know you better."

"And I crashed that shield," Thora smiled.

"You did," Angela said. "But it was also the fact that after all those years I'm debt-free."

"Hmmm, I guess my suggestion won't make you unhappy then." Thora took a deep breath. "I want to start up a cottage industry. And I need you for it."

"How so?" Angela asked curiously.

"Let me start from the other end. You know that I am kind of an environmentalist, which is one of the reasons why I quit my job."

"Right," Angela nodded.

"These days, a lot of places in Western Washington are thinking of replacing the cheap plastic bags they hand out automatically at every store with more durable ones. In most cases they do so with plastic covered fabric bags. Not much of an alternative."

"No," Angela agreed. "It's still plastic. And not everybody is able to afford these bags either."

"Right," Thora said. "And here is where my alternative comes in: simple cloth bags. They are sturdy, durable, made from renewable resources – and you can even toss them into the laundry."

Angela nodded cautiously. "But you will have to produce a huge amount of those to make it worthwhile for a store to invest in them."

"Exactly," Thora beamed. "This is why I came up with the idea of cottage industry. You need to teach me and everybody else who wants to participate how to sew. In the beginning I can rent machines. We will all sew at home. I will check with all of the Wycliff businesses who would like to jump on the band wagon."

"You might want to do this before you even rent a single machine," Angela warned, a tad of her old haughtiness blinking through.

"Of course," Thora said undauntedly. "And I would like to include especially all those people who are in need of a job. It will not pay big in the beginning, but we can dream big. My ultimate goal would be selling fancy bags and totes from a store of our own and having a B-2-B line of simple grocery bags."

Angela clapped her hands. "Girl, you are really something else! And as beggars can't be choosers, I bet you will have a lot of women lining up to learn sewing for a few dollars rather than having to pinch pennies."

Thora laughed. "I think I just found a business name, too. How about 'Bags 4 Choosers'?"

"Sounds like one of those typically fancy Wycliff company names to me," Angela smirked.

Thora laughed and gave the woman a quick hug. "Nothing wrong with fancy, is there?" she winked.

*

"Hi Mattie, it's Trevor."

"Hi." The voice on the other end of the line sounded wary. "Is everything alright?"

Trevor was sitting at his office desk, doodling blue lines onto a pad of notepaper. "Oh sure." He cleared his throat. "Listen, Mattie, I know you have been through a lot lately. But now that it's over, I thought we should celebrate the outcome. How about lunch today?"

"Trevor, I appreciate this. Really." There was a long pause on the other end now.

"But…?" Trevor frowned and drew a tiny cat with whiskers and a long tail. Then he added a couple of horns.

"I don't think we should mix business and private, Trevor." Mattie sighed. "I am your client. We can still be friends, can't we?"

"Sure," Trevor said. "Well, I was just trying."

"Right. Thanks."

Trevor hung up. His ball pen doodled viciously through the kitten, shaping spirals and finally covering up his drawing.

"Are you okay, darling?" Trevor's mother, a very patrician lady with clear views on everything, had entered the office and laid her hands on his shoulders.

"Fine," Trevor said grimly. "Just fine."

"Want to talk about it?"

He laughed bitterly. Then he rose abruptly, brushing his mother's hands off. "I prefer not to, but thanks. I will be out for lunch today. Don't keep any left-overs for me."

*

The day of the protest in front of town hall was dawning slowly. There were thick clouds in the sky, and the wind had picked up over night. Thora was not happy about this. She was also really nervous. Would there be any people from Wycliff to support her protest against the oil refinery? Would her speech be good enough to rally more people? Maybe even to win over the town council? Or would she end up alone and in the rain, an utter failure?

But the weather held. The wind calmed a bit, and though it was still a dark-grayish day, it was not drizzling either. When Thora arrived in town with Bear in tow – she took him with her for much needed emotional support – she found a crowd in front of town hall waiting for her. Wycliff town hall was an imposing building on Main Street. It took up an entire block and faced the old yacht harbor next to the ferry terminal. Built in the early 1900s, its walls were decorated with abstract friezes and stylized plants in their decorative masonry. There also was a huge balcony above the giant front doors. A teacher of the theater class at Wycliff High had set up a little lectern on the wide entrance steps for Thora, microphone and speakers included. People had crafted their own banners and placards. Some nerdy teenagers had devised sandwich-boards that they now hung from their shoulders. Thora was touched.

When the protest began, people started chorusing: "We recoil from AnCoSafe Oil!" It had not much of a content, but it rhymed and was an imaginative way of saying "No".

After a while, somebody nudged Thora. "How about you give us your speech now?"

For a moment, Thora's stomach dropped. She almost choked, but she was here for a reason, wasn't she? So she nodded, tugged on Bears leash, and climbed the steps to the lectern. She placed her short manuscript onto the table and made Bear lie at her feet. Her eyes took in the crowd which was seemingly still growing. Then she moved the microphone a little closer to her mouth and checked that it was switched on. A screech from the speakers startled the crowd into looking towards her. She laughed nervously, and the high school teacher rushed in to readjust the sound system. Thora gave him a kindly smile. Then she started with a wobbly voice that echoed over the area in front of town hall, but became firmer and firmer with the passion of her speech.

"Thank you all for coming here today," she began. A few people clapped, some whistled. "I know it is not convenient for everybody, and the weather is not all too friendly. But convenience is not what we must think about when the future of our beloved and quaint town of Wycliff is at stake."

She took a deep breath, as someone shouted "Hear, hear!"

"As everybody knows by now, the town council of Wycliff is planning to have AnCoSafe Oil build an oil refinery south of our ferry terminal. They invoke the points of more jobs, an Amtrak connection, and the more convenient refueling of the ferries. AnCoSafe Oil is also offering benefits such as free day care for the workers' children. Mind you, I'm not badmouthing AnCoSafe Oil. I actually couldn't care less which company is going to set up the oil refinery. I am arguing against *any* oil refinery being built here in the South Sound."

Applause from some in the first row, applause from an above window behind her. So even inside town hall some people agreed with her.

"Let us have just a short look on the impact an oil refinery would have on Wycliff as it is right now. Take a look to your right, towards the ferry terminal, and imagine huge fences and the pipelines and buildings a refinery typically has. Yes, you would see it from further off, because the structure would be higher than anything else in Wycliff. Our Victorian town would lose its image as quaint and turn into plain industrial. What's more – we'd see a lot more traffic. Imagine the workers commuting through Main Street, tanker trucks included. There would be crude oil trains ending up here in town. I needn't tell you about the deadly danger that comes from such transports. We have seen what happens to towns when such a crude oil transport derails and goes up in flames. In this case, the geographical uniqueness of the Wycliff bluff might also be a death sentence. A mighty explosion Downtown would almost certainly cause a massive landslide for Uptown."

"Horrible!"

"Didn't they ever think of that?!"

"Are they all dumb in the council?!"

Thora held out her hands beseechingly. People fell silent again. "There are other effects an oil refinery would have on our town. More jobs mean more people moving in. Which means that we would find more building activity. We'd have to consider whether our infrastructure would be able to manage such a sudden increase of population. The leisurely tourist aspect of our town would be lost. We'd have to respond to the demands of an industrial city. Sure, it would open opportunities for new businesses. But it would also kill off a lot of businesses that we have been living with and loving for so long."

"Shame on you, Mayor Thompson!"

"Yes, shame on you!"

Thora shook her head. "This is not a personal vendetta. This is plainly listing the risks... And these last ones were only the most blatant ones. There are other things that would creep in without our noticing at first. I'm talking about the fumes that develop when gas is flamed off. We'd breathe in the stuff without realizing. It might not even stink."

Somebody was whistling, another shouted: "Fricking creeps!"

Thora ignored them. "Another feature of oil refineries is that they are constantly at work, and that involves bright illumination at night time. Those of you living right on top of it, up on the bluff, might find that their ability to sleep deteriorates. Well, you won't be the only ones. All nocturnal animals would be disoriented and driven away from their usual routes and habitats. And the bats that see to it that we don't have mosquitos around here will starve and die out or move away. Wycliff might become mosquito infested."

She paused for effect. The applause from above and behind her encouraged her even more to continue than the eagerly listening crowd in front of her.

"Last but not least: Have our town fathers thought about the devastating effect of an oil spillage? It happens so easily. Every wharf owner, every gas station has probably had to deal with a smallish one at one time or another. The Sound is a sensitive ecosystem. How many of you can actually recall when they saw the last colorful and intact sea star around here? That's right – we are already dealing with a mysterious vanishing of the beautiful creatures. Or think of anemones. Remember the piling at our ferry terminal used to be almost infested with large white, yellow, and apricot colored anemones? Gone! An oil spillage would kill off more maritime life than just that. It would kill off everything marine here in the South Sound. Our bald headed eagles wouldn't find sea food anymore. They'd have to go for different prey. So would other birds. In the end, our entire natural ecosystem would tumble and fall apart.

There is a green adage along the lines of 'Save the planet, so the planet saves us'. I'd like to change it a little: Save Wycliff, so Wycliff saves us! – Thank you."

The crowd was cheering wildly. The high school teacher came up again and took a mobile microphone. "Thank you, Thora, for this passionate appeal not to have AnCoSafe Oil build a refinery in our beautiful town. Maybe some of our co-protesters have questions for you?" He looked into the crowd expectantly. A hand was raised. "Yes?"

"But I also heard a refinery would bring the town considerable taxes."

Thora smiled bitterly. "I cannot deny this fact. But to be honest – I think that is similar to committing arson in order to keep the manufacturing of fire extinguishers going."

"Aren't you a bit sinister about our future?" somebody else asked.

"Indeed I am," Thora admitted. "I want us to be able to enjoy this world as it is. I want our community's children and grandchildren to be able to enjoy it. Of course, things keep changing all the time. With or without us. But I wish that mankind treated Nature more empathetically. We are using, abusing, and wasting what we have. I tell you, it won't matter to our Earth. If we destroy it, it will destroy us. But it will continue turning – just without us. We'd simply be gone like the dinosaurs before us. My question to you: Is that what you wish on your children and grandchildren? And theirs?"

This rhetorical question was perceived as a perfect ending to Thora's speech, and people nodded and applauded. They started chanting again, and Thora heard the windows above her close before she had a chance to look who had applauded her from there. The high school teacher thanked her again and joined the protesting crowd. Thora wiped her brow, picked up her manuscript, and stepped away from the lectern.

The instant she did so, she felt her feet were entangled in Bear's leash. He had moved around a bit, while she had been making her speech. For a moment she swayed, then she saw the steps rushing towards her. She reached out with her right arm to stop her fall. Bear barked. Then her hand crashed onto the stone surface. As she was able to keep her head and body from hitting the stairs, she heard something crack in her upper arm and then a slow, long ripping sound. There was some insane pain going through her entire arm, but somehow she was also a rather incredulous observer of what was happening to her. "Oh no! No! No!" she kept wailing, seeing all her efforts fall apart within seconds.

Bear was barking happily and running around her, leash dragging behind. He must be thinking it was some game. The manuscript pages had fallen down and were blown about by the wind. He chased them and snapped at them.

Around her, people only slowly realized something had happened to Thora, but most of them didn't think it was more than a stumble. Until Thora finally found the power to move and simply sit on the steps, holding her right arm. The arm she worked with. The arm she did every major task with. She could have wept, but she didn't.

"You alright, dear?" Julie Dolan asked. She had pretty quickly grasped the situation.

"No," Thora managed to say. "I think I damaged my arm pretty badly. Could you help me get a ride to the hospital?"

"Sure thing," Julie said.

"And do you think somebody could bring Bear back to my house? My car is parked near the Community Center; they need to know that I'm not leaving it there just for the fun of it. And Angela needs to know that I probably won't make it to our first meeting tomorrow."

"Angela Fortescue?" Julie wondered.

"Yes, her. We have some pretty awesome plans going, and now I have messed it all up. I could cry. I wish I could turn back the clock just by five minutes!"

"Dear, dear," Julie tutted. "It is what it is."

"I know," Thora winced in pain. "I guess I simply have to think forward from here."

"Absolutely," Julie agreed, maneuvering Thora and Bear on the leash down the stairs. "You know, your speech was really good. Mind if I ask you for the manuscript, so

I can cover this event appropriately? And then, of course, I'm all ears what such a nice person as you would have to do with misanthropist Angela Fortescue. That is, if you are able to talk through clenched teeth..."

"Not sure," Thora admitted. "Gosh, I never knew something like this could hurt so badly." Then she gave a laugh while holding on to her helpless arm. "I guess you can count me amongst the fallen women now."

*

From "The Sound Messenger":

Injured Environmentalist Envisions New Business

judo. Former town hall secretary Thora Byrd gave a flaming speech intended to hinder the town council's plans for an oil refinery to be built in Wycliff. Supported by a crowd of approximately over two hundred citizens and more arriving throughout the protest event yesterday, Byrd even had back-up from some town hall employees. Her future plans for a business for herself and other less privileged people in town might lie on ice for a while though.

A break was probably the last thing she thought of when she left the lectern on the Wycliff town hall steps at yesterday's anti AnCoSafe Oil refinery protest. Unfortunately, that is exactly what happened to environmentalist Thora Byrd, who is heading the local protest movement for Wycliff staying non-industrial. A fall on the steps of town hall, caused by her own dog, left her with a painful injury to her right arm.

Byrd's speech had been greeted as a very involved and well-founded instrument in the fight against another huge refinery project in the South Sound (find a list of her arguments in the text box below). She made it a point though that she was neither in a "vendetta against the mayor" nor opposing a particular company in the oil industry. She also answered questions from the protesting crowd.

How far Thora Byrd takes environmentalism is known by now. Quitting her job at town hall because of her conscience is just one thing. But she revealed another major plan exclusively to *"The Sound Messenger"*. As cities around the Sound are contemplating a change in the policy of bagging groceries, she has an entire business concept in mind, including not only herself, but other citizens of Wycliff who might be in need of an additional job and income.

"The plastic age should finally cease," Thora said. "We have renewable resources that will work for the same purpose in an infinitely more environmentally friendly way. They wouldn't have to cost more. In the end, even fashionistas might get their fill."

As Thora Byrd is recovering at home, she hasn't lost her sense of humor, but it looks like a lot of her plans for this year are stalled. "What will become of my ideas for creating a cottage industry for and with my fellow citizens?" she worries. "But first and foremost: What will become of our protest against an oil refinery in our beautiful town?"

CHAPTER 6

The Green Maven's Tip of the Week:
Your kids got chewing gum in their hair? Pour some
Coca Cola over the gummy place, while gently rubbing
it off the strands. Then wash hair as normally.

After Julie had dropped her off at the Emergency Room of St. Christopher's and the nurses started prepping her for a doctor's examination, Thora felt all the tension of having to function properly fall off her shoulders. She had been able to stay cool-headed enough to make all the arrangements for her return home whenever that would be. She had even discussed her business plan with Julie. Now she could finally concentrate on her injury and what might happen. Finally, something of a physical shock set in, and her teeth started chattering. It was not cold in the ER, but the nurse who was seeing to her brought her a huge ice pillow to ease the pain in her limb and carefully covered Thora's shoulder with a warm, soft blanket. Alone in her curtained-off cubicle, Thora was wondering whether she would have to undergo surgery and how she would be able to afford that. Would the insurance pay at all, since it had been her own dog causing the accident? She heard a moan and a whimper and realized it was herself who finally succumbed to the pain.

Steps approached her little private space, and a tall, athletic doctor came in. His face betrayed nothing but concern. A tight smile sat in his eyes and around his lips. A tag on his white coat simply read "Burns". Thora wondered how many cases Doctor Burns might already have dealt with today and how many were probably worse than hers. She was still able to think clearly, after all.

"Are you very much in pain?" Doctor Burns inquired as he sat down in a chair next to her hospital bed.

"It's pretty bad," Thora admitted.

"Is anybody coming to stay with you while you are here in hospital?"

Thora shook her head. "I was dropped off here by one of our town's journalists. She would have stayed if she hadn't had some more appointments before her evening deadline."

"Is there anybody our hospital could call for you?"

Thora sighed. "There isn't, and actually I'm keeping enough people busy already. Anybody sitting here just for the sake of being with me might be bored to death soon enough. Then you'd have another victim on your hands," she joked weakly.

Dr. Burns flashed her an amused smile. "We'll see that you get treatment as quickly as possible. We have to wait for the result of your X-rays right now to decide what to do. For the time being, we will give you something for your pain." He rose and left the little compartment. Shortly after that, a nurse appeared and gave Thora an injection. Thora found it impossible not to moan. The pain in her arm increased by the minute. But she was also thinking of Bear. Who would look after him? Would she even be able to look after herself when she came home?

Another doctor entered the cubicle. He was slightly smaller than Dr. Burns and, in spite of some visible worry in his face, he also expressed somewhat comical despair. "I'm Dr. Reifsnyder," he introduced himself. "How did you ever manage to do this to yourself?!"

Thora ground her teeth. "So it is as bad as it feels?"

Dr. Reifsnyder nodded. "We just saw the X-ray pictures. You broke your upper arm and broke and dislocated your shoulder. How did that happen?"

"I fell on the town hall steps. I had just finished leading a protest against the planned refinery. There goes pride before the fall evidently," Thora said.

Dr. Reifsnyder shook his head as if in disbelief. "We'll take you into the hospital's trauma unit and will see what we can do for you today. We'll have to discuss amongst the team how we are going to deal with the breaks and the dislocation. We want to make it as easy as possible for you."

"Thank you, doctor." Thora smiled with a grimace as another wave of pain came and went. She hardly knew how to keep her arm in a less painful position.

After a while, Nurse Dawn transferred her to a huge examination room that had the sign "Trauma Unit" above. Thora dispassionately watched other patients being walked or pushed past in wheelchairs, nurses hurrying along with instruments, doctors checking lists. A child was howling in protest from another room. An ambulance driver was discussing something with a receptionist nurse who was looking for a doctor. It ought to have been mayhem, but the ER was so very calm and structured. And everybody was friendly and polite. Thora wondered how they could keep this up, as patients came in without a pause, some of them impatient, others outright impolite.

And then her room started filling with a big team of doctors and nurses. Dr. Burns and Dr. Reifsnyder explained the procedure she would be undergoing. "We have decided to reduce your dislocation first."

Thora cringed. She had heard that this might be as painful as the dislocation itself. But she knew there was no way around, and she trusted these compassionate doctors who were visibly worried about her physical state as well as her state of mind. She was obviously a medical case that had demanded some discussion. But without support from a family member or friend the team were equally worried how emotionally stable she really was. "I trust you," she finally said. "I know you are doing your best, and it can't get much worse than now."

The anesthetist of the team was an energetic, businesslike woman. She started explaining what medication they would inject, so Thora would stay awake, but not feel any pain.

"Sounds like an eerie experience," Thora fretted. "I've never been one for taking mind-altering drugs except maybe a glass or two of red while watching the sunset."

She had to sign some paperwork, which was pretty awkward with her untrained left. Then she let herself sink into the hands of the team. She felt the brief pricking of a syringe. Then slowly the room around her started changing. Later she would describe it as a mixture of Hubba Bubba chewing gum and SpongeBob squares shaping three-dimensional labyrinths which were encroaching on her with almost physical reality. The colors of those cubes tasted strange and started changing in ever quicker sequences. Thora still heard the doctors talk.

"I don't like this," she managed to break through her trip.

"Some people pay a lot of money for such drugs," the anesthetist answered her with a little laugh.

"Well, I'd never recommend it, for sure. You can spend your money on way better things," Thora said. Meanwhile the labyrinth oppressed her mind worse and worse. She felt it was trying to steal her soul. To kill her.

Then suddenly a voice filled the room. It sounded so familiar. It was such relief in the loneliness of the labyrinth. Thora called out: "Clark!"

"I'm here with you," she heard his voice.

Her mind was reeling, fighting the squeeze of the labyrinth. And then, as quickly as it had descended on her, the nightmare ended, and she realized that she was back to the trauma unit.

"Everything went just fine," Dr. Burns smiled. "After some more X-rays we will see how we will continue treatment. Alright?"

"Thank you," Thora smiled. Dr. Burns and his team left, and she turned her head abruptly. Her eyes widened. "You are really here, Clark?"

"I couldn't make it earlier," he smiled at her with his incredibly blue eyes. "I was in a conference while you had your protest going."

"So you didn't hear a thing of what I had to say? You didn't see how many people had come to protest against the refinery?"

"I had some spies placed in a couple of windows above," he chuckled. "Some of them gave me a piece of mind after you were done."

"Serves you right," she said with all the dignity she could muster in her hospital gown. "If you hadn't come up with this harebrained scheme…"

"Now wait… Do I deserve such treatment after I cancelled my golf game this evening just to be with you?"

Thora bit her lips. "I'm sorry. I'm sure grateful that you are sitting by my side. It's just that I'm simply overwhelmed by this situation."

"Take one day at a time," Clark soothed her. "It will all sort itself out."

*

The first morning at home was dreary and painful. Thora wore a huge, bulky sling which was to prevent her from moving her arm. But, every once in a while, she managed exactly that and was punished by some mean pain shooting up the entire length of her arm. Or she accidentally bumped into a doorframe, not being used to taking up so much space. Dressing had been impossible – she still wore the hospital gown over her jeans. She also thought her hair needed a washing direly, though she had done so only yesterday. She was frantic about looking unkempt. What she would do about her meals, was a mystery to her. She wasn't able to cut or cook anything with her untrained left. Bear whined, looking up at her. At least she had been able to put some dog food into his bowl without spilling too much of it over its brim.

Yesterday, Clark had driven her home and helped her inside. But after that she had been left to her own devices. It was then that despair hit her really hard. She didn't cry, but she stared through her favorite window across the Sound and scolded herself for the carelessness that had cost her so dearly. Her insurance was still good for this quarter. But would it be good in this case? And she wouldn't be able to drive for eight weeks. She would have to call on friends to help her go places, do groceries, even water her garden. Worst of all, her project of "Bags 4 Choosers" would have to wait until she would be able to move around on her own again. Over these sobering thoughts Thora almost forgot that she had made quite an impression on Wycliff and that, right now, word was spreading. Upset about herself, Thora would have loved to toss and turn in bed that night, but found she could only lie on her back, as her arm was lying immobile across her tummy.

Getting up had been almost a relief, even though the day started with challenge after challenge and had Thora collapse exhausted at the breakfast table. A sharp little bark from Bear roused Thora. "What's up?" she asked him.

Bear padded to the front door and whined. Thora followed him and opened the door. She looked into Clark Thompson's smiling, freshly-shaved face.

"Good morning," he said.

"You ... again?" Thora asked in disbelief. "You were here only yesterday."

"Thought you might need some help with having breakfast or lunch or whatever." Clark produced a cooler from behind his back. "May I come in?"

Thora stepped aside, holding the door wide open. Clark went straight to the kitchen and set the cooler down.

Then he started unpacking. "I brought you some fresh bagels and cream cheese. And ..." he held up a package with a mysterious smile. Thora's face was a question mark. "Gravad lox," Clark declared. "Home-made."

"You can do this yourself?" Thora asked and stared at her friend who kept surprising her more and more.

"Sure!" Clark said. "This is not my catch though. I bought it at Nathan's, then cured it. You can have it on the bagels I brought, if you like. I'll spread some cream cheese on it. I brought capers and red onions, too. I also make a mean honey mustard sauce..."

Thora sat down. "I don't get it. Why are you doing all this?"

Clark looked at her sheepishly. "I could say I miss my secretary at town hall and try to bribe her to come back." Thora opened her mouth, but he held up both his hands. "Whoa, I know that a no from you is a no! - But I also have a notion of what you are going through all on your own. I can't leave a friend alone in a situation like this. Even if she is not of my opinion or is protesting my plans."

Thora's eyes became wet all of a sudden. "I'm not sure I can make up for it."

"I'm not asking for anything in return," Clark said. "Maybe I just don't want to lose your friendship over my refinery plans. I already lost a secretary, you know."

Thora smiled weakly. "You are an awfully good friend, Clark," she said. "I just wish I could cut up the bagels and make them taste right with all these goodies..."

Clark nodded. "I can do that for you, of course."

Five minutes later, Thora was munching away on a tasty lox and cream cheese bagel, moaning softly.

"Does it hurt that badly," Clark asked anxiously.

Thora swallowed and laughed. "No, this tastes so incredibly good!"

*

"That's right, I'll be offering sewing lessons," Angela Fortescue said crisply. "You would have to bring your own machine though."

A female voice on the other end replied something.

"Oh no, you don't have to buy one. You can rent one and then figure whether this is something you would like to do. And you'd have to bring some patchwork fabric as well. The cheap stuff will do. This is just so you get a hang of feeding the thread, cutting, seaming, and basically sewing straight lines. Once the production is on, we will provide you with all the material necessary."

Something more was said on the other end.

"Sure. I'll show you, and if you decide you don't like it, I won't hold it against you."

They exchanged some more words. Then Angela hung up with a genuine smile around her thin lips. Was that really her? Had she indeed hung a note on the info board of the Community Center that she was offering sewing lessons? Was she really smiling in anticipation, as a surprising lot of women all ages had already called her in spite of her reputation as the town hag?

Angela began making a list. She had ten women on her hands who were keen to know how to sew. Some had machines handed down by their mothers or grandmothers. Most didn't know their brands nor features. Some had no machines at all. Two had tried to sew years ago, but given up, daunted by the speed of the machines. Maybe that would change. But Angela reasoned that they would also need people cutting the piecework for the seamstresses. So there might be even jobs for those who would turn out to have no sewing skills at all.

Angela hadn't conferred with Thora about her own initiative yet. At first, she had been appalled about Julie Dolan's visit which brought her the news of Thora's accident. Angela had joined the protest march in the beginning and actually enjoyed being part of the crowd, for a good purpose at that. But then somebody had given her a cold stare, and she had shrunk and walked off, never becoming a witness to the incident. When Julie had called, she had thought it was a pretext from Thora to discard the sewing project after all. But why put Julie through the trouble of searching her out and delivering the message? Besides,

Thora had the guts to speak for herself. The next day she had read about everything in the newspaper, too.

Absent of a meeting and any further directions, Angela had come up with some ideas about how to get started anyhow. The more women able to sew, the better they'd be able to implement them in their cottage industry. The more seamstresses they had, the better an offer they would be able to make to the local businesses on selling cotton or hemp bags. And they needed to find out how much buying fabric in bulk would cost them. She could do that from the computer room of the Community Center.

And then there was Meredith Baker, her next-door-neighbor, a gray and shy little mouse of maybe 35 who was scared of her own shadow. Her husband, Ron, was one of those fishermen who went away on tours to Alaska for up to three or four months, and when he came back, he usually scared the bejesus out of his little wife. He didn't beat her, but his cursing rang through half of the wharf area when he came home from the Dock Tavern. His language made her cringe and wonder where the sweet giant of yore had gone whom she had married some 15 years ago. It was just as well that they didn't have children, as they were poor as church mice due to Ron's hard drinking. Meredith could barely rub two pennies together every time he left. It was only good that his fishing corporation didn't pay their men in a lump sum, but in monthly rates, so the families wouldn't starve while the men were at sea.

Meredith would surely want to know about their plan, too. She was a sweet woman who was struggling hard to make ends meet and still stay positive. She could well use something that took her mind off daily worries and put some cash into her piggy bank. Angela also knew that Meredith was a wonderful artist. Maybe she could sketch all the models for bags and totes that they would have one day. Should she tell Meredith? Or should she ask Thora first?

Angela grabbed the phone once more. It took Thora a while to get to the phone. But then Angela spilled what she had come up with and what she also had already set in motion. "Are you upset with me now?" Angela asked cautiously.

"Upset?" Thora said. "This is wonderful. I was worried we wouldn't even get started after my stupid fall yesterday."

"How are you doing anyway?"

Thora related all the details to her future business partner. "It might take up to a year until I'm fully restored. It's nerve-racking, but I have to think forward. I can't turn back the clock..."

"No, pretty impossible," Angela said drily. "Whom are you telling?! Anyhow, I'll let Meredith in on our plan then. Maybe she can become the designer of our little cottage industry. Maybe that would put some more courage into that little mouse."

They hung up, and Angela went to her front door. This time of day, when Ron Baker was between trips,

Meredith usually was at home, preparing a dinner for two that would be eaten only by one. Angela went over to her neighbor's door and knocked. The door opened a crack, and Meredith's pale face peeped through.

"Hi Meredith," Angela said almost cordially. "Do you have a moment? I have an offer for you that you won't be able to refuse..."

*

"Hi Thora, this is Dieter. You know, the German guy from Steilacoom. We read about your accident after that speech of yours. Listen, Denise and I will be over in Wycliff this afternoon. Do you need anything?"

"Hello Thora, this is Kitty. Yes, the one from 'The Flower Bower'. I guess what with your shoulder you won't be able to take care of your garden much. I thought I'd come over whenever I finish work at the store and help you out. I'll also run with Bear down at the beach so he gets his exercise."

"How do you do? This is Pastor Wayland. Do you need someone to talk to? I'll gladly drive over and help you through this time. A tough injury like this mustn't get you down. Great speech of yours, by the way. I guess you didn't see me in the crowd. I am totally with you against that refinery plan."

"Hello, Thora. Dottie here. I know you won't be able to drive up to the store. So I packed a box of sausage ends, sliced and all. Would it be convenient if I came over after we close the deli tonight?"

"Thora, this is Paul. We were at your protest and the entire staff of 'Le Quartier' congratulates you on your chutzpah. Of course, we know that you are in a pickle with your shoulder now. So we made some special casseroles for you that just need to be warmed up and are easy to eat. When may we bring them over?"

Thora was pretty overwhelmed by the wave of helpfulness that was pouring in via phone and in quite a few cases personally. She had heard of small town solidarity. But she had always considered it a thing for people who were elderly or who had been bereaved only recently. It was hard for her to accept these offers, as she had always been so independent. Still, there were moments when she felt helpless.

One mellow evening a week after her fall, she stood on her patio, looking bleakly across the Sound. Birds were twittering their evening songs, and Bear was pressing himself against Thora's thigh, breathing heavily. Clouds were sailing across the western sky, tinted apricot and pink by the sinking sun. The Olympic Mountains stood dark blue against the ever darkening evening sky. Some boats were still on the water, making for their harbors, and a ferry was slowly turning a wide loop towards Wycliff.

A bark from Bear startled Thora out of her thoughts. Then she heard it herself. A car had pulled up behind her house, and a door was banged shut. She wasn't quick enough to get into the house and to her door, obviously, so a few moments later she heard steps crossing the lawn and approaching from the side of the house.

It was Clark, and Thora's heart made a little, happy jump. "Bear has announced you already," she said with a wide smile that belied her glum thoughts just a few minutes ago. "I've had dinner already, but I can warm you some of my wonderful left-overs, if you don't mind. I was watching the sunset."

Clark stepped up to the patio and shook his head. "No dinner, thanks." He looked grim and placed a bottle of red wine onto the table.

"Anything wrong?" Thora asked.

Clark threw her a dark look, then he started uncorking the bottle. "I need a good sip of this before I get into it. Where do I find glasses?"

"In the little hanging cupboard next to the stove."

Clark went inside and returned with two wine glasses. He busied himself for longer than necessary. "How much involved were you today?"

"Involved in what?" Thora asked surprised. Clark muttered something. "I'm sorry, but I didn't hear you. Could you repeat it, please?"

"The protest in front of town hall."

Thora looked even more flabbergasted. "What protest? What ...?!"

Clark looked her in the eyes and believed her. "Ah, I guess not. Should have known better. - Well, I might as well tell you about it, and you will probably suck it up with glee. Somebody organized another protest in front of town hall, and this time there were a thousand – a thousand! – people gathered right underneath my windows. They had three speakers, one from Green Peace even, and they brought a large petition box filled with signature lists into my office. Television covered the thing, and a radio station was there to broadcast. God knows how many newspaper journalists asked for a statement from me."

"I had no idea," Thora said tonelessly and looked into Clark's face. He was looking tired and exhausted. "And I would have to lie to say it didn't make me utterly happy that somebody has taken up the protest. But I am sorry that they are bothering you so relentlessly." She took his hand and pressed it lightly. "You are the best friend I could have, Clark. I didn't intend them to enter your office and hound you."

Clark sighed. "I guess I called it upon myself." He raised his glass. "To the town of the brave and conscientious!"

Thora raised hers too. "To loyalty and friendship in spite of controversy."

They leaned on the patio railing and stared into the sunset slowly fading into darkness. A ferry tooted its deep horn to announce its departure from Wycliff Harbor. They kept gazing at the light it threw on the glittering waves.

*

"Do you have time to see to my motorboat, please?" Daniel asked Mathilda over the phone.

"Let me check," Mattie answered, going through her books. Her office desk was looking tidy, but that didn't mean that she didn't have heaps of tasks. "It depends on how much needs to be done…"

"Oh, I don't know," Daniel hesitated. "It definitely needs some new sealing and a paint job. Also, the motor is acting up in some strange ways. Could be battery trouble. And I might want a Bimini top for it, too. Do you think that is too much at one go?"

Mattie considered his description. "Do you need the boat sometime soon?"

"Not really," Daniel said. "It might be nice to be able to run it during summer though."

"Of course," Mattie answered and scrolled down a calendar page with her right index finger. "Well, you could bring her over tomorrow afternoon. Say five? I'll have a look at her and we can go from there. She might have to sit on her trailer for a while until my people get to work on her. But I'm sure they can start pretty soon."

"Great," Daniel said. "See you then." He hung up.

Mathilda noted down the new client appointment. Repair dates were tight these days, as everybody wanted to go on the water as soon as possible. But she'd try and squeeze Daniel in between. After all, she wanted to see him again. Badly. Yet she didn't know how other than the business way.

What knowledge did she have about Daniel Harrison anyway? She remembered having read a newspaper article a couple of years ago when he had bought the disposal center near Yelm. A photo had shown the front of the business building and then a close-up of Daniel himself. Daniel had been born in Seattle and gone to school there. Sometime in his late teens, he had discovered environmentalism. It was a topic that started growing big in the Pacific Northwest. Mattie knew that, compared to some other countries in the Western hemisphere, they were still doing baby steps here. But better those than none at all. Daniel had volunteered for all kinds of projects back then – cleaning up the beaches, protest marches against drilling platforms, recycling classes for environmentally conscientious kids. And he had studied civil engineering at college.

After graduating, he had started working in his brother's recycling company in a southern suburb of the Emerald City. But he had kept looking at opportunities for himself to be more independent. When the disposal center near Yelm had been for sale – the owner had wanted to retire to Arizona – he had grabbed the chance and taken a big business loan. He had made it a point to visit with each and every client of the former owner to make sure they'd stay with him and to reassure them that business conditions wouldn't change in the next couple of years. Mattie had been one of those clients, and she had liked the man immediately. He had a mission – saving the environment from pollution and turning hazardous waste into energy. "I will burn the waste, the emissions will be filtered out. During the process water will be heated. The steam will work turbines which will create energy for my disposal center and maybe a couple of neighboring companies. I know they do this on a large scale in Europe. I want to show that things like that can work in the US as well. If you stay my client, you will be part of a project that is helping our world and the one of our ... umh, ..." Here he'd lost it and Mattie had had to laugh, as she knew he had been about to finish with the word "children", which would have caused the most improper implications. This was when she had fallen for him as a person. But she had been educated to focus strictly on business, not to betray any human interest in business partners. And Daniel had come about business only after all. So there had been no opportunity for more personal matters. Or had there?

Maybe it had been good luck in the end that Peter had stolen her checks. It had given her time to think over her business as well as what kind of an owner she was. She felt she needed to get involved more. Not the micro-managing kind of owner, but in on all the details. Her talk with Daniel had helped her. Would she be able to persuade him that more such business meetings helped both of them?

Time till the next afternoon seemed at a standstill, and Mattie didn't feel she got anything done. She found herself sitting at her desk, staring holes into the air. Or walking across the boat yard, not even remembering what she had intended to do there in the first place. When Daniel's small pick-up truck finally pulled in a bit after five, her heart made a huge leap and ended up in her throat.

Daniel got out of the car, looking nicely dressed in a leisurely outfit. "Hey," he said.

"Hey! How are you doing?"

"Good. Good."

"Fine."

They stood facing each other, not knowing what to say. Just taking each other in.

"Where's your boat?" Mattie asked finally. "Seems you didn't bring her, after all."

"Oh, but I did," Daniel said, slightly blushing.

"You must have lost your trailer then."

"No need for a trailer." Daniel walked around his truck to the passenger side and opened the door. He bent over into the leg room and retrieved something from there. Then he held it out to Mattie with both hands.

Mattie gaped as if struck by lightning. The motorboat was a motorboat all right – but a model one. It looked finished as to its construction, but definitely was in need of sealing, paint, and a Bimini top.

"What about trouble with the battery?" Mattie asked faintly.

Daniel grinned, placed the boat down on the hood, and grabbed a remote from the passenger seat. "They might just be old. I brought a pack of brand-new ones so we can try her out. Are you game?"

Now, Mattie came alive again. "Oh you ... you! How dare you pull my leg like this?! I rearranged my schedule so we could fit in your boat repair. I was even ready to put in overtime myself!"

Daniel placed the remote behind the seats in his truck. "I'm sorry about that," he said, but his sparkling eyes belied his words. "As to overtime ... would you like to go to "Le Quartier" and have dinner with me?" He stepped towards her and placed his hands onto her shoulders. "I have wanted to ask you to go out with me for a while, but I needed a pretext."

"And you found this to be a clever one?" Mattie still looked at him in disbelief.

"It is a motor boat," Daniel defended himself.

"Oh for sure, it is!" Mattie exclaimed, almost angry. Then the comical side of the situation struck her and she burst out laughing. "Daniel Harrison, you better make this overtime worth my while!"

He threw her another boyish grin. "Mattie Barton, I will try my very best."

*

It was Saturday night, and Thora was staring out of her window into a bleak and drizzly dusk. The trees were black splotches against the gray sky, and the deck in front of her window was glistening with the wetness of rain. The room felt cold. The lamp in her reading nook threw large shadows across the floor and walls. The house smelled of Bear, as he had come in wet from a run on the beach and managed to evade Thora's towel. Being one-handed, if only temporarily, had its big downsides.

Thora felt as bleak as the weather outside. It had been only two weeks since her fall, but it already felt like an eternity. She didn't hurt as much as in the beginning, but she felt extremely helpless in so many regards. Washing her hair was a pain, and she was just glad she wore it short anyway. She had to call friends to do her grocery runs. She wasn't able to open jars or bottles, so she asked her friends to open them and leave the lid on only twisted ever so slightly. She wasn't able to heave the laundry basket to her folding table, so she pushed it with her feet until she got it in place. She missed rides into the countryside. She was scared of walking too far from her home – what if she fell again? She would have loved to get some books from the library, but she hadn't dared ask anybody for such a trivial run. So here she sat, moping.

A short bark announced a visitor, before he even had a chance to knock. Thora rose wearily. She looked at her living room with the eyes of a stranger. Incredible what chaos two weeks of not being able to clean could wreak to a home! She felt a bit ashamed. Yet she walked to the door and opened it.

"You again?!" she said.

Clark stood outside with a large crate and smiled at her. "Thought your Saturday night might be a bit lonesome out in the woods…"

"It was," Thora admitted and surprised herself. She hadn't planned to let down her guard to anybody. But somehow Clark wasn't anybody.

"Well, then maybe this comes in handy." Clark went past her and set the crate down on the floor. Bear followed him, wagging his tail and sniffing the crate.

"Off," Thora said. Bear sat on his hind legs and looked at her with excitement. "What did you bring?"

"First, I thought you might like something decent to eat. So I asked Véronique for some take-out from 'Le Quartier'."

"I thought they don't do take-out."

"They don't generally. For you they did. Voilà, a three course dinner that is still hot!" Clark retrieved a few thermo boxes from the crate and set them onto the kitchen counter.

"Clark, you shouldn't have!"

"Well, I wasn't going to eat there on my own – so I thought of enjoying this with you where you are probably the most comfortable these days – at your own place."

"You are so thoughtful." Thora's eyes turned misty. "I can almost forgive you for your dreadful plans about the refinery."

Clark's blue eyes flashed amused. "Ah, there is news. Thanks to your protesting friends and their petitions there will be a hearing at town hall next week."

"A hearing," Thora repeated unenthusiastically."

"Aren't you happy?"

"I don't know," she said slowly. ""You can't expect anything from hearings. If you could, they'd be called listenings. People get all wrought up and hopeful about hearings. They expect their voices to make an impact, to even bring about change. But in most cases it is just a soothing measure from whoever sits on the other side of the table. And in the end everything stays as was planned by those in power."

Clark shrugged his shoulders. "I'm willing to listen, not just to hear. – Change of topic: I also brought this wonderful Sauvignon Blanc. It's from a new winery a friend of Eli Hayes started a couple of years ago up north of Seattle. Should be stuff you like. All ecological growth and so on ..." He winked at her and presented her with a slender bottle.

"I'm quite surprised at you."

"Ah, come on. We know that there are all these Châteauneuf-du-Pape fancy-shmancy wines out there. But the real deal is to support your local vintners ... if they are good, that is."

"I couldn't agree more."

"I also brought you some entertaining yellow press for less deep thoughts." He unloaded a pile of magazines. "Vogue, Elle, some of these VIP things, a gardening journal ... and ... tadah! ... the very latest thriller by A. J. Banner. At the book store they told me 'The Twilight Wife' was another marvelous page-turner featuring a place somewhere in the San Juan Islands." He produced a paperback with an intriguing cover photo of a broken pink shell on anthracite gravel.

"Clark!" Thora exclaimed. "Stop it! You are pampering me, and I don't even know how I will ever be able to return the favors."

Clark smiled at her mysteriously. "Maybe I don't do all this without a secret motive."

Thora blushed. For a moment she felt a bit dizzy even. Then her brain cleared again. "You must be joking, Clark Thompson."

He looked her in the face very soberly and shook his head. "Joking times are over, Thora. Yes, you have always been a dear friend to me. And I guess I have been the same for you, haven't I?"

"Of course. What a question!"

"Well, a man can be only so much of a friend usually. After a while he might be a bit more interested, if the lady is available. Do you get my drift?"

Thora swallowed hard. "I didn't think of myself as available."

Clark looked startled. "So is there already somebody else?"

Thora smiled. Then she slowly shook her head. "No, Clark. There is nobody else. And you shouldn't try either." She suddenly found herself helpless and didn't know what to do with her hands. So she hugged herself.

"Why?"

"Clark, you know that I really, really like you. Probably more than I should." He started to say something, but she held up her uninjured hand. "Don't say anything. Please. Yes, I have to admit that I do more than just like you. But back at town hall, it would have been totally inappropriate to admit these feelings. You were my boss. What would it have looked like?!"

"Like a mayor falling in love with his secretary and vice versa. So?"

Thora ignored him. "And now the situation is even worse. You have come up with a plan to build something that will destroy our environment for ages, if not all times. And I don't agree with you. Even more so: I detest the plan, and I simply don't get it that you are so hard-headed to pursue it."

Clark shook his head in defeat. "Couldn't we simply bury our hatchets?"

"No!" Thora exclaimed. "Unless you recall your plan."

Clark scratched his chin. "Can't simply do that."

"Why not?"

"It's not just me who is for the plan."

"I understand. You don't want to retract your plan."

"You don't understand," Clark said. "I would like to, just to get this darn elephant out of this room. But my hands are bound."

They glared at each other. Then their faces started to mellow. They didn't know how to leap the breach that seemed to separate them. But they knew that they would both work on it. They didn't want to lose each other over anything political.

"Let's enjoy the food you brought before it gets cold," Thora sighed and opened a kitchen cabinet. "Could you get me some of the deep dishes down, please?"

"We could eat the food right from the thermo dishes," Clark observed.

"But such food deserves better," Thora smiled. "What heavenly creations did you bring me?"

*

From "The Sound Messenger":

Mayor Wavers in Refinery Debate

judo. Last night's town hall hearing about the plans to build an oil refinery near Downtown Wycliff has taken a surprising turn. The instigator of the project, Mayor Clark Thompson, seems to be taking a new angle on things as protest grows louder in the South Sound.

Maybe it was the passionate appeal by eco-activist Thora Byrd a couple of weeks ago that caused things to fall apart at town hall. Maybe it was the fundamental support she received not just from a majority of the citizens in Wycliff, but also from cities around the South Sound and organizations such as Green Peace. The advocates of an oil refinery south of the Wycliff ferry terminal have lost a lot of enthusiasm for their arguments.

Main reason is the sudden and unexplainable turn that Mayor Clark Thompson has taken on the project he himself had originally placed on the town's agenda. "We need to weigh the pros and cons of a refinery way more thoughtfully than we handled them in the recent past," Thompson admonished town council as well as the audience. "Projects like these are quickly built, but their consequences might impact society and nature even centuries later."

AnCoSafe Oil spokesman Antonio Gepetto reacted irritated to the implications that an oil refinery might bring more damage upon the Wycliff community and the South Sound than advantages. "I thought we had discussed the matter in detail and basically were in agreement on having a promising joint venture. AnCoSafe Oil is still offering this immense opportunity to Wycliff, of course. But we only keep it open for so much longer. After that we might be looking for more reliable partnerships, if not in the South Sound, then somewhere else."

The hearing was transmitted to the square in front of town hall as well, where hundreds of protestors had arrived to support their speakers inside the building. The hearing might have brought about a landslide victory for the eco-activists after all. Now the ball lies back in the court of Wycliff town hall, who will have to come up with a decision quickly, as AnCoSafe Oil set them a deadline of four weeks. *The Sound Messenger* wasn't able to reach Thora Byrd for a comment. (…)

CHAPTER 7

The Green Maven's Tip of the Week:
No need to use poisonous chemicals when you try to get rid of ants in your house. Spread some baking soda around the areas the ants emerge from. As soon as the ants scuttle through the baking soda, they will die. This will discourage further ants from visiting what they formerly found such an interesting place.

"... and maybe we could get to know each other better while enjoying an opening night at one of the local galleries or walking along the waterfront while eating ice cream."

"Whom are you talking to, darling?" Theodora Jones entered her son's office as he was just about finished talking to his computer screen.

"Mom!" Trevor exclaimed, visibly upset. "Now you've ruined it all!"

"Ruined what?"

"My recording. Did you have to budge in at the last second? I'm pretty sure your voice is in it now."

"Well, then do it again."

"But I can't." Trevor banged the desk with his fist. He was totally frustrated. "It's been recorded and sent."

"Sent where?" Theodora coolly approached his desk and threw a look at his monitor. She froze. "Is this a dating site?!"

Trevor cringed slightly. "As a matter of fact it is."

"You don't need anything awkward like this!" Theodora was appalled. She tried hard not to frown. It would cause creases in her carefully made-up face. "You are a very attractive, young, eligible gentleman with a huge career ahead. Girls must be waiting in line for you."

"Well, for whatever reason they aren't," Trevor retorted drily.

"Aaaw, my poor baby," Theodora cooed and tried to give Trevor a hug. He evaded her. "Don't give up so easily. Maybe my idea with Patricia was bad. Kids should never be married off amongst friends' families. They should be able to make their own free choices. I see that now."

"It's not about Patricia." Trevor shuddered when he thought of the young conceited lawyer his mother had wanted him to marry barely a year earlier. Back then, he had been in love with Kitty Kittrick, the young manager of "The Flower Bower". But his mother hadn't agreed with his choice. And Patricia had ridiculed the young woman publicly at the bistro. Or tried to. Kitty had been well able to stand up for herself where he had failed. End of story. No Patricia, no Kitty. Nor Mattie either – and he didn't have a clue where he might have messed up there. Trevor felt like a miserable failure.

"Don't tell me it's still about that farmer woman."

"Can you please stop calling people names, mother?" Trevor became exasperated. "She is the owner of a business, and she happens to marry somebody who has a degree in agriculture."

Theodora raised her eyebrows. "I beg your pardon," she said. "I wasn't aware you are that touchy! Obviously you do still suffer from what that little nothing of a woman did to you."

"Mother!" Trevor exclaimed. Then he just shut down his computer and got up. "Please, for once let me handle my affairs just my way." He glared at her.

Theodora looked at him aloof. "Fine. Just don't blame me for failure."

"I certainly won't," Trevor said stiffly.

"Well then," Theodora said and turned to leave Trevor's office. "Good luck. I'm sure you'll find plenty of good wife material on the internet where anybody can pretend to be anything."

*

The sewing machines at the Community Center were whirring. Fifteen women of all ages were busy working on pieces of fabric. They kept their eyes focused on the colorful scraps of cloth running through their fingers. Every once in a while one of them exclaimed something. Then Angela would walk over and see where her help might be needed.

"Are you sure I will ever be able to do this?!" a middle-aged woman with prematurely gray, longish hair asked her desperately. Her fabric had turned into a knot underneath a strange ball of thread which had ripped in addition.

Angela smiled. It was impressive how her features had changed ever since Thora had visited her about the bag project. As if there had been lit a new light inside the old, formerly so bitter woman. "You may want to try a newer machine after all. These vintage ones sometimes act up. The newer ones self-feed their thread, so their tension is equal in every part of the machine. You won't end up with entanglements like these."

"I'm afraid I'm stuck between a rock and a hard place. I cannot afford to rent a machine," the woman said quietly.

"We will find a way," Angela said confidently though she didn't know where this confidence came from. After all, she didn't have any funds either, and Thora was operating on a shoestring these days. "Maybe we should start you as a cutter first. After our first payments, you might be able to rent a machine."

The woman sighed relieved. "I had been looking so forward to earning a tad for myself. I thought this is the end of it, now that this piece of sewing looks so messed up. My dreams go – poof! – again."

Angela nodded. She had had so many dreams go up in smoke in her past that she had stopped counting. Yet she had always somehow been able to emerge and go on.

To what purpose though? She straightened her shoulders. Maybe to prove to herself that she was worth more than that silly pregnant girl who had thought ensnaring a handsome officer might make her fortune. Maybe to prove that she didn't need anybody else but her own devices to overcome difficulties. Maybe in the silent hope that one day, one day she might find her daughter and reconcile with her.

Another call from a different corner of the room. An eager girl was sitting there with a fairly new machine and a piece that was finished. Angela inspected it carefully. "This seam is crooked, dear," she said and pointed out the line of thread. "You simply have to stop pulling at the fabric."

"But it keeps running at me so very fast."

"You can slow the sewing speed a little and speed it up again once you are comfortable with the pace. But never pull unless you really want a curve in your piece. Let the fabric run underneath the needle. It will do so straightly. You will just have to keep the fabric smooth. See, like this!" She demonstrated it to the girl.

"Where did you learn to sew?" another woman next to the girl wanted to know.

"I taught myself," Angela said. "I had to make ends meet all my life. My mother had an old machine, and I wanted some fancy items as a young girl. So I sewed them myself. Back in the day it was cheaper to make things yourself. Today, it is obviously not so anymore. Fabric is quite expensive if you don't buy it in bulk. And outsourcing industrial sewing to other countries has made clothing a lot cheaper here than creating fashion yourself. But we need to go back to when we had industry here. And if it is just a cottage industry for women like us!"

"Yay for us!" another young woman with stringy hair said.

Angela looked over the room and the women it contained. "Thora Byrd is the initiator of this project, ladies. She is a wonderful woman with her feet firmly on the ground. As she has figured this working project for all of us, we mustn't ever disappoint her."

"We wouldn't," Meredith Baker said and blushed.

Angela nodded at her. "Well, but we have to make up some rules for the sake of ourselves and the quality of our work. First thing: No smoking ever in the same room you keep your fabric and sewing materials in."

"What?!" a feisty redhead gasped from a back row. "But this is what keeps me going!"

"If you can't go without, then do it outside that room or – even better – outside your house. And after that wash your hands. Always wash your hands before handling fabric. Don't ever hand over stinky or sticky products to Thora or me. Nobody wants to buy smoky or soiled bags from anybody. You got me?"

The redhead nodded meekly.

"Second: Everybody will be handed a specific amount of cuts per week. It is up to you how many bags you will sew.

We will control the quality of each bag. And you will be paid by piece. We won't pay for messed-up pieces. We can't afford to dump money. If you deliver over ten percent of the bags messed up, you will either be removed to another task or have to get out."

"Gee, this sounds worse than that wicked English teacher at Wycliff High," one woman said.

Angela raised her brows. "Does it now? Well, then do explain what is so bad about strict quality rules? How would you feel if you bought a beautiful frozen pizza and then your daughter would burn it to a crisp in your oven?"

"I'd slap her!" the woman exclaimed.

"Well, we don't slap here. We move you to cutting. Or to distributing. Or anything else that you might be able to handle in the process until you prove you have stepped up your game. Only when everything fails, you will have to leave."

The woman kept silent.

"Any more questions or comments?" Angela asked.

"How will you be able to finance the first load of fabric?"

Angela smiled. "I managed to talk Dottie McMahon into giving us a chance. She has advanced us a nice lump sum to get us started. So we better not disappoint that generous lady. Let's make it worth her while. And as word spreads we can help it along with talking to more businesses and convincing with quality."

"Will simple square bags be enough to give us all some earnings?"

Angela shrugged. "It will not be much at first. But we can get fancier as we go. We can start backing the bags, making them into totes with special handles and with front or inner pockets. We might be able to use high-end fabric someday and create even fancier bags. Let's start small, but dream big, ladies!"

One started clapping. Then another followed suit. In the end, every woman in the room was applauding Angela. And the haggard old woman who had always felt to have messed up her life in such a massive way finally felt the tide turning.

*

"Did you find any more illegal dumps?" Julie pushed her empty plate to the side and started attacking her dessert, a Marsala poached apple crumble Dottie had created. It was another dinner at the McMahon home, and the dining room looked cozy with a candle lit in the center of the table, while the last of the sunset was illuminating the room in red and golden hues.

Luke McMahon was chewing on a bite of Schnitzel and shoving some mashers onto his fork. He swallowed. "Unfortunately, or rather fortunately, yes." He swept up the last bits off his plate and took his time, while Julie and Dottie were looking at him expectantly. "We have reports from seven more sites in Pierce County, one up in King County, and another one in Thurston."

"Dang!" Julie exclaimed. "Do you think you'll ever be sure those are all of them?"

Luke shook his head. "Unless we catch the guy who did it and he makes a full confession, I'm not sure when we will have found the last of them. It's a pain in the back, and besides it's hazardous. I just hope that Eli's picture will eventually turn up somebody who has seen the truck."

Dottie took a sip of water. "It was pretty quick-witted by Eli to take a pic, while that guy was unloading the drums kind of in his backyard."

"It was pretty dangerous, too." Luke licked his lips and wiped a breadcrumb from his chin. "You see, the guy might have been armed. We don't know that. But there is always the possibility of somebody who is committing a crime to defend himself with a weapon."

"You mean it is dangerous for anybody to approach the guy or to report him?" Julie asked.

"We will certainly keep the name of any witness confidential as long as possible."

They ate their desserts in silence. The atmosphere had darkened just as the room had. Dottie switched on a lamp on a side table.

"How big is the probability that the guy who unloaded the truck and Peter Michaels are one and the same person?" Julie asked.

Luke stopped chewing his last bite of dessert for a moment as if in consideration. Then he leaned back in his chair. "Listen, Julie, this is all off the record, you understand?"

"I won't breathe a word until you give me permission," Julie promised. "Cross my heart and hope to die."

There was a tiny twinkle of humor in Luke's eyes at this childish vow. Then he became very serious again. "We surmise that Peter Michaels is identical with the person who dumped the hazardous waste illegally, just as he is definitely John Minor's blackmailer."

Julie exhaled deeply. "Wow. You got any proof? I mean, that police drawing of the blackmailer was certainly as close a likeness to Michaels as it gets. But it doesn't necessarily mean that it was him committing the other crime, does it?"

Dottie rose and started clearing away the dishes. Julie offered her help, half-heartedly collecting some cutlery from the table cloth, but Dottie stopped her with a wave of her hand. "I know you want to discuss this in more detail," she winked at her daughter. "You're a good journalist, and I won't get in between you and your work with a petty request for helping me with the dishes."

Julie blushed. "I'll make it up to you, Mom."

"Sure," Dottie said. She knew that Julie was likely to forget any promise to help in the household. A certain strain of selfishness was simply part of her daughter's character. She didn't know how it had ever made it past her and her first husband Sean's parental awareness, but there it was. And now it was too late to change her. Ah well, other children obviously turned out worse. Did Peter Michaels' parents know what he was up to these days? Could they have ever prevented it to happen with a good spanking or two? Or was he one of those kids from a dysfunctional family who would be excused even by the judges because he had been abused as a child?

"... no sign yet." Luke had finished his answer to another of Julie's questions. "He might still be around. As is often the case with criminals, they don't necessarily move far from their crime scenes. They seem to be comfortable in these areas. And they might even return to check whether they have been found out."

"How dumb!" Julie said.

"Makes it easier for us good guys to catch them, trust me," Luke said.

"How did Mathilda come to fall for his offer of collection service anyhow?"

"Easily enough." Luke stretched his arms and folded his hands behind his head. "Mind you, Mathilda is no fool. Nor is any of the other clients of Harrison Disposal Center who had Michaels come and collect their waste."

"Why hire a disposal service in the first place?"

"It is tough work heaving heavy drums onto a truck bed. So if you are not physically strong enough to handle the job yourself, you need to have enough people to be able to spare a person for loading and delivering the waste."

"Sounds pretty easy to me," Julie said. "Mattie certainly has quite a few people at her wharf."

"Not when business is tight and she needs every man to work on her clients' boats. Peter Michaels came in very handy indeed. So she grasped the opportunity."

"Did he ever show her his license?"

Luke sighed. "She even had him make her a copy of it to keep with her paperwork."

"Hm," Julie said. "She's obviously got more sense than I thought."

Luke raised his eyebrows. "Just because she fell for a fraud doesn't mean she is stupid. This guy did it in such a clever way that nobody would have suspected anything if Thora hadn't stumbled across that dump in Wycliff Forest. Now, the choice of that site was stupid. But Mattie? No."

"Was the licensing paperwork for real then?"

"It looked legit," Luke said and rubbed his hair. "It had all the right stamps and illegible signatures you'd expect from such paperwork. But the watermark was stamped on instead of in the paper. And when we checked out the address it gave for his business, it turned out to be a vacant lot in a residential, not a business area in Lakewood."

"So the business was a fraud from the first." Julie drew circles on the table cloth with her index fingers.

"Absolutely." Luke rose and walked over to the window. "Peter Michaels was no legal waste collector ever." He fell silent and turned around to Julie again. "Through the grapevine, we heard of a fitness trainer he had actually lived with in one of the seedier places in Lakewood. She recognized the Dodge RAM as his and the clothes the person wore in the picture as 'maybe his'. I don't know how much the girl can be trusted though. He dropped her before he left the area, and she might have some thoughts of revenge."

"Or she may have told you the truth," Julie ventured.

"Sure, or that," Luke admitted.

"What if Peter Michaels isn't even his real name?"

Luke snorted a short laugh. "That, my dear, is one of the things that might have to wait until we have caught the man."

"Have there been any similar cases in other counties or states?" Julie asked curiously.

"We are looking into that, but so far we come up with only dead alleys."

Julie bit her lips. "Something feels so utterly wrong about this. He turns up only about half a year ago. But he knows this area like the back of his hand."

Luke stared at her. Then he took a deep breath. "Gee whiz, Julie! I took that for granted, but you are right. You might be onto something here."

*

Thora bit her lips in pain. Her arm was still in that huge, bulky sling that hindered her from moving it. But every once in a while, she was permitted to remove it from there and turn her wrist and bend her elbow to keep both from becoming stiff. It hurt as if somebody was trying to cut off her arm, but she was willing to get her full mobility back one day. Even if it made her wince.

Bear sat on his haunches in front of her and observed her with big dog eyes. He didn't understand what Thora was doing there, flapping her right arm like a hurt bird. In between he yelped.

Clark sat at Thora's dining table, writing a paper. He had been at her place in the evenings more often than not these past weeks. Finally, he laid down his ball pen, took off his reading glasses, and rubbed the bridge of his nose. "Quite a few things happening at once, aren't there?" he said, half to himself.

"Could have done without some of them," Thora replied. Then she counted on, "Eighteen, nineteen, twenty. Done." She let her arm sink and carefully started placing it into her sling again. A sound of pain escaped her as she moved the elbow in its place.

"I wish I could take over that pain from you."

Thora looked up from the sling and at Clark's worried face in surprise. "Why, Clark?! I wouldn't want to inflict any pain on you at all."

Clark smiled grimly and looked away. "It just hurts me to see you suffer, and I wish there was something I could do about it."

"But you are!" Thora smiled widely now and walked over to him, placing her left hand on his shoulder, squeezing it gently. "I wouldn't have known what to do without you most of the time. You have been showing up almost daily, running errands, bringing goodies, cutting my food, even helping me keep the house clean! What more could anybody do for me?!"

Clark sighed, but didn't answer. Instead, he pushed his chair back and rose to walk to her reading nook to take a look out of the window. Thora followed him. She, too, looked out of the window, but her thoughts were turned onto something different.

"You have been working hard tonight," she said quietly.

"We will have yet another town council meeting on the refinery project."

"How did the town hall hearing turn out? I mean, yes, I have read the papers."

"You could have been there and seen for yourself. You had enough offers to drive you there," he said, taking in the outside drizzle in an ever denser dusk.

"You know I couldn't have done this," Thora contradicted calmly. "How could I bite the hand that is tending to me? I instigated the protest, but I'm not sitting with the attacking crowd when you are seeing to me in such a kindly manner." She looked at him sideways with an impish grin. "Maybe you took that into your equation, huh?"

"What?" Clark asked and turned to her.

"That I wouldn't go against you if only you took care of me."

Clark raised his eyebrows. "That is not what you're really thinking, is it?" She looked at him mischievously. "You know, even without your presence there were enough protesters at the hearing. They even stood outside the building, and we had to install loudspeakers in the town hall windows."

"That must have been pretty tough for you."

"Yes, well …" Clark faltered. "All in all we got flooded with 30,000 signatures that protest the building of a refinery in Wycliff."

"What?!"

"You heard me."

"But this is more than double the population of Wycliff, which means more than double of those people are not eligible to vote on this!"

Clark turned his face toward the window again. He stared at his reflection in the glass. He didn't look like a defeated man. He looked calm enough. But inside he wasn't. "There were a lot of people from around, apparently interested in the subject as well."

"But then their votes don't count. They are not Wycliffians!"

"I guess here is where the town council has to overcome the factual numbers that would have counted. We need to consider the fear of all those, after all, whose petition as out-of-towners should not matter by law."

"Taking it to another level?" Thora asked softly.

"Taking it to the level of common human interest and thinking of our responsibility towards the people we live with."

Thora smiled, but it was not triumphantly. "You have come a long way in a short time, Clark," she said and leaned against him with her healthy left side.

He put an arm around her. "I should have listened to you from the first. It would have saved me a lot of trouble."

"You are not afraid of losing face?"

"Life is a learning process. If we lost face every time we had to step back from an idea or a task that turns out not to be for us or not right or not … I don't know what …"

Thora nodded. "So you are not afraid of telling town council and AnCoSafe Oil to retreat from the refinery plans?"

Clark chuckled. "I wish it were that easy! I can give my recommendation to the town council. But we still have to have a clear decision that is to be delivered to AnCoSafe Oil."

"So we aren't sure yet that the refinery won't be built after all?"

"No, we aren't. Let's hope that the concerns of the people of Wycliff and the people around will be taken seriously enough to drop the plan."

"Clark! You are about to vote against your own idea?"

"I have always wanted only what is good for the people who elected me mayor. If my idea is not what they want, then who am I to fight it through against them?"

They stood side by side, looking out into the dark.

"I am proud of you, Clark."

"I am not," he said. "I thought I was doing the right thing, and I stirred up a lot of anger and even problems for people."

"You made us all aware of what we have in the beauty of Wycliff and the nature around it. We were in a state of mind where we took it all for granted."

"You think so?"

"Yes, I do! Besides, it has kicked off more environmental awareness in general. Which means that my little cottage industry project might not find it as difficult to grow as I feared it might at first."

"Your bag thing? Tell me a bit more about it."

Thora took a deep breath. "Where should I begin? ..."

*

"What do you mean by you're out?!" Peter shouted into his phone. He had had to turn into a Walmart parking lot to take the call. There were people all around. He was livid. "And why the heck are you calling me?! Are you out of your mind?!"

"I had my mother bail me out."

"So she's in on us too, now?"

"No. Not at all. It's just the usual thing a mother does." Julian Teal tried to sound tough, but failed miserably. "Hey, isn't it great?! Man, I gave them nothing, and I'm free to do whatever I want to do."

"That's what you think, moron" Peter hissed. "First big mistake is that you are calling me at all. Are you sure they didn't tap into your phone?"

"I'm not that stupid, partner. I'm calling from a booth."

"There are no more booths in Western Washington that are in working order."

"Well, I'm not sending you smoke signals here either. This is definitely a working booth, man."

"Did anybody follow you?"

Silence on the other end. Peter pictured Teal turning his head in all four directions, trying to figure whether anybody around was looking suspicious. "Nope. Street is clean. Nobody in the windows across either."

"Right," Peter breathed in and found that he was slightly shaken. He searched his pockets for cigarettes with one hand, while holding on to his cell phone. "You're lucky to reach me anyhow."

"Why? You not around the area anymore?"

"Got no reception where I'm living these days."

"That's those darn old flip phones for you," Teal said dismissively.

"It's good enough for my purposes," Peter answered. "Be that as it is. You must have a reason to call."

Teal cleared his throat. "As a matter of fact, I do. I'm running a bit low on money these days. My mother bailing me out doesn't help much either."

"So you are calling me about my never-receding funds, huh?" Peter mocked, while lighting up and inhaling the smoke deeply.

"Well, I didn't mean to be so blunt."

"Then don't act like a cat on a tin-roof. You want me to give you some money? What securities do you have?" Teal was silent on the other end. "None. I thought so. And I am not a welfare institution." Another pause. "Do you have a piece?"

"How do you mean?"

"Well, a gun? A pistol, a revolver, whatever?"

"I got an old hunting rifle from my grandfather."

"Yeah, big deal," Peter snorted. "That will help us."

"It will?"

"You understand sarcasm, dude?!" Peter drummed his fingers on the steering wheel.

"Oh!"

"So you don't have one."

"I got ..."

"That doesn't work for the job I was planning. Okay. Now listen closely: You will be my driver in this, okay?"

"That it?"

"Sweet Jeez, what do you want? Don't play the hero – you're not cut for that stuff. So just shut your trap and listen. I will pick you up at your place. I'll let you know the date."

"Got it."

Peter rolled his eyes. If Teal had sat next to him now, he might have throttled him. "You drive from there."

"Whereto?"

"I'll give you the directions. Then I'll get out and leave for a few minutes. As soon as I come back, you will hit the gas."

"With or without you inside?"

"Teal, how did you ever become something like a bookkeeper?!"

"By being meticulous," Teal answered sourly.

"Okay." Peter inhaled his cigarette. "Okay. ... I get into the car, you hit the gas, and you keep going wherever we will decide to go right then and there."

"And there is money in this for me? Just for driving you?"

"Fifteen."

"Grand?"

"Oh for God's sake, how would I know?!" Peter spit. "Fifteen percent."

"Thirty."

"Twenty then."

"Twenty-five and I'll drive you."

Peter sighed though he had Teal exactly at the point he had wanted him. Teal wouldn't be able to say he had been underpaid. "Okay. Done deal. I'll call you as soon as I'm ready to start on this business. Be at the ready."

They hung up. Peter banged the dashboard. Now for all those little details that had to be planned. Wouldn't some people wish they had treated him nicer when he had been living in Wycliff way back when?!

*

"So good to see you again, Thora!" The store owner of "Ultimate Crafts", Marylou Webster, was beaming. "How is your shoulder doing? Does it hurt much? How long will it take to be fine again?"

Thora smiled weakly. She had heard and answered the same questions so often these past few days when she had let Clark drive her into town. "Thank you, dear. It still hurts off and on, but it's bearable. I'm just lucky I won't need any surgery. All it takes are time and patience – and I'm running short of patience, I have to admit."

"Yeah, well, I know what you're talking about," Marylou smiled. "I had meniscus surgery some years ago. It was painful, and I was not supposed to stand on my legs working."

"What did you do?"

"I sat," Marylou grinned. "But, you know, I had only started out with this store back then, and I couldn't afford any extra staff. Couldn't afford to be closed for the duration either. It was a tough time. But after a while you look back and say, 'oh wow, I did it!'- You'll see."

Thora nodded. "I guess. It's just that I started a project. And now I'm kind of letting everybody down if I don't do my part."

"You mean the refinery thing? Sweetie, that has been taken care of for sure! There are so many people speaking out against it - they won't be able to ignore it. You started it, we will finish it. All of us!"

Thora shook her head. "Actually, that is not what I meant. Though it is truly amazing how the protest has grown and gained momentum."

"Isn't it? But what are you talking about .... Oh! Oh!!! The bag thing?"

Thora pulled a folded white cotton bag from her handbag, which dangled from her left shoulder. Her right hand held onto it though it was still in the sling. Thora bit her lips. Every tiny movement that her right arm was involved in cost her so much time and pain these days. Then she held the bag out to Marylou.

"This is only the beginning," Thora stated. "Angela and I have started a cottage industry project that will sew grocery bags to order. This is a sample of what we are selling to 'Dottie's Deli', for example. It's 100 percent cotton and therefore washable as well as fully compostable or recyclable."

"It is quite neat," Marylou admitted. "But I'm sure they cost quite a penny, right?"

"They are not as cheap as the plastic bags that stores usually have," Thora admitted. "But think of what a favor we do our environment and future generations in not using fossil, but regrowable materials for grocery bags."

"Is anybody else buying into this product of yours?"

"How do you mean?"

"Any other businesses. Or is Dottie the only one?"

"Well, the tourist office has ordered a box of a hundred and will have it printed with the Wycliff tourism logo."

"Yeah, well, but that's probably your friend Clark, who has a finger in this as the mayor, right?" Marylou winked.

Thora blushed. "It's not at all what you think! Anyhow, he hasn't even seen these bags yet."

Marylou bit her lips and turned the bag over in her hands. "They are of good quality. How much would you sell them for?"

"A dollar a piece," Thora said quickly. "I know you won't make much of a margin on these. But they last so much longer than even the one-dollar sturdy, reinforced plastic supermarket bags. And ..."

"Yes, I heard you. You can wash them."

"Indeed you can," Thora said stiffly.

"How many would I have to take?"

"We sell them in units of 50."

"Not much to be gained for any of your ladies at all, is there?"

"Not really, no. But we are only at the beginning. 'Nathan's' is considering taking on our bags as well."

"The supermarket at the Harbor Mall?"

"Well, that one and the three affiliates in Lakewood, Tacoma, and Olympia." Thora massaged her right elbow slightly. It was a bit numb, and the sling felt heavier by the minute. "That is, of course, if they decide for us..."

"Of course." Marylou handed Thora back the bag. "I suppose you will need this again?"

Thora took the bag and stuffed it back into her handbag. "Well, thank you for your time and for listening anyway."

"You're welcome," said Marylou.

Thora turned around and started walking towards the exit, past maritime decoration items and canvasses, past a display of brushes and another large one of watercolors, oil paints, and acrylics. She was almost at the door when Marylou called her name."

Thora turned around again. "Yes?"

"I would like to order a box of 50 for a start, please. I think I have an idea."

Thora stood as if hit by lightning. "You what?"

"You heard me alright, dear. I would like to have 50 bags for the beginning – and if my idea goes well, I might even reorder."

"Seriously?"

"Seriously."

Thora's started to beam. "Oh Marylou, thank you. We can use any support we get. You will not regret this!" And her step was so much lighter when she walked back to the counter to fix the details.

*

Susanne Bacon

From "The Sound Messenger":

Cotton to a Greener Environment

judo. **Sustainable materials are the resource of one of Wycliff's latest companies, "Bags 4 Choosers". The fledgling enterprise relies on cottage industry only, as founders and Wycliff citizens Thora Byrd and Angela Fortescue stress. Their hope is to make it into every household in the South Sound area by the end of the decade.**

For most Wycliffians, the teaming up of Angela Fortescue, 75, and Thora Byrd, 42, for a business must seem as unlikely as the success they hope for with their new cottage industry project. But they have already engaged fifteen local women to cut, sew, and distribute grocery bags made from cotton or hemp, either bleached or untreated. Whereas Fortescue takes on the practical angle of breaking in employees, buying of materials, and quality control, Byrd is managing marketing, sales, and distribution as well as PR.

"We do not expect to earn big dollars with our initiative at first," Byrd admits. "We need to shift people's minds from getting free plastic bags to buying sturdy, reusable grocery bags that are environmentally friendly. That takes baby steps, as the first common answer to any revolutionary ecological idea is usually no. It may sound expensive for some people right now. But if we keep wasting resources as we are right now, we will pay a price that will hurt us way more one day."

In the long run, Bags 4 Choosers, as the young company is calling itself, will produce bags of all kinds, especially in the design section. "We plan to work with brocades, velvet, silk, and even materials such as cork or birch rind," Angela Fortescue says. "Customers will also be able to bring their own materials to have a bag made that is one of a kind."

For now, the business operates decentralized, every employee at her own home. There won't be an outlet in downtown Wycliff until the enterprise starts paying off, which will be a long time from now. But, so far, the business has created hope for a lot of women whose lives seemed to have had not that much of a perspective lately.

What is Wycliff businesses' response to the B-2-B offer of Bags 4 Choosers? Actually quite positive. "Dottie's Deli" is handing out free bags next weekend and, after that, will sell them a dollar a piece until further notice. "We simply handle them through," owner Dottie McMahon says. "If we have a chance to change our children's future for the better, this is one at hand and at no high risk." The tourist bureau has their bags customized and sells them with the Wycliff logo at their information center. Nathan's four supermarkets in the South Sound will start selling cotton bags as of the first of next month.

A very special effort has been made by "Ultimate Crafts" on Back Row. "Crafting has a tradition of the sustainable," owner Marylou Webster says. "And we need to honor the *ultimate* in our business name." She tenders a competition for all of her customers to create Wycliff's "ultimately creative cotton bag". For this purpose she has assembled kits containing a cotton bag, fabric paints, and glitter glue. The deadline is this up-coming July 31. Ask for more information at her store or call …

CHAPTER 8

The Green Maven's Tip of the Week:
Re-use cardboard egg carton as start-up planters. Cut the box into single compartments, fill with soil, add the seed, and keep moist until the seeds sprout. You might want to place the compartments in a saucer to catch surplus water. Transplant the sprout including the cardboard into potted soil. The egg carton will disintegrate.

"Le Quartier" had a busy Thursday night. Véronique was ushering in people and taking bookings at the hostess table. Paul and Barb were busy in the kitchen, and Christian was rushing between expediting and serving the hungry guests.

At one of the more quiet small tables in a back niche, Daniel and Mattie were enjoying a piece of Quiche Lorraine each.

"I was serious about helping you with your boat the other day," Mattie said, her eyes full of glee.

"Even after I showed you the real deal and it was so much smaller than you had expected?" Daniel asked surprised. "I had actually just needed an excuse to see you again."

"But the boat really needs some work," Mattie insisted.

"It's not that important though," Daniel said. "I built it with my dad when I was about 15. It sat in a box in his attic for years, and I only took it down when I moved out from home. Ever since, that box has been shoved to places where it was least in the way."

"But wouldn't it be nice to see your motorboat afloat?" Mattie insisted.

"Are you sure?" Daniel asked. "Usually girls are not that much into technical stuff."

"You forget that I am running a wharf, and I know what I'm talking about, because I really learned the job." Mattie took a sip of Chablis. "Wouldn't it be fun to work on this together and make it look perfect? Just like you wanted it to be in the first place?"

Daniel looked into her eager face and started feeling mellow. Was this the woman he had hoped might take a permanent place in his life one day? Somebody with whom he might share not only his business worries, but also his favorite activities, his hobbies, his dreams?

"You wouldn't even need any more excuses to see me," Mattie smiled at him.

"Aren't I a lucky man?!" Daniel exclaimed. "Sure. I would love to work on the boat with you."

"Good. Then it's a done deal."

They both continued eating in silence, eying each other with ever growing fondness. Véronique sensed their mood, and presented them with a tiny amuse bouche as an in-between course. "It's on the house," she whispered and winked. Mattie blushed, and Daniel thanked her profusely.

A couple of tables away, Luke and Dottie McMahon were enjoying a date night dinner. They were sharing a colorful tasting platter with diverse delicacies and a carafe of dry red wine. Luke was just feeding Dottie a flavorful tidbit when Véronique approached their table. Her face broke into a huge smile.

"Seems like we are having quite a few lovebirds in tonight," she observed. "How wonderful – I can never get enough of people like you."

"Who else is getting fawned over like I am?" Dottie asked with a twinkle.

"Looks like Mattie Barton has hooked up with Daniel Harrison." Véronique nodded slightly in the younger couple's direction.

"So something good has come out of that nasty story after all," Luke observed. "I just wish they had been spared the fraud that brought them together."

"Ah, there is no great loss without some small gain." Dottie patted his arm. "And you helped them so well."

"Wish we could apprehend people who are up to no good before they have even done it," he muttered. Then he concentrated on a petit four created from smoked trout, honeyed cream cheese, horse radish, and a tad of pink pepper and dill. "I usually never have anything as fancy as this. But I have to admit these are really something else."

"So glad you like them," Véronique said.

"So how about *your* love life, sweetie?" Dottie enquired. "I know I'm too curious, but as a friend with a business next door I can't help observing how busy you all are in here. Are you sure you find enough time to tend to your more private needs at all?"

Véronique blushed. "I don't know whether it is too early to say. And maybe I'm getting it all wrong, after all. But, yes, I think Paul and I might be heading into a certain direction…"

"Really?!" Dottie was utterly excited and hushed her voice immediately. "You and Paul? How wonderful! And how discreet you are handling it!"

"Yeah, well," Véronique hesitated. "It wouldn't do to exhibit our love in front of the guests, would it? And Paul hasn't said yet whether he wants to tie the knot."

"Ah, he will, he will," Luke grinned and lifted his glass to toast her. "He would be insane to let go a pretty, intelligent, and diligent young lady like you. Here's to you!"

"Thank you," Véronique said. "I just wish Finn could be here when it happens. Where is he these days? We haven't heard from him in a while."

Finn Rover had been an 18-year-old run-away orphan when he had arrived in Wycliff a few years ago. Caught by Dottie in the act of stealing from her deli, she had offered him a home in exchange for working off the money he owed her and other stores in town. The team of "Le

Quartier" had offered him a position as a bus boy. While he was conscientiously tending to his tasks, he quickly became as good as a family member to Dottie as well as to the bistro team. Another turning point in his fate had been his rescuing a tiny boy, Bobby Random, from tumbling under the wheels of a float at the Tulip Parade that same year. The kid's grateful parents had awarded Finn the education of his dreams. He was well on his way of becoming a restaurant chef these days.

"I wish we heard from him more often, too," Dottie sighed. "He has been so very busy last semester, he barely came home for Christmas. But then I guess that he had to work so hard."

"Is he still in Seattle, by the way?"

"No," Luke answered for Dottie who had teared up a little. "He was on the East Coast till last week. He said he needed to learn about different regional leanings in the American cuisine. As there is a college specialized in cooking in New York City as well, he went there. And the Randoms pay for him generously."

"He obviously emails them more often than us," Dottie said and seemed a bit disappointed.

"Well, he will have to, as they sponsor his studies," Véronique observed, ever the practical one.

"He was cooking as a line cook at an exclusive restaurant on 9th Avenue," Dottie told her. "And the chef there recommended him to another chef over in Europe."

"So he might be going over there?"

"He already is, and he is tickled to death, of course," Luke confirmed. "Imagine his boss telling him to learn more on the other side of the Atlantic. I hope he won't allow it to go to his head. Sure, he wants to travel all over Europe this up-coming summer and, depending on what might be happening over in the Old World, he will go from there."

Véronique swallowed. "I hope he will come back every once in a while. He's like the younger brother I never had. Our bistro family misses him."

Dottie stroked the young woman's arm. "Don't I know it? We all do."

Véronique smiled wistfully, then she became all business again. "Got to go back to work again. I hope you enjoy your evening."

"We will," Dottie managed to say before Luke gently stuffed her mouth with a marinated clam.

*

Main Gallery was lit festively that same night. Owners Mark Owen and Harlan Hopkins had invited to an opening night with a newly discovered local artist, and people had been flocking in to see for themselves. Now they were meandering through the exhibition, noshing on finger food, sipping beverages, and talking in that strangely low tone that seems to be reserved for museums and galleries in general. Some people were presenting themselves as pieces of art, flaunting interesting costume either extremely over-the-top bohemian or elegantly subdued. Others had come in as they were. Trevor had chosen something a bit dressier, as he was expecting to meet one of his internet date choices tonight.

As he pretended to be engrossed by the strange abstract oil paintings he thought might be looking better if hung upside down, some maybe even better face to the wall, he scanned the entrance nervously every once in a while. He saw Mark and Harlan greet some Wycliff VIPs. He saw John Minor take notes and a few photos for "The Sound Messenger" and was wondering what he made of the paintings. Well, John was known to be truly sophisticated, so he'd probably find something to say that made the artist as well as the gallery happy and had some people return there to take another look and maybe even buy a piece.

He turned back to the canvas in front of him and stared at it.

"Do you like it?" a fresh, young voice asked him. He was startled a little. Then he found himself looking into an almost angelic face framed by long blond curls. The face belonged to an elfin woman in a burgundy colored dress that seemed to come from another era.

"Umh, I am not really sure," he stammered and blushed. "I am not a connoisseur, you know."

Silvery laughter. She shook her head, and her curls flew. "I could give you a tour if you want."

"In fact, I'm waiting for somebody I had a date with…" Trevor felt he was in the wrong place at the wrong time for all the wrong reasons.

"What a pity," the pretty lady said. "Well, maybe another time."

"Sure." He felt oddly bereaved when she left his side with a friendly smile. Had he messed up again?

There was a bit of a bustle in the doorway as some people tried to get in at the same time, while offering the others to enter first. There was laughter, and Trevor felt even lonelier and more excluded. But with this little crowd a tall, pretty lady had entered who reminded him of the internet photo he had responded to earlier that week. As she was searching the room their eyes met and a flash of recognition sparked. They approached each other.

"Hello," Trevor said and suddenly felt very gauche. "So nice you could make it."

"Hello," the brunette answered and pushed a strand of her sleek hair behind her ear. "It sounded interesting enough." She gave him a businesslike smile.

"It?"

"The opening night. There are usually a lot of interesting people in these places. And there are good networking opportunities."

Trevor was almost speechless. "Well, I thought we'd get to know each other first..."

She gave him a pitiful smile. "Trevor, right? Nice meeting you, but I don't think we'd be happy with each other."

"But you have only met me a second ago."

"Right. And I'm sure you will think the same. Was that your mother walking in on your dating video?"

"As a matter of fact, yes. But what does this have to with it?"

"Trevor, I'm a business woman. I don't know what kind of a lawyer you are. And to be honest: I don't want to know. Obviously, your life is still run by your mother. And no woman – at least not a woman like I – cares to share a man with his mother. Believe me. So let me give you some good advice: Grow up before you start dating." She gave him a wink and walked off, introducing herself to Mark, who exchanged business cards after a few minutes of talking to her.

Trevor felt horribly humiliated. How could she have shown up only to ridicule him and to stand him up? What cruelty! What opportunism, too. She had apparently liked his suggestion to come out to Wycliff, but all along it had only been about her, not him. He found himself walking towards the door.

"She didn't come?" the friendly voice from earlier asked and he felt a light touch on his shirt sleeve.

"No. She didn't," he said and threw a bitter look back into the room.

"Maybe we could talk some other time then?" The young woman slipped a card into his hand.

"Maybe," he said, and she didn't press further.

Later, when he was sitting alone in his office in the darkened house of his parents, he remembered the card and lifted his face from his hands. He rummaged through his pockets and came up with it, only slightly crumpled at one edge. The print was fine and curvy. The name was the opening night's artist's.

*

On Friday afternoon, Mildred Packman, the retired Wycliff High School teacher, was hobbling up Main Street. Though her mind was still very alert, she felt age creeping up on her, beginning with her legs. Today was not a good day for walking. But she didn't want to go through the hustle of finding a parking space on Main. Still, she had to pay a visit to the bank. She needed to get some money to tide her over the weekend. She was expecting some other teacher retirees at her house and wanted to do something more special than just the few brownies she usually had herself on weekends.

*

Thora and Angela walked from the wharf area towards Main Street. They were talking happily about their future dreams.

"So Meredith has sent off her husband to another four months off the coast of Alaska this morning," Angela told Thora. "Good riddance to him. Now she can finally start designing some totes with a front pocket. I also told her to make the inside pocket with a zipper and to shape it big enough it can hold an iPad and a wallet."

"Wonderful," Thora said, bag over one shoulder, immobilization sling over the other. "And to be able to cash in the very first checks today – what a reward for everybody's work! Even though it is just peanuts."

"Every bit counts," Angela said confidently. "Remember that some of these women haven't seen a penny of their own in years. They may not be able to splurge big time, but with orders coming in even from the farms in the Farmers Co-op, I mean – farm stores all over Western Washington... isn't this something incredible?!"

"We are certainly growing," Thora said. "One day, we might even have our own bag lines in boutiques and gift shops."

*

"I will hop over to the bank quickly to get some more change," Pattie May said with joy in her voice. "Obviously our customers have BBQ season in their bones. We need a lot more change." She grabbed a couple of hundreds and pushed them into an envelope.

"Maybe you could also deposit some of today's cash already," Dottie suggested. "I'm never really comfortable with such amounts of money sitting in the office while we are all serving customers. Rather have that in the bank quickly."

*

Julie was driving the long way around from "The Sound Messenger" towards downtown Wycliff. Today had been payday, and she desperately wanted to reward herself for the success that her latest series about environmental incidents in the area during the past 50 years had brought her newspaper. John Minor had even given her a bonus for more ads coming in than ever.

Maybe she would get herself that cute little summer dress she had spotted at "La Boutique" earlier this month. If it still fit her. She had gained a few pounds, because in her loneliness she kept treating herself for her success with chocolate and other goodies at night. There was still no man in her life, and she needed to have something for her creature comforts at least.

*

"Paul, we need another oven, desperately. It's the fifth time this month that it blew the fuse while I was baking only a Tarte Tatin in it." Barb pouted. "If it goes on like this, I cannot promise to make pâtisseries of quality in it anymore."

Paul turned around to his friend and colleague. "I know this oven is not state of the art. Can you work it just a couple of weeks longer, please?"

"As a matter of fact, I can't. Listen, it is not just my name standing for our desserts and cakes. It is also the name of the bistro. If we mess up and we serve guests raw dough just because of this flawed appliance... What if they end up with salmonella?"

Paul sighed. "You know that we don't have enough money to exchange all the old equipment at once. We are still paying off the walk-in freezer."

"Well, that is why there are banks," Barb insisted. "They know us, for Heaven's sake. We are local. They eat at our place. Don't you think they can give us another loan? They know we are paying back punctually."

Paul lifted his hands. "Can it wait till Monday?"

Barb stood with her arms akimbo. "Paul Sinclair, why is it that men always try to procrastinate things?! The earlier we get their go, the better. We might even be able to look at a new oven this weekend!"

"Alright," Paul said. "I'll drop over quickly and try to convince them to give us another loan. Gee, Barb, I'm glad we only do business together."

"Well," Barb countered. "So am I. By the way, the sooner we get all these loans done and over with, the sooner you will be able to buy that ring you're planning to give Véronique. A new oven means more capacity ..."

*

Peter was looking into his rearview mirror. Nobody had been following him so far. But then he had taken extra care to take tiny backroads only. His truck had been all over the news after all. Now that the novelty of the search warrant had died down and people had stopped looking at the posters in supermarkets, post offices, and other public buildings, he deemed it safe enough to go on his mission.

This morning, he had changed his hair to a buzz cut with his electric shaver. He knew it didn't look like a professional cut. But it sure had changed his looks. He also had decided not to wear his green contact lenses. So now his blue eyes were gleaming dangerously from his cleanly shaven face. No, nobody would recognize Peter Michaels in the man who was driving this Dodge RAM. Nobody would expect him to pop up anywhere in Western Washington anyway – period.

Peter Michaels chuckled. He had warned Teal about his changed looks. Teal had understood nothing about it, but he would be ready by the time he got picked up. Peter patted his jacket where it was slightly bulging. The hardness of the item underneath felt more than reassuring. It simply felt right.

*

Julie was slowing down, checking Main Street for parking slots. Eventually she spotted one and pulled into it. She was just about to unbuckle, when a dark-gray Dodge RAM drove past her and double-parked outside the bank. Julie stared.

She read the license plate and immediately recognized the number. A slight sound escaped her mouth. She had written down the plate number often enough to recognize its import. Feverishly she dug in her handbag for her smart phone. She hit the speed dialing button for Luke and had him on the other end after only two ring tones.

"Luke?" she asked breathlessly. "You need to come to Main Street immediately."

"What's up, Julie?" Luke asked. "I'm not in my office, but in Uptown."

Julie moaned. "Send somebody else then. Peter Michaels' truck is double-parking outside the bank."

"You sure it's his?" Luke's voice sounded wary.

"Absolutely. And I don't know why, but it gives me the creeps." She took a deep breath. "There is somebody getting out from the passenger side now."

"Michaels?"

"No. Somebody with short hair and no beard."

"Is the driver getting out, too?" Luke's voice sounded as if he were walking very fast now.

"No, and the motor is still running. – Oh my God!" Julie's eyes widened with horror. "He's pulling out a gun!"

"Oh goodness," Luke said. "I'm coming as quickly as I can. Stay on the phone with me, Julie. I'll alarm my guys at the office." Julie heard him open and close a car door and start the motor, while he was calling for reinforcement via his police radio. Then he was back on the phone. "You still there, Julie?"

"Yes," she said, and she was trembling. "I just heard something like a shot."

"Sit tight, Julie. Stay in your car. Don't do anything dumb!"

*

Teal had gaped at Peter when he had pulled up at his apartment. "Gee, dude! I almost didn't recognize you!"

Peter grunted. Idiot. He had probably only identified the car. Fair enough. If his disguise worked so well, he would pull this one off without anybody being the wiser. He got into the passenger seat, while Teal fiddled with the mirrors and the position of his seat.

"Are you done yet?" Peter asked exasperated.

"Hey man, if I am to drive fast, I need to feel good in the driver seat, okay?" Teal looked at him with pleading eyes. Peter lifted his hands in mute frustration. Finally, they drove off.

They took I-5 and exited near Parkland. From there they chose tiny streets and backroads. "Where are we going?" Teal wanted to know. "Do we really have to take these weird detours?"

Peter didn't answer. That fool would know soon enough where they were headed. And that it wouldn't help to draw any attention to their truck too soon.

Half an hour later they entered Wycliff from the south and kept going towards Downtown. "Park outside the bank," Peter said. "Keep the motor running. I'll be just a few minutes."

"Jesus, Peter!" Julian Teal exclaimed. "Are you doing what I think you are going to do?"

Peter looked at him. "What do you think I'm going to do?"

Teal's face turned white. "Shit! Oh shit!"

"Listen, Teal," Peter said. "You shut up and sit tight. There's money in it for you after all." Peter left the car.

Teal looked through the side window in desperation. What had seemed like such a good idea first, had become a nightmare. Wasn't everybody already staring at their truck? Or was it just his imagination that they did?

Peter pulled out his Sig P 320 as soon as he reached the bank entrance. He didn't don a mask. He felt safe enough as his undisguised self.

Inside the bank, there were several people waiting in front of the three counters. He wasn't sure whether he recognized any of them. He certainly didn't care if he would. He quickly stepped past a man and a woman. Someone behind him opened their mouth to protest his cutting the line. Then he heard a gasp. "Oh my God! Oh my God! He's got a gun!"

He smirked. The power was all his. He jostled the lady with the flaming red hair at one counter to the side, shoved an empty garbage bag over the counter, and pointed his gun at the cashier. "Don't push the alarm button," he commanded. "Get me all your money and that from the other counters, too. Make it quick."

To emphasize the seriousness of the situation he shot into the ceiling. One woman screamed. The acrid smell of gun smoke was filling the hall. The cashier was stuffing the bag with flying fingers. His face was deadly pale. His colleagues at the other counters were standing and staring helplessly.

"No pushing alarm buttons, you hear?" Peter shouted and focused on them.

There was a tiny movement behind his back, and turning around, he saw an elderly lady point at him with a trembling hand. "I know you, don't I? You are Prosper Martinovic."

A red curtain was drawing over his eyes. He was furious. He pulled the trigger. Another shot rang out. He grabbed the bag, but the bag wouldn't give. He grabbed an arm, but he didn't know whose. He pulled the person the arm belonged to towards the door, ignoring the sounds of panic behind him. He rushed out. He raced to the truck. He pulled open the door. He thrust the person whose arm he was still gripping into the middle seat and jumped in himself. He banged the door close.

"Hit it!" he screamed.

The tires screeched. Horns were honking behind them. They almost ran over a couple of teens crossing the road. Then everything turned quiet in Peter/Prosper's mind. The world was turning an angry dark gray. His plan had utterly failed.

*

Inside the bank, people had thought they were in an ugly dream. First they hadn't even realized that an armed bank robber had come in. When they did, everybody tried to become as invisible as possible. The poor cashier who had the gun pointed at him was near fainting. He hoped his colleagues would press the alarm button under their counters. Instead, they seemed paralyzed and about as incapable to do anything as the Biblical pillars of salt.

Angela Fortescue, who had been shoved aside unceremoniously by the bank robber, was not sure whether she was more upset by the way he had treated her or by the fact that she found herself in the middle of a bank robbery.

Thora, who stood right next to her, warned her with a finger to her lips not to make a sound. She was seemingly calm, but she was quavering like the rest of them.

Paul had been waiting in line behind Mildred Packman. He figured they would just have to be quiet and let the robber succeed in order to get the ordeal over with quickly. He was only hoping that nobody else would enter the bank, unaware of the situation inside.

Mildred Packman had been exchanging some kindly words with Pattie May, when the robber had entered. Something about the man triggered a memory with her. Whether it was his overly confident gate, his stature, or his facial features and the piercing color of his eyes (or maybe all of these together), she'd never be sure.

Everybody was startled and shrunk even more when the robber shot into the ceiling. Some plaster fell down, and a bit of dust drizzled right behind. The neon lights flickered slightly. Somebody had gasped aloud. And in that moment, when she smelled the gun smoke, Mildred remembered who that man reminded her of. Almost a decade and a half ago that man, then a teenager, had sat in her history class. Back then she had taught them about the naval battle at Salamis, and the boy with the fierce face and bright blue eyes had lit paper ships on his desk. He had enjoyed himself hugely when the black powder he had poured into them exploded with little "Pops". Mildred had managed to douse the fire and then sent the boy to the headmaster. The boy had been suspended for a couple of weeks, and his parents had had to pay for the damage that he had wrought. Prosper Martinovic. The no-good kid, then teenager who became worse and worse by the year. And look where he had ended up.

When she called the man by his name, a flash of angry fear had passed over his face. She saw the muzzle of the pistol move into her direction. Later she wouldn't really remember what happened afterwards. Except that there was another shot, she ended up on the floor, and all hell broke loose. She had blood all over herself, but she felt no pain apart from the knee she had landed on first.

People were screaming. They were all around her and fawning over her and the person next to her. The robber was gone. The bank siren was howling and adding to the insane cacophony. The blaring horns of police cars could be heard approaching outside. Somebody shrieked: "Call an ambulance! Call an ambulance! Oh my God, he might be bleeding to death!"

It was a nightmare filled with frantic faces. Then the calming sight of police uniforms broke the scene. Somebody switched off the alarm. People were led to the side and made to sit down on the floor or on chairs. Angela

Fortescue was sobbing loudly. Since when was that woman capable of such human emotions?!

When the bustle by Mildred's side thinned out a little, she was able to catch a glimpse of the very pale face of Paul Sinclair. His eyes were closed. He was lying in a puddle of blood. He was breathing weakly, and the policeman who was holding him gazed nervously at the clock on the wall above the door. "Why does this damn ambulance take so long?!"

"What happened?" Mildred asked softly.

"He saved your life," an elderly man said.

"He saved my life?" Mildred asked aghast.

"That bastard had the gun pointed at you, and that young man there pushed you over so the bullet wouldn't hit you. Got in the way of it himself though. If you ask me, he's a darn hero!"

Mildred stared at Paul. Her teeth started chattering loudly.

A minute later, some paramedics burst through the door with large emergency kits. They went to work on Paul immediately. But one of them also saw to Mildred, who was shaking badly, and covered her with a foil to keep her warm. He gave her a tranquilizing shot and band aided her knee.

"How is Paul?" she asked the paramedic.

"That the guy who got shot?" he asked with a look at the young man who was in and out of consciousness now and got tended to by three paramedics at once.

"Yes. He saved my life," Mildred said, only now realizing what Paul had done for her. It was as if she slowly woke from a deep, deep daze.

"Can't say, Ma'am," the paramedic answered, and his face didn't tell her much else either. He was probably not supposed to say anything bad or good. "But a prayer for him can't be wrong, huh?"

Mildred nodded, while she was feeling close to tears. "I guess not." Her eyes were following the gurney on which they were rolling Paul outside now.

"Will you be alright?" the paramedic asked.

"Sure," Mildred said automatically. "Sure."

*

Julie thought it took the police ages to come. Though she knew that it was only seconds seemingly stretching into hours. Hearing the shot had rattled her badly. Her hand on the smart phone shook. What was going on in there?

"Just stay calm," Luke's voice sounded warmly through the phone. Julie felt its soothing effect. "Is anybody else approaching the bank yet?"

Julie looked around. "You mean, will anybody else walk into this?" She swallowed hard. "I can't see anybody. As a matter of fact, I think I can hear sirens from the direction of the police department now."

"Good guys – they are up to par with their fastest training results obviously," Luke said proudly.

In that instant, Julie heard a second shot. "Oh gosh, no please!"

"What's the matter now?"

"There was a second shot just now."

"Sit tight, sweetie. Don't be scared."

"I'm not scared for myself," Julie said. "I'm worried for the people inside the bank."

Suddenly the bank door opened, and she saw the man come out again, literally racing. He still held the gun, muzzle pointed to the ground. And with him he was dragging a person whom he shoved into the truck.

"Oh no!" Julie shouted into the phone.

"What now?!" Luke asked. "I'm almost Downtown."

Julie closed her eyes for a moment. Then she opened them again to see the truck speed away.

"It's awful," she said. "He just left the bank. They got Thora."

*

From "The Sound Messenger":

Robbing Attempt Ends with Kidnapping

jomin. **Though the bank robbery attempted yesterday afternoon at the Wycliff Bank failed in essence, the robber, identified as 30-year-old Prosper Martinovic (aka Peter Michaels), escaped. One person was seriously wounded during the incident, another Wycliff citizen has been kidnapped.**

The town of Wycliff is shaken by the brutal bank robbery attempt yesterday afternoon an hour before closing. At the time the robber entered the bank on Main Street, there were 20 people inside.

After retired Wycliff High teacher Mildred Packman was able to identify the robber as Prosper Martinovic, the robber tried to shoot her. Chef Paul Sinclair from "Le Quartier" saved Packman in throwing himself in the line of fire, while pushing her to the ground. He is now critically injured at St. Christopher's in Wycliff where doctors are still fighting for his life. Packman remained uninjured.

In order to get away unhindered, Martinovic took environmental activist Thora Byrd hostage and managed to escape in a dark-gray Dodge Ram that was driven by an accomplice so far unidentified. Up to yesterday's editorial deadline, Thora Byrd has not been found nor have any demands for ransom been made.

Prosper Martinovic, formerly a citizen of Wycliff, was lately involved in a series of fraud committed in the business of hazardous waste disposal. He has also been investigated for probably being the person who dumped hazardous waste in the region in at least ten cases. Furthermore, he was at least partly responsible for the fund theft from the Wycliff Victorian Christmas a couple of years ago. As he is also wanted in other states for fraud, hold-ups, robbery, manslaughter, and attempted murder, the FBI has taken over the case. The Wycliff Police Department (WPD) is co-operating in the local cases.

Both WPD and FBI are hoping for tips from the population. If you see a Dodge RAM as in the photo below or know the whereabouts of Prosper Martinovic (see current police drawing below) and his accomplice or of victim Thora Byrd (see photo to the right), please inform WPD immediately by calling 911. The FBI warns citizens to beware of Martinovic and his accomplice, as both might be armed and are obviously willing to shoot. "People should not try to approach either of the persons mentioned," warns Luke McMahon, Chief of WPD. "We don't know yet whether Thora Byrd is used as a human shield. Any direct encounter with those men might endanger her life."

CHAPTER 9

The Green Maven's Tip of the Week:
Don't throw vegetable cut-offs away, but make stock from them. Boil the cut-offs in lightly salted-water, then discard the now flavorless solids and freeze the stock. Do similarly with poultry fish carcasses. You will receive flavorful bases for all kinds of stews, soups, sauces, and/or gravies without any waste.

"It is all my fault," Barb wailed as she sagged onto a chair in the bistro. She, Véronique, and Christian had just been briefed about the bank robbery by Chief McMahon. He had worded the message very carefully, but the full impact of what had happened needed to sink in yet.

Véronique closed the bistro door and locked it. She was as pale as a ghost.

"I guess we keep the restaurant closed tonight," she said tonelessly. Then she walked towards Barb and laid an arm around her shoulder. "Don't blame yourself. This was simply a horrible coincidence..."

She didn't cry. She was numbed by the news. She needed to get things into the right order and do something. She needed to go see how bad it was. She needed to figure how to continue without Paul until he would be back on his feet again. She wouldn't need to call Paul's parents. They would have received the terrible news from the police, too. They would have gone to the hospital immediately. She would probably meet them outside the ER. She would be able to talk to them there.

Christian was cleaning tables vigorously. It was his way of dealing with a situation that blew his mind. A friend of his shot? Friendly, peaceful Paul? When he had only gone to get another fricking loan from the bank?

The three friends looked at each other mutely. Barb's eyes were red, Véronique's dry, Christian filled with rage.

"I will drive over to the hospital," Véronique decided.

"You can't drive," Christian observed.

"I am totally calm," Véronique claimed.

"It's because the physical shock hasn't set in yet. You will be a bundle of nerves once you're behind the wheel."

"I'll do just fine."

"Please," Barb implored. "Please, don't argue. It's bad enough already. We are worried you might get hurt, hon. Can't you just catch a bus?"

Véronique looked at the two and sighed. "Very well. I guess we have been scared enough today already. You don't need any more worries on top of that." She left for the staff room and got her coat. "I'll call you later. I hope they let me see Paul." She gave them a sad little wave and let herself out through the kitchen back door.

An early diner was knocking at the bistro door.

"Chris," Barb said faintly, "could you please deal with him?"

He nodded. His mien betrayed no emotions whatsoever. "Write a sign for the door meanwhile."

She nodded, and he went to unlock the door to explain why "Le Quartier" would be closed tonight. The man was visibly shocked. After a short exchange of words, Christian locked up again, and he taped Barb's handwritten note to the glass door.

"What now?" he asked.

"I don't know," Barb started wailing again. "It's all my fault, because I didn't want to wait for a loan until Monday." She began shaking seriously and kept repeating that it was her fault. Christian was helpless. He sat down next to her and just listened. He simply couldn't grasp that an hour ago their world had been turned upside down.

*

Clark was at his town hall desk when his new secretary, whom he still hadn't really warmed up to, cautiously knocked on his office door and then peeked in.

"Mr. Thompson," she said, her face totally drained of color. "There's Chief McMahon for you outside."

"Well, send him in," Clark said friendly. "Oh, and make us a cup of coffee, please!"

She nodded and disappeared. A second later, Luke entered the room and bit his lips. The message he had to convey was something he couldn't deliver gracefully or diplomatically. The situation was entirely new to him, and he wasn't sure how to handle it.

Clark rose and came around his desk, shaking his old friend's hand, while giving him a manly hug at the same time. "Luke, old boy! What brings you here?"

Luke hemmed and hawed. "Can we sit down maybe?"

"Sure, sure," Clark answered cordially. "Let's drop in the armchairs over there – much more comfortable than these monstrosities of wooden chairs by the desk." He led Luke over to the lounging area and sank into one of the recliners. "So, what makes you spend your Friday afternoon at town hall instead of picking up your lovely wife from work and enjoying the weekend?"

Luke sighed. "I don't even know how to put this."

Clark finally realized how worried and tired Luke was looking and became very sober. "Anything bad happening in town?"

"We've had a bloody bank robbery about an hour ago."

"Here in Wycliff?"

"Wycliff Bank."

They were staring at each other.

"How are the bank people doing?" Clark asked.

Luke sighed. Clark was obviously a wonderful mayor, asking about the people involved rather than the amount that might have been robbed.

"They are shaken, but okay."

"Good, good."

The secretary came in and placed two cups filled with coffee onto the table between them. Her hands were shaking, and some of the hot liquid spilled over the rim into Clark's saucer. "Sorry about that. Shall I ..."

"No," Clark interrupted her. "It's fine. A napkin will do."

She almost fled out of the room.

"You are not here to tell me about a bank robbery that is of no consequence, Luke. Why are you here? What happened? Spit it out."

"One of the bank customers was critically injured in the event." Luke moved uncomfortably. Clark look at him with an unspoken question in his face. "Paul Sinclair. The young chef from 'Le Quartier'."

"Good God," Clark groaned. "That will be a blow for Dottie, right? I mean, she and those kids have been so close to each other from the very beginning. She must be horribly worried."

"She doesn't know yet," Luke said through clenched teeth. "Paul is at the ER at St. Christopher's now. The doctors can't say much so far. He suffered a huge loss of blood. Other than that I have no idea what damage the shot gun wound may have wrought."

Clark cursed. Then he apologized. "I will contact the parents later and check with them," he said. "Maybe there is something we can do for Paul or them."

Luke nodded. The worst part of the message was still to be delivered. Clark sensed it from the tight look in the chief's face.

"This isn't all of it, is it?" Clark asked softly.

"Unfortunately not," Luke conceded. "There is another victim in this." He paused and swallowed. Then he decided to put it bluntly, because he wouldn't be able to disguise or soften the facts anyhow. "They have taken Thora with them."

"They what?!" Clark's jaw dropped in horror, then he got a grip on himself. "This is not really true, is it?"

Luke shook his head as if in slow motion. "It is though. I am utterly sorry to have to bring such news to you. I think I know what she means to you."

Clark covered his eyes with his right hand for a moment. Then he wiped it over his face. "And there was no chance that anybody would have intercepted the robber who did this?"

"None. You cannot argue with somebody with a loose gun, Clark. People were already shocked by Paul lying on the ground. It would have been madness to stand up to the man and try to talk him out of it or wrestle Thora away from him."

"Do we know what car they escaped in?"

"There is the hook," Luke said. "It was Peter Michaels' truck."

"The one that was involved in the illegal dumping cases?"

"The same." Luke rose and paced the room. "Somebody was even able to identify the robber. It was Prosper Martinovic, according to Ms. Packman, our retired high school teacher."

"Prosper Martinovic?" Clark almost laughed. "But this is bizarre! He has already been sought for being involved in stealing the Christmas fund from the Chamber of Commerce a couple of years ago. Now he comes back to rob the bank and kidnap a citizen? What the heck?!" He beat his fist on the tiny table, at which the cup of coffee made another jump and spilled over some more. Then he also rose and walked to the window. Putting his hands into his pant pockets he was staring blankly into the falling dusk outside.

"The FBI have taken over this case. The Wycliff Police Department is on a co-operating level only. I just know that they are having a search warrant longer than my arm for that man. As to Peter Michaels – he might have been the driver. Unfortunately, nobody paid attention to that person."

"Do they have any idea where they have gone?"

"Left the town in the northern direction," Luke said quietly.

"Did you give them chase?"

Luke sighed. "We contacted all the police departments in Western Washington immediately. So the alert is out. But you know how it is – somebody has to see them in order to be able to report on them."

"So Thora is out there all by herself with two armed robbers..." Clark spoke more to himself than to Luke.

Luke didn't answer. He stepped to the side of his friend and looked outside as well.

"Is there anything that I can do?" Clark asked, and his voice finally cracked.

Luke patted his shoulder. "The FBI and we are doing everything possible to get Thora back safe and sound," he tried to console.

Clark nodded and swallowed. Then he looked at Luke with moist eyes. "I was going to ask her this weekend whether she would marry me ..."

"You will have to wait just a little longer, that's all," Luke said quietly. "I'm sure she will be back sooner than we dare imagine right now." Clark nodded mutely. "Meanwhile, I promise to keep you updated wherever I can, okay?" A friendly slap on the mayor's shoulder, and Luke turned to leave the office. The room had turned dark meanwhile. The coffee stood on the table, cold and unconsumed.

*

Véronique had arrived at the hospital only half an hour after she had left "Le Quartier". She had to admit to herself that Christian had been right. She wouldn't have been able to drive. She wouldn't even have been able to start the motor of her car. For by now shock had set in, and she shook, weak to the bone.

At the reception desk in the hospital lobby she barely got out the words. The receptionist didn't look too impressed that she wanted to see this afternoon's shooting victim. Wouldn't people come under all kinds of pretenses, after all, to catch a glimpse of Paul Sinclair and to satisfy their curiosity? Also, as an out-of-towner the receptionist rarely made it into Wycliff at all, and to be honest - the fare of "Le Quartier" would have been too exotic for her to even go there for a meal. She preferred places like Pizza Hut at the Harbor Mall, the Harbor Pub, or - and that was as far as she went as to food adventures - the Southern BBQ place that had opened south of the ferry terminal only recently. So she wouldn't have known what half of Wycliff already suspected - that Véronique and Paul were indeed an item.

"Sorry, Ma'am," she said. "I cannot let you even near the ER. You are not family or have power of attorney. Besides, he is probably still in the operation theater."

"Could I just sit there in the Emergency Unit waiting area, please?"

The receptionist rolled her eyes. "I don't know what good that would do. And the doctors won't tell you anything either."

"But his parents will be here, I'm pretty sure."

"I hope you don't want to add to their sorrow."

Véronique was exasperated. Just as she was about to give up, the receptionist waved her off with one hand. "Ah well. You might as well go and see for yourself that there is nothing you can do."

Before there might be time for any reconsideration, Véronique rushed towards the hall that led to the wing with the Emergency Unit. Her mouth was dry when she entered the unit's waiting area. She didn't know why she had expected there would be only Paul's family and she in there. The world was full of accidents and incidents, and the waiting area was teeming with worried faces, pacing feet, clinging hands, and every once in a while a sob. Doctors were dashing in and out, nurses were busily looking at patient files. The coffee maker in one corner was constantly busy.

Véronique scanned the room for Paul's parents, but she didn't seem able to find them.

"Can I help you, hon?" a nurse asked softly.

Véronique swallowed. "I am the girl-friend of the shooting victim that was brought in earlier."

"Which one?" the nurse asked.

"There's more than one?"

"The nurse smiled tightly. "Unfortunately some people don't know how to handle their weapons right. We sent one with a grazed arm home earlier. So if you are looking for him…"

"No," Véronique said huskily. "No, the man I mean was injured in the bank robbery this afternoon."

The nurse's face fell, and she gave Véronique an empathetic nod. "He's still in the operation theater."

"Are his parents here yet?"

"They are waiting in a different room," the nurse said with a sober tone. "For situations like these we like to keep them in a more private area. Would you follow me, please?"

Véronique felt an ice-cold shiver creep down her body. "Is Paul ... I mean, he is still ..."

The nurse looked at her in a businesslike way. "I am not supposed to say anything about any patient's state. That is up to the doctors only. I'm sorry. But if there weren't hope, they'd not keep operating, right?"

"Of course."

There were two doors in the little hallway between the operation theater and the waiting area. One was closed; it was a staff room. The other door was slightly cracked open, and Véronique sensed movement in the room behind. The nurse knocked and pushed her face through the opening. "You have a visitor." She held the door for Véronique.

"Véronique!" Mrs. Sinclair exclaimed. She was a broad woman with an ample bosom and a kindly, if not very striking face. Tonight, she was looking awful. Her face was covered with hectic splotches, her eyes were red-rimmed, and her hair was a crow's nest as if she had torn it in despair.

Mr. Sinclair was tall and pale. Nobody could deny that Paul was his son – their similarities as to looks were too obvious. He now strode over to Paul's girl-friend and shook her hand. "Thank you for coming," he said curtly. Then he turned around and studied the pictures on the wall again. "How is it possible that a perfect day like this is all of a sudden filled with such chaos and grief?"

Véronique didn't even try to answer. Mrs. Sinclair was crying again. She dabbed at her tears with a Kleenex that was already soaked, and Véronique handed her a fresh one from a box at a side table.

"Thank you, dear," Paul's mother whispered.

"How is Paul doing?" Véronique asked after a small pause.

"We don't know that yet," Paul's father answered. "We know that he had to have some blood transfusions, because he lost so much. And they have to figure what damage the bullet caused. The doctors have been working on him ever since we came. We haven't seen any of them, just one of the nurses. She told us it could take some hours."

Véronique sobbed drily. "He only went there to take care of a loan for a new oven for the bistro," she said. "He loves the bistro so much…"

Mrs. Sinclair cried more openly now. "Why him?!"

"Because he is a hero," Véronique said quietly and stroked the other woman's arm. "He saved a life today. He never thought of himself. He was just thinking of saving Ms. Packman."

"What if ..."

"Don't even think of it!" Mr. Sinclair interrupted his wife. "The doctors are still in there with him. I take that as a sign of hope."

Mrs. Sinclair pressed her Kleenex against her mouth to stifle her sobs. Then she let her hand sink into her lap. "I remember when he brought home the stray cat when he was three. Turns out the cat wasn't a stray. It belonged to somebody in Uptown who was frantically searching for her, while kitty was getting pampered in our kitchen." She laughed hysterically.

"See what a big heart he has?" Véronique said, quickly preventing Paul's father from saying anything harsh. "I'm pretty sure he will pull through. And we will all help him to get well as quickly as possible. We have closed the bistro tonight, so we can be at hand if you need anything. And if Paul needs anything ..." Véronique's voice broke.

"We appreciate this so very much, Véronique," Mrs. Sinclair said in a wobbly voice. "God knows, you are a good girl-friend. Paul loves you so ..."

"You should go home to your folks, dear," Paul's father said.

"They know where I am." Véronique stood firm. "I need to be where you and Paul are. I couldn't imagine being at home or with my parents while Paul is fighting such a fight."

Mr. Sinclair searched her face, then gave her a slight nod of approval. Mrs. Sinclair squeezed her hand.

They paced. They had some sandwiches from the food court in the hospital basement – it might have been something delicious, but it tasted like rubber, and every bite seemed to grow bigger in the process of chewing. They spoke rarely. They stared at the photos on the walls. They sat down. Worry kept their eyes open. Until one after the other nodded off.

It was past midnight when an exhausted doctor entered the room to report the results of the operation. Mrs. Sinclair's hand flew to her mouth, Mr. Sinclair wiped his eyes. Véronique never realized. She was fast asleep, her arms hugging her body as if in self-comfort.

*

Dottie had heard about the robbery attempt gone wrong as soon as Christian and Barb left the bistro. They had dropped by the deli and told her in her office. When they had left, Dottie had sunk down onto her office chair and remained there for five minutes, gazing at nothing in particular, staying mute and tearless, stunned.

That was how her sales assistant Sabine found her after she had started missing her bustling around the aisles and continuing stocking up the shelves. "Are you alright?" Sabine asked her.

Dottie nodded, but she didn't say a word.

"I just saw Chris and Barb leave. Is anything wrong over there?"

"Paul got shot at the bank," Dottie said, and her own voice sounded like a stranger's in her ears.

"What?!" Sabine gasped.

"He was caught in an attempted bank robbery. And the robber shot him. That is, he didn't actually aim at him, but at Ms. Packman. Paul saved her life."

Sabine's hand flew to her mouth. "That is awful! How is he?"

"Chris and Barb didn't know much more than that. Véronique went to the hospital, of course. And they decided to keep the bistro closed tonight. They were simply too upset to try to keep things going."

"Of course," Sabine breathed. "Oh my God! And I always thought Wycliff was such an idyllic place where nothing like this could happen!"

"Yeah, well. It's not an island all by itself, but part of this country. We have just been lucky so far."

"Did they catch the robber yet?"

Dottie shook her head and sighed. "This is where it gets really nasty. They took Thora hostage when they left."

"Thora?!"

"Yes. She probably just stood in a spot where she was easy to get to. It could have been anybody else as well. But now she's with them." Dottie hugged herself for warmth, as she had started shaking. "As if she hadn't been through enough already this year what with losing her job and breaking her shoulder."

Sabine leaned against a sideboard used for additional storage of products in the office. "And to be in that situation with the sling ... how brutal of them!"

"Well, we can argue about what is more brutal – kidnapping somebody rather helpless or shooting at people." Dottie shook her head as if trying to wake from a nightmare. Then she rose. "I guess I should continue my tasks out in the shop. Can't let this affect me too much for now. And I guess we won't see Pattie tonight anymore. She will be questioned by the police as a witness."

Sabine patted Dottie's shoulder as she went past. She was upset. But she was more angry than worried. All they could do about Paul was pray right now. But she wished there could be done something about criminals turning Wycliff into a place that it simply was never meant to be. Wycliff was peaceful and beautiful, not a stage for crime and violence.

Dottie and she went about their work as usual again. When they closed the deli later, they talked it over with others. By then rumors had spread. But nobody knew more than what Christian and Barb had already told Dottie.

With a heavy heart Dottie went home. The McMahon house was lit up in the kitchen and dining room, which meant that Luke might have prepared dinner already. Dottie's heart made a little leap at the thought of her husband. What luck she had had to find such a kindly and caring man after her first husband, Sean, had passed so early and suddenly. Luke was the rock in her life now, and masculine as he was, he kept surprising her every once in a while in taking over a task of hers.

She wasn't surprised, therefore, when she opened the front door and the hallway was fragrant with the aromas of garlic and vegetables. "Mmmh!" she said. "Smells like my favorite vegetarian pizza."

Luke came from the kitchen and smiled at her. "Five more minutes. I just got it out of the oven."

Dottie hugged him and almost vanished in his bearlike arms. "It's so good to come home to you. Especially on a day like this."

Luke's face turned serious. "It has been awful, and I am just glad that I can take a break for now, because the FBI is on it. I will have to be on stand-by though."

"I am so upset about what happened to Paul."

"Quite some heroic action there," Luke agreed. "It's a bloody shame though!"

Dottie didn't scold him for cursing in this situation. If he needed to vent this way, let him for once. He must have had some tough past hours, dealing with victims and their families, organizing shifts around this special case, and working with the FBI. She stroked his five o' clock shaded face. "Time for you to sit down and get pampered, huh?"

He smiled lopsidedly. "I don't really feel like sitting," he admitted. "Though I laid the table in the dining room. I feel rather like standing while eating."

"Well, then let's eat in the kitchen, and you can pace and stand as much as you want," Dottie indulged him. "Though you know that it is much healthier to sit while eating."

Luke winked at her, but the wink lacked its usual lightheartedness. He went back into the kitchen. "You wouldn't guess what we found out at the office once we poured over the FBI data and the police drawing we have," he said over his shoulder.

"What?" Dottie wanted to know. She followed him into the kitchen and watched him push a cutting wheel across the pizza steaming on the counter top. He placed a large slice onto a plate and handed it to her. "Sit down and eat. I'll tell you."

Dottie climbed one of the bar stools at the kitchen counter and dug into her pizza. "So good!" she mumbled between two bites.

Luke started pacing the kitchen, while biting into his slice. He chewed, watching his tiny wife enjoy one of her favorite meals. He needed to have her eat first before he'd break news to her that would be even more disturbing than what she already knew.

"Well?" Dottie asked curiously.

"Well," Luke smiled grimly. "Turns out that Wycliff knows the bank robber pretty well from years and years ago when he was a mischievous, at times even criminal kid and teenager."

"Prosper Martinovic," Dottie nodded.

"Right. Ms. Packman identified him. It gets even better. After the truck in which the robber arrived turned out to be the same as the one Peter Michaels owns, we placed the computer images of both on the monitor next to each other." Luke paused for effect and saw that he got Dottie's whole attention. "Turns out that, by 98 percent of the similarities between the two, Prosper Martinovic is one and the same person as Peter Michaels."

"What?" Dottie sputtered out.

"Yep. He must have worn contact lenses when being Michaels. He grew his hair longer and wore a beard. Apart from that there are so many similarities that there is almost no doubt about the true identity of Peter Michaels."

Dottie wiped her mouth with a paper towel. "I can't believe it!"

"You better."

She pushed the plate away. "I'm not hungry anymore."

"Really? No second slice?"

"No thanks. This whole story is so sordid."

Luke nodded. He scrutinized her face and went for the rest of his story. "It gets even nastier."

"Thora ..."

"Martinovic dragged her to his vehicle and pushed her in. Then they drove off."

"So there was another person driving?"

"There was. We don't know yet who."

"As long as you get them. So, are the FBI following them?"

"Sort of."

"How do you mean?"

Luke sighed. It was so hard to tell her. And yet he must. "Obviously we arrived only when Martinovic's truck was already gone. The FBI arrived even later – they'd been stuck in one of those infernal I-5 traffic jams on their way down from Seattle. But ... the truck has been followed ever since, alright."

"If not by the police and the FBI, then by... Oh God, no!" Dottie gasped and turned as white as the wall behind her.

"Yes, Julie." Luke came around the counter and took Dottie into his arms to hold her tight. "She was actually on her way to the bank when she witnessed Martinovic double-park, get out, and pull out a gun."

"No. Not Julie!!!" Dottie whimpered.

"As soon as she saw it happen, she gave me a call and kept briefing me. I was in Uptown on a minor incident, and

I was filled in on the shooting and Thora's kidnapping by her, while I was racing to get to the bank. My fellow officers were there a tad before me, but they also arrived too late."

"And Julie?"

"Julie kept her phone on for a while yet. She told me she was following them. I warned her to be careful. She said she tried to keep a couple of cars between her and the truck. They went northeast."

"Mt. Rainier?"

"There is a lot northeast," Luke said quietly. "We don't know yet."

"Oh Julie, my child," Dottie wept. "Why is she so stupid to follow such dangerous people?!"

"Because she felt she had to help Thora." Luke cradled Dottie softly, and she sobbed silently.

"But she could get killed if they find she's following them."

"She knows that, sweetie, but she wouldn't let Thora alone in this. That is what she said before she hung up on me."

"She hung up?"

"She was busy giving chase and hiding at the same time."

"That silly, unthinking girl!" Luke didn't answer. "I hope she loses them. I hope she gets to be safe."

"She will be safe," Luke answered. "The FBI are onto her phone GPS by now. They know exactly where she is."

"Where?"

Luke swallowed, but his throat stayed dry. "Somewhere on Route 410 east of Enumclaw."

*

When Julie saw Thora being dragged to Peter Michaels' truck and pushed in by the man who had obviously been wielding his gun only a couple of minutes ago inside the bank, she was aghast. She started her motor and slowly moved out of her parking spot as the truck sped off.

Thora was in danger. She was still injured and probably even more helpless and uncomfortable in this horrendous situation than any physically fully capable person would have been. And hadn't it been her after all who had found the first illegal dump? This might make it doubly dangerous for Thora. Who knew what Peter Michaels and the bank robber might be able to do to her?!

"Talk to me, Julie." Luke's voice sounded through her phone again.

"Thora was pushed into Peter Michaels' truck, and they are off on Main Street towards the north now."

"I hear you started your motor."

"I'm following them."

"No, you won't do nothing of the kind!"

"You can't make me not follow them," Julie countered. "Besides this gives us a real advantage in knowing exactly where they are. I know it will take you a while to contact other police to try and stop them. Meanwhile I will chase after them and keep you current."

"This is crazy, Julie."

"It's not what I would normally do," Julie admitted, threading herself into the Harbor Mall round-about and checking which of the three exits the truck two cars ahead of her would take. "But it's the best option to get Thora out of the truck as quickly as possible."

"You don't even know what to pay attention to when giving chase to armed gangsters."

"True, but I'll do my best."

She heard how Luke switched off the motor of his car. She heard him open and close his door. "I'm at the bank now. Listen, I'll call you in a little. As soon as I know what has happened inside the bank and have taken care of that. Meanwhile, I'm contacting other police stations. Sit tight, and don't do anything more stupid than you're already doing." He hung up.

"Yeah, very encouraging," Julie said to herself and switched off her hands-off device.

At first, it was easy enough to follow the truck. Julie had read and watched so many whodunits that she knew she must not be too obvious in following the RAM. She kept a couple of cars between them, once or twice even a third one. It was the evening rush hour, and there were plenty of other things to take care of for the truck driver than check his rearview mirror to see whether they were followed.

At the outskirts of Wycliff, the truck veered off into a smaller country road with less traffic, winding through prairies and woods, through sloughs and less densely settled area. Julie didn't even care to look where they went. She knew this part of Western Washington like the back of her hand. As long as Thora's kidnappers stayed around here, she wouldn't have any trouble describing her whereabouts to Luke or any other police person.

Sundown was gorgeous. Mt. Rainier stood out against the Cascade Mountains like a majestic white giant, now tinted with soft hues of pinks and blues. The rivers and lakes Julie passed were shining bodies of quicksilver, with waterfowl dipping in and out, catching insects or small fish. A raccoon hurried across the road in front of Julie's car, and she braked for the cute little animal. The world could have been such an idyll…

Julie was hoping that the police would catch up with her sooner or later and relieve her from this hellish chase. But for whatever reason no car with flashing lights showed up behind her. And by the time Luke finally called her back, night was falling quickly.

"Are you still okay, Julie?" were Luke's first words.

"Yep," she said between clenched teeth. She was miffed that so far there were no signs of any attempts of intercepting the truck which was now half a mile ahead of her.

"Where are you at?"

"Just passed the gas station at Buckley."

"Do they take any of the turns east?

Julie scanned the road ahead for the truck. Traffic had become denser again. But there it was, a bit closer to her again. "Nope. They are still on the main road. - Listen, don't you guys set up any road blocks anywhere?"

Luke snorted. "Listen, Miss Smarty Pants, whose job are you doing? Your mother will be worried sick by the time you come home. Road blocks ... Do you know how many we would have to build in this area? We need to make sure which direction they go, before we spend people, time, and money on road blocks."

"Well, they're on their way to Enumclaw now," Julie said and hung up. Really! Had he just called her Miss Smarty Pants when she was all the police had right now to spot the kidnappers? She'd show him.

A few miles later, the truck chose the route towards the National Park. At first, there were still quite a few cars coming from the other direction, but about half an hour into the drive, a bit past Greenwater, traffic had let up. Julie felt hungry. She had some granola bars in the back of her car, but she wouldn't be able to get to them unless she stopped and got out. She also needed desperately to relieve herself. But she couldn't let anything happen to Thora. Unless it had already happened to her. The thought alone made her sick to the stomach. So much for being hungry. She wouldn't be able to get down a bite.

Julie drove on. She didn't have the radio on, as she didn't want to miss any phone calls. She wouldn't have been enjoying any kind of music right now anyway. And she wouldn't have been able to digest anything that was news, documentaries, or radio entertainment shows. The humming of her car and the deep darkness around had an almost hypnotizing quality.

Suddenly, Julie had to break very sharply. The truck was gone as if swallowed up by the ground. Dang! She hadn't seen it take a turn. Where could they have gone? Julie carefully slowed down, until the car ahead that had been separating her from the truck was just two red shining dots which finally expired in the night.

With no car behind her, Julie could afford to drive even more slowly. And there it was: a very small turnoff into the woods, barely paved and quite rutted. Julie shuddered. Looking down the small road, she observed something that could have been truck lights. She pulled over and frantically searched for her big map. Her fingers were shaking as they were flying to turn over page after page. She hardly dared switch on her indoor light to read the particular map she had looked for. Was this the turnoff? Was it that? Julie hadn't checked the milestone she had passed only recently. Big mistake. On the other hand, either turnoff looked pretty much the same according to the map. They both led into the middle of nowhere. Hopefully that also meant that the truck would have to return the same way as it had gone.

Julie was shivering. Should she follow? Or sit in her car waiting until the truck came back and then pick up the chase again? She tried to reach Luke on the phone, but she only had one bar on her display. Not enough to make any call or to receive any. Julie bit her lips. She was all by herself now, and she wasn't sure what she should do. One thing was certain though: She couldn't leave where she was. She wouldn't leave Thora alone with her kidnappers somewhere out in the wilderness of Mt. Rainier. She'd stay and wait, no matter how long it would take.

*

When the robber had snatched her left arm and torn her away from Angela's side, Thora hadn't made a sound. The cry for help that she wanted to let out somehow stuck in her throat like a bit of gluey food. She wasn't able to swallow, to utter a noise, or to protest. She was propelled through the doors faster than she could get her wits together and then thrust into the middle seat of a truck that somehow seemed familiar to her.

The bank robber slumped into the seat right next to her, pulling the door shut, slamming into her right arm. She moaned. The robber shouted something at the driver next to her, and the truck screeched forward, horns honking behind. Only then did Thora fully realize what had happened. And screaming now would not help her at all.

Quietly she tried to figure what to do. Hold still for now, she decided. Look how they are reacting to each other. The one to her right obviously was trigger-happy. Even now, he was still pointing his gun at her. As if she could have moved from the middle seat and made for a dash over his legs or the driver's, for goodness sake!

The driver ... He struck Thora as somebody who didn't fit into the situation at all. He was well-groomed compared to the obviously self-applied buzz cut of the robber. He looked wistful, almost as if he was caught in the situation against his will, similar as she was. But maybe she was just interpreting things as she wanted them to be.

"Where's the money?" the driver asked.

"Didn't get it," the robber said through clenched teeth.

"What the heck?!"

"Shut up and drive!"

They kept the silence until they were outside Wycliff and turned into a small country road. Thora had always loved this road for its scenic views. Now it would be tainted with these memories forever. She moaned, as the gravity of taking a steeper bend in the road pressed her kidnapper against her right arm again.

"Shut up, woman," he said roughly.

"She's hurt," the driver said with a sideways look at Thora. "Can't you see that bulky sling? She's probably in pain."

"What are you? Defending that ...?" He bit his lips, swallowing the obscene word he had been about to say. Somehow Thora didn't fit his usual bill of women, and he felt he needed to change his wording.

"Hey man," the driver said, and in Thora's ears it rang like cheap gangster imitation. "I was in for the money, but not a kidnapping."

"Well, you are in one now," the robber snapped.

"At least put that gun away," the driver said. "She won't be able to do anything with that fat sling of hers. And if you try to shoot her, you might even accidentally hit me."

"Think me a fool?" the robber grumped. But he put his gun into its holster under his jacket anyway. Thora heaved a sigh of relief. "Now, lady, this is no carte blanche for you to do anything stupid, hear me?"

"Yes," Thora said meekly.

"You got anybody who could pay ransom?"

"No," Thora said.

"No family? Parents? Brothers or sisters? A husband?"

"None whatsoever."

The robber stared at her in disbelief. But Thora's face stayed calm, and he turned away disgruntled.

"You okay, Ma'am?" the driver asked.

"Thora," she said. "Kind of, under the circumstances."

He glanced at her. "You in pain?"

"Hey, what are you playing at?!" the robber shouted at the driver. "Good cop, bad cop, or what?!"

The driver stared hard at the robber. "You know that I wasn't planning on any of this. - You must believe me, Thora."

She almost laughed with despair. The robber was dangerous. The driver was obviously just some money-greedy idiot who got himself into a mess. Big mess. Then she looked at the man on her other side. He looked worried and strained. The robbery had gone so wrong for him and he had to keep face. That was all it was about for now. She kept silent and stared straight ahead.

At one point - it was somewhere at a traffic light in Bonny Lake - she looked into the rearview mirror to check whether any police was trying to catch up with them. There wasn't any police car in sight. But she spotted a sky-blue VW beetle that looked quite like Julie Dolan's. Her heart jumped into her throat. Then she discarded the notion. What would Julie want, following them like this? Besides, she was the step-daughter of a chief of police. She'd know better than to chase armed robbers and kidnappers all by herself. And how many sky-blue VW beetles must be there in Western Washington anyhow?!

At the big bend of the main road in Buckley, Thora ventured another tentative look into the rearview mirror. Indeed, the VW beetle was still behind with a few cars in between them. Thora sent up a silent prayer. If only it were Julie! If only somebody, anybody knew where she was taken to... She needed to catch the two men's attention and distract them from the car that might or might not be following them intentionally.

"What are you planning to do with me?" she asked.

"Don't know yet," the man in the passenger seat answered.

"The old school teacher called you by a name," Thora went on. "Prosper Martin..."

"Prosper Martinovic," the man said. "Damn it, it's all her fault this thing went wrong."

"How did she know you?"

"She was an old teacher of mine," Prosper said.

"Wait," the driver interrupted. "I thought your name was Peter!"

"Kind of like a pen name," Prosper replied almost proudly. "Same initials, same signature, if you make it illegible enough."

"You mean you never gave me your real name?!" The driver was visibly upset.

"What's in a name, Teal?!"

Thora listened up. Teal?! Then she was not only with the team that had tried to rob a bank this afternoon and had Paul's blood on their hands. They were also the people who had committed check fraud and dumped hazardous waste illegally. She needed to step really carefully now.

"Is that why you shot at her? Because she recognized you?" Prosper kept his mouth shut. "Because she endangered you?"

"Listen, lady, you don't know a thing!" it burst out of Prosper. "I grew up here. My parents came from Communist Eastern Europe. They were so adjusted, they had lost any identity. If you want to describe my father ... he was gray. His opinion was gray, his ambition was gray, even his dreams were gray. He was colorless. That was what I was taught to be at home: Be colorless so you fit in. But I decided to be a leader. If you can't be a leader, because people tell you that you don't belong with them, you make up your own laws and try to be a leader for people who like your laws."

"Meaning you became a rebel?"

Prosper laughed, but he didn't sound happy. "You can call it that. And, of course, my parents tried to smooth it over. Again and again and again. In smoothing things over, they tried to turn my life into the same grayness as theirs. But they didn't succeed. I came up with bigger and bigger ideas."

"But has it made you happy?" Thora asked carefully.

Prosper laughed again. "Ah well ... What is happiness?!"

"To be at one with one's conscience. To live without being infringed nor infringe others. To have everything for your creature comforts. To love and be loved..."

"Love!" Prosper snorted. Thora was almost waiting for a "bah, humbug!" "You know what kind of women you run into once you have decided on the path I have taken? They sell themselves for money, for drugs, for material things. None of them love me. They love what I can provide them with."

"Sad," Thora said, and stealthily checked the rearview mirror again. There were still lights there, but far behind in the distance. Thora wasn't even sure whether this was the beetle anymore. She glanced at Teal. He was driving in a very concentrated fashion. Obviously he was not comfortable with driving through the dark. Also, the subject they were discussing seemed to upset him.

"I'm sure you just haven't found the right person yet."

"Oh sure," Prosper mocked. "Maybe one day. One of those semi-holy women who think they can make me turn my life upside down and change me back to gray again?"

"What is so wrong about wanting to fit in?"

"It's boring. It makes you size down all of your potential into a certain frame. It takes your individualism. - Lady, I don't even know why I am discussing this with you."

Thora gave him a smile. She tried so hard to make it look friendly and innocent. She needed them both on her side. "Because I asked for the person who is underneath the robber costume with the gun?"

"Yeah, right." They drove on for a short while. "Turn left after this little bridge," Prosper said to Teal.

They turned off the main road and into a one-lane forestry road. It was hardly paved and quite bumpy in places. Thora bit her lips, but couldn't help moaning when Prosper bounced against her in one particularly bad pothole.

"Sorry," he said.

"It's okay," Thora managed.

It was a rough ride, and they went on for a good hour, taking twists and turns through the dense rain forest. Branches brushed against the truck, puddles spit their wetness up against the windows. The lights cut through the darkness and illuminated lichened boulders and tall, wide tree stems next to the ruts. A bewildered deer stared at them. Then it stepped cautiously into the shade of the trees. At one time, there even seemed to be a bear cub sharpening its claws on a young spruce. But that might have been just an illusion.

The ruts grew wider. They crossed a narrow board bridge. Then the road ended in a roughly smoothed turning area.

"Stop here," Prosper ordered Teal. Teal did. The motor was running smoothly. The gas tank was still half-full. Thora started worrying. Stopping in the middle of the woods at night didn't give her any good forebodings.

Prosper opened his door and hopped down. "Out!" he said to Thora.

"What?"

"Out! You heard me."

Thora gave Teal a worried look. He pretended not to see. Thora climbed out cautiously. She knew this would become an execution now. She felt bile rise in her throat. She thought of Clark whom she hadn't ever thanked enough for his care, his friendship. Whom she had never really shown how much she loved him. Oh, how she loved him, even if his economic views clashed sadly with her ecological ones. But oh ... She sobbed drily.

Prosper stepped past her, climbed back into the truck, and closed the door. Thora looked at him, not comprehending. He let the window down. "Consider this your lucky day!" he said to her in a hoarse tone. Then he ordered Teal to turn around and left Thora standing alone in the dark in the middle of nowhere.

*

Susanne Bacon

From "The Sound Messenger":

Kidnapping Has Lucky Ending

jomin. **Environmentalist Thora Byrd, who was kidnapped on Friday afternoon during an attempted bank robbery, was found safe and sound in the foothills of Mt. Rainier later the same night. The identity of both robber-kidnappers could be confirmed. The escape vehicle is assumed to be on an easterly route.**

"They just let me go!" Thora Byrd, citizen of Wycliff, still cannot believe she was released unscathed by her kidnappers late Friday night. She had been inside the Wycliff bank where she witnessed an attempt at bank robbery going south. During the incident (we reported in *The Sound Messenger's* Saturday edition), Chef Paul Sinclair was shot in the heroic act of saving retired high school teacher Mildred Packman's life. Immediately after, and without any loot, the bank robber now identified as former Wycliff citizen Prosper Martinovic kidnapped Thora Byrd and held her together with his accomplice until approximately ten o'clock at night.

Thora Byrd describes the kidnappers as rough, but humane. "This is not a case of Stockholm Syndrome," she says. "I am certainly not sympathizing with these people. But they treated me decently under the circumstances." Byrd was taken towards the Mt. Rainier area where she was set free at the end of a forestry road some six miles away from SR 410 near one of the National Park Entrances. She started walking back through the dark when she was picked up by *The Sound Messenger* editor Julie Dolan, who had been able to follow her without being spied by the kidnappers.

Dolan had parked her car near the turnoff until the kidnappers' truck returned. "It was plain luck that they came back the same way. I could have been left waiting for ages, had there been a connection to another forestry road," she states. She observed the truck leave in the direction of Cayuse Pass to cross over the Cascades, then drove up the forestry road to find Byrd.

Thora Byrd was not only able to identify her kidnapper, bank robber Prosper Martinovic, as identical with the illegal dumper and check fraudster Peter Michaels. His accomplice in the scam turned out to be also the driver in the bank robbery, Julian Teal. "He was obviously not aware he would be part of a kidnapping on top of the robbery," Thora Byrd says. "But he was definitely upset about the failed robbery."

The FBI have taken measures to hunt the escapees down. Anybody who might see or even encounter Martinovic and/or Teal (see description in text box below) should not try to approach them, but call 911 directly. Both men are most certainly armed and willing to shoot.

Meanwhile, Thora Byrd is recovering from the shock of her kidnapping experience at her cozy beach cottage. "I'll just try and focus on my fledgling company 'Bags 4 Choosers," she says.

The other victim of Friday afternoon's crime is not so lucky. Paul Sinclair is still hospitalized and in critical condition. (…)

CHAPTER 10

The Green Maven's Tip of the Week:
Remove wax spots from textiles by using a warm iron and a paper towel or toilet paper. Make sure you don't use the steam function of the iron. Place the paper onto the wax, then cautiously move the point of the warm iron across the paper. The paper will absorb the wax, and your textile should be wax-free after repeating the process.

Thora didn't know how many tears of relief and joy she had been shedding ever since she had been released by her kidnappers. At first, she had been too stunned to feel anything. Her only thought had been how to get out of the wilderness in the dark and back to the road. Anybody who has ever been in the woods at night knows how bewildering and treacherous every move can be. The rain forest of the Pacific Northwest is dense and usually gives you a feeling of walking through dusk even on a bright day. Though there was a bright moon in the sky, it barely penetrated the thick foliage and needle trees around the turning area at the end of the forestry road. Thora was all alert as to where she ought to step next. She was worried that people might search for her and pass the little takeoff from the road. In addition, the sight of wild animals earlier had her keep eyes and ears wide open.

Her steps were hesitant. Every once in a while she slipped or stumbled in the uneven rut she had chosen to walk in to keep her direction. She heard something rustling in the underbrush and saw it dash across her path, a smallish creature that she prayed was as wary as she. She was hungry, too, but she didn't have anything on her. Besides, the urge to reach the main road was bigger than anything.

When she thought she'd been searching her way through the dark for hours already, she was suddenly blinded by bright car lights. Thinking her kidnappers might have reconsidered setting her free, she dashed into the underbrush where she twisted her ankle. Then she heard Julie call for her, and she limped out, starting to sob with relief to have been found. Julie wrapped her in a blanket and fed her a granola bar, then drove up to the point of release again, turned around, and went for the main road as quickly as possible.

Reaching Greenwater meant being back in civilization and to a full number of bars on her phone again. Julie stopped by the General Store and called Luke to let him know they were on their way back to Wycliff.

Thora was shaking with shock the entire way back, though Julie switched the AC to full heat. When the lights of Wycliff came in sight, Julie drove straight for Thora's beach cottage. There were two cars there already – Luke's and Clark's.

The front door opened, and the light from inside spread invitingly across the lawn and the narrow tiled path towards the car. Bear came dashing through the door and started barking and howling with joy, barely giving Thora a chance to open the car door and get out. In his ecstasy to have Thora back again, Bear almost threw her over, jumping at her and trying to give her something like a dog hug, while wagging his tail and whining.

Thora looked at the door. Clark stood on the threshold and watched her with a smile that still bore the traces of the past hours' worry. Thora finally managed to calm Bear and walk toward her home.

"Clark," she said, and her voice broke. Then she ran the last few steps and ended in his widely spread arms. "Clark!"

"You're home." He whispered tenderly and held her tightly. "I'm so glad you are safe."

Luke cleared his throat behind the two of them. "I don't want to disturb you or keep you from each other any longer. But I have to take a first report, Thora. Sorry."

She nodded without looking at him.

"Can't that wait?" Clark asked. "She's been through so much."

"Actually, this might help her to deal with the experience even better. You might be able to sleep more tightly once you have talked about it, Thora. Besides, the FBI needs our support." Then Luke spotted his stepdaughter and frowned. "You better give your mother a call now! She has been up all night long with worry."

Julie stifled a smile. He wasn't really angry about her having helped out. He had misgivings that she had given Dottie a really bad time. She lifted her phone to show she was dialing and retreated to her car again.

"Thank you!" Thora called after her. Then they went inside.

It was three in the morning when Luke finally said good-bye. Clark insisted on staying with Thora, and she was quite grateful. His presence kept her from turning her kidnapping over in her thoughts again and again. Instead, she was able to enjoy him pampering her with stew he had found in her freezer and heated up for her.

"Mmmh," he said. "I call this soul food."

"It's just a white bean soup with spinach," she smiled and dipped her spoon in. "I also have some meatballs somewhere in the freezer. Want some of those in?"

He shook his head. "I just want to sit here with you and pretend that it is entirely normal to eat hot soup with the woman I love at almost four in the morning."

She didn't gasp. He had told her what she had been knowing, but somehow ignoring for so very long. She smiled at him, and she felt a soft warmth slipping into her mind and body, something that simply relaxed her, yet made her heart beat wildly, too. "I love you too, Clark," she said quietly. "I don't know a better man than you, and I hope you forgive me for having lead you a dance like this."

He grabbed her hand across the table. "There was no dance. You were right to keep our relationship and our jobs separate. You were right about this terrible idea of mine with the refinery. And I rather had you act somewhat restrained than be available too easily."

They looked into each other's eyes. They finished their stew. They cleared the dishes away together. It was the most natural thing in the world that they shared Thora's bedroom for the next few hours. Hugging each other tightly, they slept the sleep of utter exhaustion. Once in her dreams Thora moaned softly. But Clark pulled her against him even a bit more closely, sling and all, and she snuggled up to him without ever waking.

*

Julie had a hard time explaining to Dottie why she had put herself into danger's path. "Don't you see that it was utterly unnecessary?" Dottie wanted to know. "There was the FBI involved. They would have brought Thora home. They know how to follow criminals and deal with negotiations if need be."

"Mom, I had no choice!" Julie insisted.

"Tell me you didn't do it just for the sake of the story!"

Julie looked at Dottie incredulously. "You think I had that in mind in the first place? Mom, do you really think

I'm capable only of thinking of myself?" She slammed the door behind her, and Dottie sank on a chair.

Her child was back, safe and sound. So why did she hold the excursion up against her? Because all could have gone so dead-wrong. Because she was still a mother, even though her child was a grown and independent woman by now. Because she hadn't been involved, but had to watch from the sidelines with no chance of interfering with fate at all.

Luke came in and saw her looking bleakly at her folded hands. "Another fight with Julie?" he asked softly, gave her a hug, and kissed her brow.

"I guess you can call it my fault," Dottie said miserably. "I simply want her to think before acting. And it seems it is not my place to say anything anymore."

"Not when it comes in the shape of a belated scolding," he gave her to consider. "You must let go, hon. She will ask you for advice if and when she needs it. But not if you judge her as if she were a willful child."

Dottie nodded. "I know. I messed up."

Luke gave her one of his lopsided smiles. "You know, between us, she deserved a scolding. She shouldn't have gone off as if there were no people who knew how to deal with such a situation."

Dottie gave him a half-smile. "That's what I tried to tell her."

"I told her when I had her on the phone yesterday afternoon. - Enough said. The case is over and done with, and we have to pick up the pieces."

"Paul," Dottie said sadly. "Do you have any news of him?"

"Nothing too precise yet. The doctors just say that he has been upgraded from critical to serious condition. They wouldn't tell anybody anything more. It might take a while yet to figure how badly the bullet damaged him."

Dottie sighed. "The poor parents."

Luke nodded. "Being proud of a child sometimes comes at a price." He took a bottle of milk from the fridge and poured some into a glass. "Want something to drink, too?"

"No, thanks," Dottie said. She paused, then changed her tone, indicating a change of subject. "Are there any news of Prosper Martinovic? Did they catch him?"

"No news other than that the FBI are on his heels. But they found Teal by the roadside somewhere east of Leavenworth."

"He was simply sitting there?"

"Basically. He was walking towards the next few houses up the road when they found him. He surrendered without resistance."

"So he had separated from Martinovic? Being a better person after all?"

"Not really." Luke shook his head. "Apparently Martinovic kicked him out. Teal would have stayed on otherwise. He admitted that much."

"I hope he gets what he deserves," Dottie said.

Luke emptied his glass in one long draught. "That's up to the courts, not the police or the FBI, dear," he said.

"And I hope they finally catch that Martinovic, that gangster, that ..." Dottie broke off her tirade. She didn't want to betray her true feelings in juicier language.

"Just give it another day or two. It won't take much longer once they are so close on a felon's heels."

*

Trevor was sitting on the garden porch with his parents, enjoying some late lunch sandwiches. At least Theodora and James were enjoying theirs. The garden was in full bloom, and the white wicker furniture gave the scene something of a romantic setting. Trevor was listlessly chewing, wondering how to put the news out there. He glimpsed into the sunlight as if the panoramic view of the Sound might inspire him. After a while he cleared his throat.

"Can I talk to you, Dad?"

"Right now?" James asked.

"After lunch in your office?"

"Do you have a secret from me?" Theodora asked a little piqued.

Trevor sighed. "No, Mother, of course I don't."

"Then why don't you talk right here?"

Trevor shrunk inwardly, but then he straightened his back. Nothing would ever change if he didn't embrace change first.

"Alright then," he said. "I am going to move out."

James looked surprised, but Theodora was aghast. "Don't you like it here anymore? Did we do anything wrong?"

Trevor shook his head. "No, you didn't. Except that you should have kicked me out a long time ago."

"But we love having you. The Joneses are an old Wycliff dynasty. There have always been several generations under one roof."

"Well, then I am the first to change the pattern," Trevor said.

"But why?"

"First, I need to spread my wings and learn to fly on my own. That doesn't mean I'll not come in for work anymore. But it will be just that. No more regular meals with you either." Theodora tried to interrupt, but he warded her off. "No, Mother. I will gladly come as a guest every now and then, but I need to establish my own house in my own right."

"James!" Theodora pleaded. "Does this make sense to you?"

James chuckled. "Very much indeed. And I think I'm not entirely wrong to assume that it has to do with that date you had the other night. You returned in such a black mood that I didn't even dare to offer you a drink to down the pain."

"What date?" Theodora asked. "Did anybody hurt you, darling?"

Trevor shook his head in despair. "I'm an adult, Mother, not a 13-year-old who needs protection in this. I can fend for myself. Which is actually what I'm doing in moving out."

"Of course, you are grown-up…" Theodora said faintly.

"And that is exactly the point," Trevor interrupted her. "I have been told I was not. And in a way that lady was right. I thought our short conversation over very carefully, and I found that I wouldn't want to date anybody either if it meant I would end up in my in-laws' household and had to put my feet underneath their table."

"But what's wrong with that?" Theodora tried once more.

"Theo!" James laid one hand on her beautifully manicured ones and patted them gently. "Remember how tough a time you had with my mother? She constantly tried to run your life, and you tried to modernize hers. She treated you like an unwelcome child when all you wanted was a husband. It only stopped when we had to place her in a nursing home. Do you want the same thing for a future wife of Trevor's?"

"But I am different from your mother!" Theodora protested.

"Of course, you are, darling," James conceded. "But those girls out there don't know this. And they are not willing to give it a try either. Understandably so. The times of large dynasties under one roof belong to the past, Theo. Give Trevor a chance to meet a woman who loves him. And over time she might come to our house more and more often, not because it is the home of our son, but because she feels friendship for us old farts.

Theodora snapped for air, probably more because of the flippant choice of words than their content. Then she calmed herself down with visible effort. Still with hurt in her mien she asked Trevor: "Is that what you think, then?"

Trevor nodded. "I'm afraid so."

Theodora's eyes suddenly became moist. "Here goes my baby..."

Trevor rolled his eyes. James winked at him. "Only to maybe bring you another one into our house one day," he said and took a sip from his water glass. But as he was chuckling at the same time, he got some water into his windpipe, had to cough violently, and quickly fled the scene.

*

"I hope you know why you are deciding against the refinery all of a sudden, as it was your idea from the very first!" Walter May was upset. The Town Council meeting was barely into a quarter of an hour, and the agenda had just mentioned "New Business", not that it would be a swing of opinion with the Mayor. Clark had explained he was refraining from his refinery proposal due to environmental considerations as well as economic ones.

Now he was sitting in his chair at the head of the long table and facing the reactions of his fellow Councilors. He had expected Walter to be angry, so he was ready to parry. "Walter, be sure that I am. And I am a bit embarrassed about it myself.

"I am sure that we all know the reason why you changed your mind," Dr. Ajith Katkar said with a fine smile. "And actually I am glad that you reconsider rather than follow your first opinion just because it was your idea."

"What do you mean?" Walter stared at the oriental-looking man belligerently.

"That changing one's mind is sometimes more honest than just hanging on to a stale thought."

"Stale?!" Walter's face turned deeply red with anger. "A refinery means progress. It means growth. It means opportunity."

"Forgive me," Ajith said quietly, placing his slender hands against each other, fingertip on fingertip. "It wasn't my intention to aggravate you. And I see your point. But maybe the consideration of ecological destruction against economic development has become weightier to Clark. I abstained from voting last time because I needed to reflect it more deeply, and I have to admit that I have looked into the idea more closely."

"Well, so have I," Philip Nouveau, the firefighter, admitted. "As a family man I would love to see more job opportunities than only those in public safety and the tourist business in Wycliff, of course. Umh, but I can't close my eyes to the undeniable danger of crude oil trains ending up downtown and the risk of a fire in the refinery."

"I thought you were in favor of our idea!" Walter stared at Philip with a confused expression. "When did you change your mind?!"

"Does it matter when?" James Jones, the attorney, tried to calm the waves. "What really matters is that we need to be clear about what we want in order to be able to give a clear message to AnCoSafe Oil."

"I thought that in order to get a synopsis of our arguments I'd put the pros and cons on one sheet." Clark grabbed a pile of photocopies and handed them around. "I wrote down my former arguments on as well as those that I have now. I won't hide from my change of mind."

Walter mumbled something, but shut his mouth as soon as he caught the questioning look from Clark and a very amused one from Bill "Chirpy" Smith.

"Maybe we start with the pros and discuss one after the other," Clark suggested. "If we come up with a con, we'll note it on the other side if it's not already there. Later, the same goes for the cons, of course. So, let's start with more job opportunities ..."

They were discussing as calmly as possible what might mean a decisive change in Wycliff's future. They argued for three hours, leaving aside any other "new business" on the agenda. And in the end they voted. It was not a unanimous vote, but Clark knew what his orders were now.

*

Angela was visibly nervous. Her hands shook slightly as she laid her camping table for an afternoon coffee and cake German-style. In a moment, her guests would arrive. She heard a car approach, Thora's voice, and then a car door banged. A minute later, there was a knock on her door. Angela opened.

"Hello Ang...," Thora stopped in the middle of the word. She gaped. "What did you do to your hair? You look beautiful!"

Angela smiled and blushed. "You think?"

"Most certainly." Thora gazed at the stylish new haircut that was still a rich red, but by far more fetching than the artificial ruby-red Angela had worn before.

"I thought that if we want to sell fashion I need to up my game," Angela said shyly. Another knock on the door. "Come in, Meredith – it's open."

Meredith slipped in and gave Angela a hug. She was a little more cautious about Thora whom she still didn't know well enough for such cordial greetings.

"Sit down, sit down," Angela urged. "I got us some nice German cake from 'Dottie's Deli', and the coffee is brewed, too."

"That is such a treat," Meredith said. She pulled out a chair and sat down, placing a paper wrapped object on the table.

Angela brought the coffee and cake, and then she and Thora took a seat, too.

"How do you feel?" Meredith asked Thora.

Thora smiled. "I'm okay, thank you."

"Angela and I were wrecks after you were dragged off like this." Meredith faltered. "It must have been worse for you."

"It's nothing I'd care to go through again." Thora laughed nervously. "I think I might abstain from forest walks for a while yet."

"Those men ought to be punished severely!" Angela exclaimed.

"I trust in our justice system," Thora said calmly. "It's not like they will get off the hook once they are caught. And they have Teal already."

They took their first bites of cake in silence.

"Well," Thora said after a sip of hot coffee. "You made it such a secret why I ought to come and see you today. You got me all excited."

Angela smiled mysteriously, and Meredith pushed the wrapped object towards Thora. "It's all about this."

Thora looked at the package with curiosity. "What is it?"

"Open it up," Angela beamed. "While you were gone, we thought we needed to make sure that your dreams start getting real and put in an overnight shift."

Thora fiddled with the tissue paper. Her mouth suddenly went dry. She glimpsed an inch of brocade through a rip in the paper. She gasped when she saw the entire object. A beautiful handbag, complete with a flap and a gorgeous and unique decorative button, a strap that could be adjusted, silk lining, and an inside pocket with a zipper. The colors of the fabric were subtle browns and ochres, accentuated with teals and turquoise, in a geometric pattern. "This looks simply stunning!" Thora exclaimed, holding it at arm's length to have a better look. "When did you do this?"

"Meredith made the design here at the table while I was bawling my eyes out," Angela said with a smirk.

"Then Angela remembered that she still had some wonderful fabric from back in her German days," Meredith tossed in.

"We called in one of our cutters to take care of the pieces, and one of our seamstresses had time enough on her hands to do an extra-project."

"I checked how well the design was realized," Meredith continued. "And Angela did quality control."

The two women looked at Thora expectantly. Thora was speechless. She put the handbag down on the table and stroked the fabric. "You make me almost cry," she whispered.

"Have some more cake then," Angela laughed.

"This is even more beautiful than I thought we'd manage."

"Thank you," Meredith smiled, and a tad of self-confidence shone through her plainness.

"This is most certainly a start to our new line," Thora said with dreamy eyes. "Which means that from now on you have to let your imagination run whenever it comes up with something, Meredith. We should also look into similar fabrics to re-create the design in different colors and patterns. And I will definitely show this to the gift and fashion stores here in Wycliff. I'm pretty sure that they will adore this kind of accessory."

Angela lifted her coffee cup. "To 'Bags 4 Choosers' then!"

Thora and Meredith lifted their cups as well.

"This is the best outcome I could have hoped for on my bad adventure," Thora smiled. "Thank you, ladies."

The three looked at each other. There could hardly have been three women more different at one table. Yet their passions and dreams had started to weave a tight band of friendship between them.

*

Daniel rose when Mattie approached the table he sat at in the Bair Bistro in Steilacoom. He smiled. Mattie was looking beautiful in her flaring summer skirt and sleeveless blouse. It was a Saturday, and as she didn't work this weekend - a freedom she took every once in a while - she had been able to dress up. Daniel had cleaned himself up nicely, too. He pulled out a chair for her, waited until she sat, and took his seat again. The bistro was busy with late guests for breakfast and early ones for lunch.

"Lucky that we got a table at all," Mattie observed. "In the window niche at that! I know this place can be terribly busy." She gazed out at Lafayette Street and watched people go to the café up Wilkins or return from the recently opened veggie store with their bags full. Some people were also obviously only taking a stroll through the beautiful little town, pointing out houses as old as the very founding of the State of Washington.

"I feel like a glass of champagne," Daniel announced to her. "We are back to the place of our first date, after all."

"It didn't feel much like a date," Mattie admitted. "I was angry about my business. I was worried what you had going on in yours. I felt all these butterflies, but I was scared of what was lying in the wharf's future. I was scared of losing my reputation. And I was a bit scared of you, too. I'd only known you as a business partner, after all." She smiled at him, tilting her head to the side a little. "I'd love a glass of champagne, but I need something to eat and a cup of tea first. Otherwise you'll have a very tipsy Mattie hanging on to you later."

"I wouldn't mind having you hanging on to me at all," Daniel grinned unabashed. "Let's see whether they have a special this morning."

They looked into their menus, and a little later, Daniel made eye contact with bistro owner Sarah Cannon. She came over with energetic steps.

"Good morning, guys," she said and smiled. She had her hair in two cute little pigtails, bound with ribbons printed with pink and red hearts. "Nice you are back. What can I get for you?"

Daniel ordered eggs Hemingway and a side salad. Mattie asked for Belgian waffles and a berry topping. "And a cup of Earl Grey, please." Mattie leaned back and returned the menu to Sarah. She missed seeing the glint in Sarah's eyes, as she was smiling at Daniel.

"I'm sorry, we are out of Earl Grey," Sarah said and batted her eyes. She stifled the laugh that wanted to bubble out of her mouth, and Daniel frowned at her.

"Well, anything but Lapsang Souchong tea then," Mattie said.

"We have some very nice Lady Gold tea," Sarah managed barely without a giggle, and Daniel looked at her with another frown.

"Never heard of that, but ... well, let's give it a try."

Sarah rushed towards the kitchen, and Mattie heard her burst into merry laughter.

"Did I say anything wrong?"

"Not at all, sweetheart." Daniel shook his head. He frowned.

"Why are you frowning?"

"Am I?" Daniel coughed.

Sarah was returning with a beautiful china mug that was decorated with a big red rose and had a lid that would hold the aroma of the tea while steeping. She set the cup in front of Mattie and stepped back.

Mattie looked at the cup, then at Daniel. "Isn't that some neat china? I wonder what the tea will taste like." She carefully lifted the lid, and a cloud of steam came out. Mattie sniffed, eyes closed. "Apparently the flavor has to develop yet," she mused. "Lady Gold ..." She opened her eyes, lifted the teabag a bit to move it in the cup, and gasped. The teabag held a ring with a set of beautiful small diamonds.

The next moment, Daniel was on one knee in front of her, grasping her hand. "Mattie dearest," he said huskily.

"Would you do me the joy and honor to become my wife? I know it is early to ask. But the past days have shown me how quickly something bad can happen. So I thought we might as well make something good come about."

Mattie teared up. "Daniel," she whispered.

"If it is too early for you, you may just as well keep the ring and think it over."

"No," she said decidedly.

"No?" Daniel blanched.

"I mean, no, I don't have to think it over. And the flavor of this special tea won't have to develop any more. - Oh Daniel, of course, it is yes!" She flung her arms around his neck, and their kiss was drowned in the applause of the other guests and the plopping sound of a champagne bottle being opened.

"Champagne is better than tea sometimes," Sarah grinned and handed the newly engaged couple two flutes of golden bubbly. "You gave me a hard time to not laugh out loudly, Daniel. Your idea with the ring in the tea cup was really something else." She winked. "I hope we keep getting tea with this kind of flavor more often from now."

*

Susanne Bacon

From "The Sound Messenger":

Mayor Nixes Refinery Project, Gets Engaged

judo. Wycliff and its aficionados may heave a sigh of relief as Mayor Clark Thompson announced the AnCoSafe Oil refinery project null and void in last Friday's press conference. Instead, the town will invest in more environmental-friendly concepts that may enhance the South Sound's future.

Activists involved in protesting the AnCoSafe Oil refinery project planned to be built south of the Wycliff ferry terminal greeted Mayor Clark Thompson's announcement with cheers. "We had hoped at least to be able to delay construction by a few years in sending petition after petition," says a citizen who asked not to be named. "We would have put in a lot of effort to have courts deal with it. That the project has simply been dropped is more than we had dared hope for."

Town Council hadn't voted unanimously against the project; actually, there was one abstention. Yet it shows how valid the cons were - abstentions are not nays, after all. Part of the outcome is obviously due to activist Thora Byrd's strong voice that set off the protest movement and in the end even turned the mayor's opinion.

"What danger lies in hazardous materials, we have seen in the illegal dumping of hazardous waste that occurred in the past months in the South Puget Sound region," Thompson said. "The effort to cleanse such sites and to keep the population safe is time and budget intense. And it is literally unpredictable. We were lucky enough to find all the dump sites and secure them. We are barely able to foresee all of the impact the building of a major refinery would have had on the South Sound. And I'm not even talking any catastrophic scenario."

The budget that the Town of Wycliff might have invested in new infrastructure and an increase of public safety and services will now be turned towards environmental-friendly and preservative measures. Next week, members from the Chamber of Commerce as well as Town Council will be discussing possible projects with the Department of Wildlife and Fishing as well as with the Department of Transportation in order to make Wycliff even more attractive and ecological.

Thora Byrd, who made the headlines with her kidnapping last week, received a huge extra-applause when she was spotted amongst the audience. She declined any comment, but later was seen to congratulate Thompson on the Town Council's decision.

Though the refinery project is off the Mayor's desk now, he won't win back his former town hall secretary jobwise. Instead, rumors have it that Thompson is hosting an engagement party with his bride-to-be at a so far undisclosed location at the end of this month. *The Sound Messenger* wishes Clark Thompson and Thora Byrd all the best.

EPILOGUE

Thora was leaning on the banister of her deck, enjoying the mellow breeze that was coming from the water. The sound of soft waves lapping at the beach was soothing. A gull was screeching above in the air, and Bear sat on his haunches next to Thora, his plush teddy under one paw. He had hardly left her side ever since her kidnapping.

"The mail just brought a letter for you," Clark said and approached her from the cottage. He handed her a plain white envelope that showed no return address. "I opened it for you."

"Thank you, dear," Thora said, caressing his face with her eyes. "I wouldn't know how to handle things without you. This sling is really bothering me."

"Shhhh," Clark gave her a tender kiss on the lips. "Just a couple more weeks, and you will be back to normal again. Besides, it helped us get to where we are standing with each other now."

"On my deck," Thora teased, knowing he meant something way less tangible.

He chuckled. "Never short of an answer, are you? Well, I'll leave you with your letter then."

"No, stay. I wonder – let's just look at it together."

Clark placed his arm around her shoulder as she pulled a single white sheet of paper from the envelope and unfolded it.

"Dear Ms. Byrd," she read aloud. "When a child goes down the wrong path in life, there are two parties that are touched by them ... their parents and their victims. I am Prosper Martinovic's father, and on behalf of my son I need to ask your forgiveness for what he did to you. Believe me, nobody is grieving more about who Prosper has become than I. If I may offer anything to make up for your dire situation in any way, please have your say in *The Sound Messenger*, and I'll know how to reach you. Sincerely, Michael Martinovic."

"Mike Martinovic, the former treasurer who cheated the Chamber of Commerce out of their Christmas budget," Clark stated in wonder.

Thora nodded. "It's just as Prosper said to me, while we were driving towards Mt. Rainier. His parents always cover up for him and try to smooth things over."

Clark nodded pensively. "It won't be necessary any longer," he said and handed her this morning's newspaper, pointing at a headline. Thora's eyes widened. Then she read the article and crumpled the letter.

"He killed himself right in front of the FBI?"

"Slammed his car through the side railing of the road and dropped down into the canyon some hundred feet," Clark confirmed. His face was serious.

Thora gazed across the water. "So he defied them once more," she stated. "He didn't ever want to fit in. He wanted to stand out. As he couldn't lay hands on what he thought would be the success of his life, he chose a dramatic exit. What a waste!"

Clark pulled her towards him. "Not even *his* existence was in vain though," he said softly. "Giving us the shock of our lives, he pushed us together."

"Oh Clark," Thora scolded. "Are you making something good from something awful?"

"Might as well." His deep blue eyes sparkled with boyishness. "How about some lemonade from Life's lemons?"

Recipes

Dottie's Chicken Fricassee

1 tbsp. butter
2 tsp. all-purpose flour
Juice of ½ lemon
200 ml chicken stock
1 tsp. mustard
½ cup sour cream or yoghurt
Tarragon to taste
½ tsp. sugar
½ tsp salt
Pepper to taste
1 lb. of boiled or fried chicken meat, cubed, and boiled or fried
½ lb. white asparagus, peeled, sliced, and slightly boiled
½ lb. mushrooms, peeled, sliced, and fried

Melt the butter and dissolve the flour in it (roux). Add some lemon juice and let boil up. Whisk stock in and dissolve the roux well in it. Add sour cream, mustard, tarragon, sugar, salt, and pepper. Add chicken meat, asparagus, and mushrooms. Add water as needed. Taste and re-season as necessary. Serve with rice.

Clark's Cured Salmon (Gravad Lax) with Honey Dijon Mustard Sauce

2 slices of salmon filet, at least ½ lbs. each, skin on
½ cup of salt
½ cup of sugar
½ bouquet of fresh dill

For the sauce mix:
5 tbsp. Dijon mustard (no matter if ground finely or not)
3 tbsp. liquid honey
2 tbsp. vegetable oil (no olive or nut oil)
1 tbsp. rice vinegar
1 pinch of salt

Roll out a large sheet of aluminum foil. Mix the salt and sugar and strew a third of the mixture onto the foil, add a third of the dill. Place one salmon filet on the mixture, skin down. Spread another third of the mix and the dill onto the salmon. Place the other filet on top with the meaty side down. Spread the rest of the salt & sugar mix and the dill onto the top. Fold the aluminum foil tightly around the salmon. Place the package into a deep dish and let rest in the fridge for at least 3 days. Turn package about every 12 hours (it will leak, so handle with care). After 3 days, you can unwrap the salmon and wipe off the excess sugar and salt from the filets. Slice into thin slices in an angle, following the salmon structure. Serve with honey Dijon mustard sauce and baguette or with hash brown patties.

Susanne Bacon

Thora's Spinach and Bean Stew with Meatballs

2 cups of navy beans
1 small bag of baby spinach, chopped
1 clove of garlic
1 box of Knorr jellied beef or chicken stock
Salt
Pepper
Marjoram
Oregano
1 tbsp. sour cream
Olive oil

For the meatballs:
1 lb. ground beef or turkey
1 egg
1 onion, finely chopped
½ cup of breadcrumbs
¼ lb. carrots, finely shredded
Salt
Pepper
Garlic powder to taste

Soak the beans in water in a large pot over night. Bring to a boil and let simmer for one hour. Meanwhile mix the ingredients for the meatballs. Shape into tiny balls and fry in a separate pan. You can freeze in what you don't want to put into the stew later. When the beans are soft, add the stock (beef for beef meatballs, chicken for turkey meatballs), garlic, seasoning, and herbs to taste. Also add water until you have achieved the desired consistency of your soup. Let the meatballs soak in the hot bean soup for five minutes. Add the spinach and sour cream only shortly before serving. Some rustic bread and butter on the side go well with the dish.

Thora's Tip for Vegetarians:

Instead of the jellied meat stock use a cube of vegetable broth. And, of course, leave out the meatballs.

Acknowledgements

First and foremost, I'd like to thank everybody who has bought my Wycliff novels so far, read them, maybe recommended them to others via reviews on Amazon.com or on their own homepages, and/or morally supported me on my Facebook page www.facebook.com/susannebaconauthor.

The AuthorHouse team outdid themselves to help create another book in the Wycliff series, giving dedicated and creative input as well as fast support whenever needed. You rock!

Dieter and Denise Mielimonka are priceless friends who gave me constructive criticism, helped edit my first draft, and took me for walks when I needed a break.

Dr. Samuel Burns and Dr. Jeremy W. Reifsnyder, real doctors in the South Puget Sound region, have helped me incredibly when I had broken and dislocated my right shoulder. So have Dr. Julie Spataro, the PT team, and quite a few nurses, X-ray technicians, and staff at Madigan Medical Center.

Without Arnie and Gary, two real USPS employees at the Steilacoom post office, Wycliff would still be without a post office of its own.

Thanks also go to Chef Sarah Cannon of the quaint Bair Bistro in Steilacoom (www.thebairbistro.com). From scratch is the best!

Thanks for all the inspiration to the wonderful people from Hess Bakery & Deli – without you I'd never have started the Wycliff series.

Hugs and cheers to my friends and supporters belonging to the Steilacoom Historical Museum Association for giving me a wonderful platform for book signings.

A shout out goes to my unbelievably supportive friends Katerina Delidimou (http://culinaryflavors.gr/), Linda Shapiro (www.mealplanmaven.com), and the talented hobby cooks of The Kitchen Cabinet. You all encourage me to try new recipes and to think "outside the bowl". Special thanks go to Karen Lodder, who keeps recommending my books on her wonderful website (http://germangirlinamerica.com).

Hugs to my inspiring author friends Anjali Banerjee (aka A.J. Banner), Janine Donoho, Dia Calhoun, and Donna Lee Anderson for encouraging me and for sharing thoughts.

Thanks also to my family in Europe and in the U.S, but especially to my husband, Donald. You give me all the time I need to create and revise, lend me your ear, support me in so many ways in so many situations, and often enough make me laugh tears. You're truly my biggest inspiration.